The Emancipator

TRACY WINEGAR

OMNIFIC PUBLISHING

LOS ANGELES

Omnific Publishing
2355 Westwood Blvd, Suite 506
Los Angeles, CA 90064
www.omnificpublishing.com

First Omnific eBook edition, September 2016
First Omnific trade paperback edition, September 2016

The characters and events in this book are fictitious.
Any similarity to real persons, living or dead,
is coincidental and not intended by the author.

Library of Congress Cataloguing-in-Publication Data

Winegar, Tracy.
The Emancipator / Tracy Winegar – 1st ed.
ISBN: 978-1-623422-45-5
1. Civil War — Fiction. 2. Historical Romance — Fiction.
3. Union Troops — Fiction. 4. Female Soldiers — Fiction. I. Title

10 9 8 7 6 5 4 3 2 1

Cover Design by Micha Stone and Amy Brokaw

Printed in the United States of America

For Ben

Chapter 1

"You left Sam?" The man was incredulous. I remembered feeling the same once upon a time when I was called upon to actually do the leaving. I felt as though my world might end with Sam's absence and wondered if I could go on without him. When you are so immersed in tragedy it is difficult to see there will be anything beyond it, that life will go on and somehow right itself again.

"On record it will say I deserted the army, but you can see that it was not my choice to do so, it was out of necessity. I was having a child and couldn't continue on."

"Yes, but…"

"That is really the only part of the story that pertains to you," I said. "You can see that I did indeed serve my country in the war."

"It would appear so," he said with an emphatic nod of his head.

"Can you tell me when I can expect to hear back from the pension board?"

He sputtered about, collecting his papers, pulling his leather case from the floor and stuffing things inside of it. It was a direct contradiction to the meticulous man who had arrived in such a precise way. He was flustered. "It will take a thorough going over. You seem to have knowledge and information that could only be gathered through a firsthand account, but I am not at liberty to share my personal sentiments. It is the pension board that will rule on it. I will present your case to the board, and you should receive a letter shortly after stating the outcome of our ruling."

"I have a list of the names of the men I served with that are still living. I hope it will aid in the investigation." I pulled a neatly folded piece of paper from my apron pocket and presented him with the list of names I had acquired, together with their addresses where possible.

"That will certainly help me in the matter. Thank you," he said, accepting the list from me.

He acted as though he might get up to leave, but paused with his case in his hand, leaning forward in his chair as though he wanted to share something with me, some juicy bit of gossip that required delicacy.

"Was there something else?" I inquired.

"I am just curious," he admitted. "I must know-what happened? I mean after you left Sam, what became of him? Of you?"

"I went home and Sam went to Libby Prison."

He was astonished. His eyes grew wide and his mouth fell open as though he were in shock. "Libby Prison?" he gasped. Who had not heard of the infamous Libby Prison? The name was said as a hiss, as an expletive. It was a dirty foul place where men went to waste away and die terrible agonizing deaths. "Please," he implored, "tell me what happened."

He wanted to know what happened. I found myself reluctant to speak of it. All of the other business I had gone over with him, that was the easy part. The things he wanted me to speak of...They were things I kept buried deep within. They were things that brought sorrow, and remorse, and I did not want to remember all of that.

Many long months I was with Sam as a soldier, as a boy. We fought together, we suffered and struggled together for the most basic of human needs. In many ways we grew to rely upon one another as friends so often do. But when he discovered I was a girl, that I had deceived him, there was a time, albeit short, when he wouldn't speak to me. It hurt. It hurt to think of his distaste for me.

And yet somehow through all of this, we transformed into lovers. I became his wife. I shared the happiness of being his lady through the blessed winter in 1863 in the camp with the Army of the Potomac. That was before I discovered I was with child, and Sam would have no more of me tramping about with the army knowing I carried his babe within my womb.

When I left him, when I got on the train, I believed the promise he made to me. I believed he would come back to me. If I only knew what his future held I would have sacrificed all to stay with him, to keep him just a little longer for myself.

I was alone. Not very much more can be said about it. Some people are comfortable in being alone, content in solitude and with their own thoughts. Perhaps they like who they are enough to find comfort being with themselves and don't need others to fill the emptiness within. Maybe they do not experience those moments of self-doubt and terrible fear that creep in with the quiet, with the isolation.

I did not share that sentiment. I thought of Sam and how he made me whole. Without him I was nothing. I was her again, that girl that no one cared to know. The train kept me steadily moving back to the beginning, and I felt the tangible defeat of losing ground as the changing landscapes passed by my window.

Heading home again, I felt forsaken and afraid of what I must face. I was surrounded by strangers' faces and places that were unfamiliar to me. I was a pilgrim in foreign lands, confronted with a great unknown that loomed ahead. Oddly enough I had the strongest desire to close my eyes and sleep and sleep and sleep. But I was frightened to do that. I was frightened of what might happen if I did go to sleep. The thought made me hunch my shoulders and clutch my bag closer, hunkering down and making myself ready for an attack.

My eyes were wide, and I was alert. I watched everyone around me. I observed them as I would the characters of a play. I tried to remove sensation and emotion from it and look at them objectively. There was a woman with a young boy who was noticeable upset and flustered with him, who repeatedly scolded him as he sat with his wide eyes fixed upon her as though he was alarmed by her behavior. While I was aware of her frustration and his discomfort, I did not feel anything in regard to it because I was merely a third party, withdrawn and aloof and only watching. There were others that I studied as well, until my neutrality gave me a feeling of numbness that made me forget where I was and where I was going.

When the train stopped in Washington I scarcely knew how I had gotten there or where the time had gone. I waited politely to exit, feeling my legs cramp and my back ache from sitting so long. I was not use to being idle, and my body rebelled against the hard bench and the confinement of the passenger car. It was a relief to have a moment to stand up and walk about. I made my way across the platform teaming with people and soldiers-a general mass of excitement and confusion-and went to the ticket window where I purchased a ticket for the next leg of my trip to Philadelphia. After that I went to the meal stop and paid for some Indian bread, pea pudding, and boiled mutton. I rushed to finish it, wanting to make sure that I had plenty of time to board.

I had eaten better, but at least I could eat it without having to fish the maggots out. It was a good meal compared to some of the food I was fed in the army. I had only twenty minutes to swallow it down and get back to the train before we departed. As I made my way to the passenger car I noted a man in Cavalry uniform who was bending down and searching with his hands along the ground. He had dropped his cane. I went to him, picking the cane up so that I might hand it back.

"Do you need help, sir?" I asked as I straightened myself up holding the cane out to him.

He raised his head toward me with an expression that made me think I had startled him. But then I got a good look at his eyes, and the food I'd just eaten churned in my stomach. I swallowed hard a few times, willing it to stay down.

The man's eyes drifted back and forth in their sockets, as though he had no apparent control over which direction they traveled. I also noted there was substantial scaring on each of his temples. It threw off the appearance of his whole face-one I was certain had been very handsome before his accident. I saw now the cane was to help him navigate because he was blind. I experienced what you generally experience during such times-a sense of overwhelming sympathy. How could you not feel sorry for someone who has experienced such misfortune?

"I hope I didn't alarm you," I said softly. I took his hand in mine and placed the cane in it. "Here is your cane."

"Thank you, ma'am," he said with a smile. "It seems I am in your debt."

"Not at all, it is I who owe the debt," I replied. "May I help you to your train?" He hesitated. I wasn't sure if he was wary of me or felt uncomfortable with the fact that he needed assistance.

"If it isn't an inconvenience, I'd be very grateful," he finally agreed.

"Not at all, sir," I assured him.

He fumbled in his pocket. "My ticket."

I looked over the ticket and saw that he was headed for Cincinnati, Ohio. "Would you mind taking my arm and I'll show you the way?"

He gripped my arm above the elbow, and I began moving him through the crowd. He shuffled his feet slowly, as though afraid I might lead him off of a cliff and he was doing his best to find the edge. My curiosity was piqued. I thought I must know what happened to him.

"Where are you coming from?" I asked.

"Field hospital. I've spent many months there. But they've now deemed me fit enough to travel."

"You're going home?"

"I'm going home."

"Where did you fight?"

"Droop Mountain. That's where I lost my sight. But we licked 'em good."

"Yes, I heard it was an overwhelming victory. Brigadier General Averell led the engagement, did he not?"

"You are well read, ma'am," he replied. "He did indeed."

"And I see that you were in the Cavalry?"

"You are correct again. Dismounted during the battle. The last thing I saw was the mountain, covered in all shades of red, and yellow, and orange. The colors were brilliant, more beautiful than anything

I've ever seen before. All of those trees turned by the fall, against the bluest sky…I am blind, but I can yet see it. And then a bullet entered through here." He indicated with his finger where the bullet had gone through his temple. "And came out here," he said tapping the other side of his head.

"It's a miracle you're alive," I said in a reverent tone.

He had a strange half smile on his lips that contained no humor. "Yes, a miracle."

I thought to tell him I'd been at Rappahannock Station, but I realized he would think that was odd, since I was a woman. I thought better of it and kept my mouth closed. Once we had made it to his train, I put his hand upon the railing and stepped aside so he might access the stairway.

"I hope you have a safe journey." I wanted him to hear the sincerity in my voice.

"Thank you, ma'am," he replied as he put his foot tentatively onto the first step.

I left him there and went to find my own train. I was lucky to make it just in time. I ran up the steps and found an empty seat next to the window, leaning my forehead against the cool glass. No sooner had I gotten situated than the train whistle blew, and we pulled away from the depot.

It occurred to me that I hadn't even thought to ask the soldier's name. He remained more of a mystery than not. But I felt changed. Here I was feeling so very sorry for myself and my circumstances, when there were others who suffered greater disappointments and heartaches than I dared to imagine. I should be ashamed. I remembered my mother telling me that the quickest way to get over feeling sorry for myself was to find someone else who had it worse and render them service, and just then, I knew it to be wise counsel.

Thinking of my mother made me wonder what it would be like to be home again. Was she really growing better, as my father had indicated in his letters? Maybe he was just saying that to ease my worries. I was soon to find out. I would see for myself if she had improved. But I dared to hope.

Chapter 2

I didn't have sufficient time to write and tell my father I would be coming home. By the time he received such news I would likely already be there anyhow. After a solid week of travel by train and river steamer and then on foot, I found myself again in Richfield as the evening was setting in, with no one to welcome me.

After my wanderings and worldly experience, Richfield seemed, in my eyes, to have shrunk. Perhaps that is how it is for any person accustomed to the small surroundings of a pocket-sized town. They've never been anywhere or done anything, then travel abroad and get some life experience, only to return to their origins again and find it is not what they remembered it to be. I stood at the corner of the main street looking this way and that, observing the diminutive spread with a mix of familiarity and peculiarity, marveling at the phenomenon.

I knew this place well. Little had changed since I'd left nearly two years ago. Yet those two years had made it seem all new to me. There was the mill Sam's father owned, where Sam worked before he left with the army. There was the modest little school house and the white clapboard church with the bell tower looming above it. But it was as though I saw it through the mist of dream. A sense of already having experienced this moment engulfed me, causing eerie goose pimples to rise upon my flesh as I wandered along in a trance-like state.

I headed down the dusty road, into the lane that would lead me home, passing the mercantile and the milliner's shop. *Millinery and Fancy Goods* the store window read. A new shop that I didn't remember was next to the smithy, where Mr. Haney's brother still worked, where Mr. Haney himself would hopefully work again someday if he should return from the war. It was a saddle and harness shop advertising that they used the best leather around.

Eventually I passed all of the shops and then a few town homes before the road was nothing more than a path through solitary stretches of trees and fields. I had walked for roughly four miles when I came upon the farm, old widow Derringer's home. With no lights flickering in the windows it was dark and seemed somehow sad to me. Perhaps the place was as lonely as I was.

The two story brick could be seen from the road, and I followed the lane to the front yard. There was the great tree which had been struck by lightning. At one time it had probably been a wonderful shade tree. Now it was a hulking dead thing, with branches splintered and scorch marks where bark had once been.

The porch ran the full length of the front of the house, with five posts holding it up. The roof above the porch needed to be redone, the black shingles looking much deteriorated by the elements, patches of green moss growing in some parts. The posts and awning and window casings were all a faded white. There were two windows with twelve panes in each window on the second floor and two smaller windows on the main floor each with a set of shutters. A chimney ran up the left side of the house, made of the same red brick as the structure itself.

This is my home now, I thought. And the only thing that could have made the moment any better was if Sam had been there with me. I didn't see the sagging porch or the crooked shutters or the overgrown yard with the shrubberies so large there was no decent view of the front door. I saw a house Sam and I would live together in and raise our child in. I saw rooms filled with memories of us, and windows that would witness our joy, and doors that would open to great possibilities. I stood leaning against the peeling picket fence missing some of its boards, with black gaping holes randomly sprinkled, and I looked at the house and saw potential. I saw what *could* be, not what was, and the place developed into a charming cottage right before my eyes.

I would sew curtains of cheerful calico, paint, trim back the overgrowth, and plant flowers. There would be a rocking chair on the porch where I could sit and rock the baby in the cool shade in the evenings. I'd have Sam build a swing to hang from one of the trees that our boy could play on while I watched at the window as I worked in the house. And there would be lilac bushes to leave a sweet scent upon the breeze in the summer. I could see it all.

In the midst of my daydreaming it grew late, and I grew tired. I eventually drifted away from the fence and continued down the road, instinct showing me the way as twilight grew into darkness. Another seven miles passed before I reached my childhood home. I walked up the path, feeling anxious, but I couldn't say exactly why I felt that way. I knew this place well. Shouldn't I feel peace?

Over near the barn was where I fell and broke my leg. There was a pond a short ways away where Caleb and I went fishing and collected frogs. A wooden ladder bridged the gap between ground and leaf cover in the tree that Caleb and I climbed, where we had a bird's eye view of all below from the small platform we had built there. Just behind the house was the garden I had helped my mother tend every spring and summer. Why should I feel apprehensive? Then it dawned on me. I didn't belong here anymore.

Caleb was gone. I had only memories of him now. My mother was no longer the same person, and my father was nothing more than a survivor, brave in his misery. I'd been gone for two years and was nothing like the girl that left this place. Everything was changed. Everything was different now.

I approached the door, lingering on the step as I collected myself, straightening my jacket, smoothing my skirt before I knocked softly. Soon the door opened and my father stood before me. When he caught sight of me a look of amazement fell over his face. He was older, thinner, his hair more gray, but he was the same man I had always known.

He let out a deep breath and blinked rapidly a few times before he said in astonishment, "Serena!"

"Hello, Father."

Chapter 3

I could see that my father was in shock. He looked me over, as though he weren't sure it was really me. After a brief moment of uncertainty, he stepped forward, collecting me in his arms, and clasped me so tightly I felt as though I might pop out of my skin. I dropped my bag and wrapped my arms around him too, and I began to cry. I was not only very glad to see him but relieved that I was home, that I felt safe in his arms, as though I were a little child again, and the moments of uncertainty I'd experienced just a short time ago seemed to flee when his strength enfolded me.

After a while he pulled away from me, looked me over again long and hard with a tender smile, and said, "Well, look at my girl-all grown up!" He bent down, picked up my bag, and then ushered me into the house. "Come in! Come in!"

Everything was as it had been before I left. This was both reassuring and frightening. Surrounded by all of the things I had known since my youth, I began to feel as though perhaps the last two years hadn't happened at all. It was all a false recollection, and I was back where I'd been the day I resolved to leave.

I sat down at the table with my father and he gave me some cold leftovers from supper that I did my best to swallow down. As I ate he asked me questions, which I answered mostly in half truths. His joy at seeing me again gave me a moment of guilt, for I had left him and misled him, although I couldn't help but feel glad also to be with him again.

"Why didn't you write to tell me you were coming?" he asked.

"There wasn't time. I thought I'd go on with the 121st. But Sam didn't want it. I left camp the same morning they did."

"Are you well?"

"I am. It was a long journey and I'm tired. But I'm well."

"Your mother and I got your latest letter. But it was nearly three weeks ago. We wait for news and try and keep up with what's going on in the papers."

"Sam and I got word on the fourth that the whole army would be moving out. They abandoned winter camp at Grant's order. There'll be a battle soon, of that I'm sure. When Sam heard the order to move out, he said he was worried for my safety. He wanted me to come back home."

"That was wise of him."

"I hope you don't mind, but I'll stay with you, until I can get things figured out."

"Yes, of course."

"Did you receive my letter about the place Sam arranged to purchase? I mean to get the house together and move in as soon as I can," I told him.

"The Derringer place?"

"Yes, that's it. I stopped by there on the way home. I can't be sure how much work it'll take, because I only saw it from the yard, but I have plenty of time to work on it now, don't I?"

"Sam did the right thing, sending you home," Father said thoughtfully. "I've long worried of the dangers you've faced, out there at the front. I've felt like the worst sort of coward allowing it. But you are no child anymore. I can't choose for you."

"Coward?" I was surprised.

"Me here, a strong and able man, and you there, doing what you could for our country. It shames me."

"There's no shame in it, Father. Someone had to look after Mother and the farm. With Caleb gone there was no one else," I reasoned.

"Well now, your mother is doing well. You'll see. She's gone to bed, but in the morning you'll see."

"I missed her very much. And you, Father. I missed you very much too."

"You sitting before me now, I can hardly believe it," he smiled broadly. "I'm just so pleased."

"It is good to be home again," I said half-heartedly. And I *was* pleased. I was happy to see my father, because I truly had missed him, but Sam was there, lingering at the back of my brain, casting a shadow over my joy. I wondered where he was and what he was doing at this very moment. I wondered how long I must go on without him, before he returned to me and made me glad again. Perhaps my father could read my thoughts.

"He will come home soon enough," Father said.

"Who, Sam?" I dropped my eyes and fiddled with the fork on my plate. "I hope so, Father. It hurts my heart to be apart from him."

"You are young and feel things more deeply. When this is over, you'll see it is but a brief moment in life's great passing."

"Father…" I began. I leaned back in my chair, my eyes dropping. How do you speak of delicate things to your father? It was never natural for me, even when he was all I had and I didn't have a mother to speak to. I wasn't sure what to say, but I knew I must tell him. I wasn't strong enough to carry the knowledge of it alone.

"What is it, daughter?"

"There will be a baby in the fall," I said softly. Again, I had stunned him. His mouth fell slightly open, and his eyes widened. He rubbed the stubble on his chin and then smiled slightly as he cleared his throat.

"When Sam wrote me in the winter to tell me he had met up with you, how he found your company agreeable, and wanted to ask my permission to marry, I thought it was a good thing. I knew Sam Barlow to be a good boy. I believed Caleb would've been proud and glad for it too. Two people he loved the most, together. He thought so highly of Sam. And it was no secret to me how you felt about him."

"It wasn't?" I asked in surprise. I didn't think anyone knew how much I loved Sam, how much I pined for him. I thought it was a secret I'd kept well, that I had hidden from everyone.

"When you left, I figured it was… well, that you couldn't stand to see him go," he revealed. "So I was glad for you and for him when you were married. It is a father's greatest and only wish that his children have joy. It pleases me you'll now have a family of your own."

"Oh, Father-" I began, tears pricking my eyes. "What if he doesn't come back to me? How will I go on?"

I knelt before him, resting my head on his knee. My father put his hand on my back and rubbed it tenderly. I stayed there for a long time, crying and letting him console me. Everything I felt from the moment Sam had told me I must leave burst through me and out of me. I felt like a draining sieve, rushing emotions pouring through every crack. I knew I was being selfish, but I didn't care. I embraced my vulnerability and let it wash over me until I was spent and there was nothing left.

Chapter 4

I could sense someone near, watching me. I have never understood how it works, how you can physically feel someone's eyes upon you without a touch to alert you to it. But there it was, the prickle of my hidden mind alerting me someone was there, someone besides me. I struggled to lift my eyelids, resenting the bright morning as it burned my eyes. I blinked rapidly and did my best to focus and grow accustomed to the light. There, sitting on the edge of the bed, was my mother.

She reached out shyly and stroked my hair, studying me closely. "What happened to your beautiful hair?" she whispered, as though she were afraid to break the silence between us. I noted she avoided looking me in the eye as she spoke to me.

It was the first time in such a long time that I had heard her voice I was speechless. My eyebrows furrowed, and I looked at her curiously. "Mother?"

"Why did you cut it?" she asked.

"Lice," I lied.

"Oh. I see. No matter, you are still my pretty girl. And you've come home."

"Yes, Mama." Emotion made my voice waver. "I am home."

"I should've let you sleep, but I couldn't wait to see you," she admitted. "When you were a baby, I would tiptoe to your cradle to make sure you were breathing. You were so still, and I would grow frightened trying to see the rise and fall of your belly. And then in a panic, I would nudge you awake to make sure that indeed you were still breathing." Her expression was tender and forlorn. "Just now, I had the same terrible urge."

"I don't mind," I told her. "How are you?"

"Well," she said simply.

I drew her hand to my lips and kissed her palm. "I have missed you, Mother. Oh, how I have missed you."

After breakfast I rifled through my things, disappointed to see the moths had gotten at some of them. Three of the dresses were useless to me now, ravaged by the winged pests. I had a skirt and blouse and one of mother's old round dresses, which I chose to wear. I put my wedding dress out to air, thinking I'd give it a good washing when I got the chance. I presented myself to my mother, who was taking care of the dishes.

"Let me do that for you," I offered.

"I am nearly finished now," she insisted.

"Well, I've just looked through my old dresses and there isn't very much can be salvaged. I'll have to see the dressmaker."

"I can help you sew some things," she offered. This took me aback. It was true that mother had been a gifted seamstress, but that was before… I studied her closely. She hadn't really smiled since I first saw her. Her face was shrouded in an almost frown, and her eyes conveyed the pain she must be constantly carrying. There was no joy in her, but at least she was among the living again. I consoled myself with the thought she may perhaps find happiness again somewhere down the road.

"If you wouldn't mind, I'd be very grateful. You know I'm not exceedingly good at needlework." There was a pause before I said, "I've asked Father to take me to town."

"Yes, he's hitching up the horse and wagon."

"Would you like to come too? You could help me choose some fabric."

She seemed to hesitate, as though she were unsure of herself. "No, I have things to tend to here."

"All right, then." It grew awkward, as I didn't know what to say or do. I thought I should move in to give her a hug, but she wasn't expecting it, and it went very badly. I ended up trapping one of her arms to her side and then pulled away quickly before it grew any more uncomfortable.

When I came outside into the yard, I saw Father pulling the wagon around to the door.

"What happened to Gus?" I asked, seeing that this horse was not familiar to me.

"He's gone to meet the maker," Father told me. "This here is Dandy. Bought him about a year or so ago."

He helped me climb up the wagon, where I situated myself on the bench, and off we headed down the lane. The weather was already warm, and I had to shield my eyes despite the shade of my bonnet. It was silent, but for the rhythmic clopping of the horse's hooves as we traveled down the road.

Eventually, I said what I was thinking, "You were speaking the truth about Mother."

"Yes."

"I thought perhaps you were just saying she was better so I wouldn't be worried."

"No, she is gradually recovering day by day."

"I'm glad. But I don't understand it. When I left she was… well, I thought then she might never return to us."

"After you left, things were hard."

"I'm sorry, Father."

"You are your own person. No use in you feeling sorry for living your life. I want it that way. There was nothing here for you. I understand. But after you left, I couldn't stand it any longer. I wasn't doing your mother any favors by letting it go on that way, and I knew it."

"You were doing the best you could, Father." He cocked his head and gave me a look that said, *don't patronize me*. I hadn't meant to, but

I had misspoken. Father was not a child, and I had no right to treat him like one. "I'm sorry," I apologized.

"The truth is sometimes hard to hear, but isn't it better to live in truth than to lie to yourself, to everyone else around you? There ain't no favors in it. I can tell you that."

I was surprised by his speech. Was this the man who was afraid to finish his sentences, who allowed my mother a steady diet of Laudanum to keep her from experiencing her grief? That was not the only thing I was thinking. I was thinking I'd lied to him about where I'd been and what I'd been up to in order to spare him. I wondered if he would feel the same if I was to tell him my truth. Would he be angry, or disappointed, or ashamed, or all of them mixed together?

Again I said, "I'm sorry."

"You shouldn't be. You leaving made me see it clear. I gradually gave you're mother a smaller and smaller dose of her medicine until she came out of it. It wasn't easy. Near the end she took it hard, got the shakes and begged and begged…but eventually she came through it."

"I asked her to go into town with us."

"She said no, I'm sure. Mother is still working through some things. And the thought of town frightens her a bit. She says she's not ready to face all them people. I suppose she worries about what they think of her."

"What about you, Father?"

He looked at me in confusion. "What about me?"

"How are you?" He acted as though he didn't know how to answer such a question. I seemed to have caught him by surprise.

"With the good Lord's help, I'm making it day by day. And I'm mighty pleased you're home now, mighty pleased."

We spent the remainder of our trip in relative silence. When we got to town I hesitated but figured that perhaps my father would understand when I made a request of him. "Would you mind getting the key to the house?"

"I'd assume John Barlow has it," my father replied. "If he's the one made arrangements."

"Yes, I would think so," I stammered. "I just don't know that I'm ready to see him yet."

Father studied me suspiciously. "Why not?"

"I don't know," I said, although I did know. I was afraid to face him. It had been a long time now, nearly a year and a half since we'd last met. But when I'd seen him at winter camp, I had been Frank. He was sure to recognize me. Maybe I could manage to put it off for a time, until my hair grew long again, until I looked more like a woman. "I just don't feel like answering a lot of questions. He'll want news of Sam, and I don't feel up to talking about him right now.

He nodded sympathetically. "All right. You take care of what needs to be taken care of, and I'll go see John Barlow."

He headed toward the mill, and I went the opposite direction to the hardware. Once I was finished there, getting paint and nails and other things I knew I would need, I went and picked out some fabric and thread for some clothing and for the curtains I intended to make. I put them in the wagon and headed over to the mercantile to purchase some food goods. When I was finished, I went back to the wagon again.

While I waited, I looked over a newspaper that I had purchased, hoping there would be some news on the movement of troops. There seemed to be nothing noteworthy, which frustrated me. I wondered how I would live through Sam being gone, with nothing but secondhand news to keep me informed. Everything that was happening right now would take days for me to find out about. It left me feeling somewhat helpless.

I tossed the paper aside in frustration, stewing over it. Father returned, clutching the key in his hand. He climbed to the wagon seat and sat down heavily next to me. Taking my hand in his, he placed the key in my palm and curled my fingers shut over it. I waited for him to speak but he didn't he gave the reins a little tug and the horse took the lead.

"How did it go?" I finally asked.

"Fine. John says he hopes to see you soon. He was just as surprised as I was by your return." Father looked at me out of the corner of his eye, as if he were measuring my reaction. "He said he'd like to come by the house next week to call on you and see what he might do to help."

"It's really not necessary," I responded a little too quickly.

"Mind telling me what you got against John Barlow?" Father asked. This time he didn't look at me. He kept his eyes safely on the road.

"Nothing," I insisted. There must be *some* perfectly good explanation for my not wanting to see him. I thought about it a moment before I began. "I just...I just worry about whether he will like me or not. I'm certainly not Prudence Sayer or Cora Hendricks." I fleetingly wondered what those two girls thought about Sam marrying me after he had told them he couldn't have a steady girl because he wasn't sure what would happen while he was gone. They were probably pretty sore over it. I knew I would be.

"What they got that you ain't?"

"Lots of things, Father. They're both beautiful girls. Beautiful... beautiful and well-accomplished girls. I don't know that I ever would have caught Sam's eye, if I hadn't been the only girl for miles around. That there is the whole truth of it." Thinking about it made me squirm. If I had them as competition, and Sam was able to choose from us all, I wondered if I would be Sam Barlow's wife at all right now. It made me feel miserable and small.

"I don't like to hear that kind of talk. I raised a good, sensible girl. But you ain't acting much like her." His words were not angry or meant to condemn, but I felt the sear of them anyhow.

"I was hoping my hair would grow out some, that I would be more presentable. I just don't want to make a bad impression."

"If Sam found you agreeable, I'm sure that his family will too. John's a good man. Never known him to be the uppity type that thinks he's too good for others. Give him a chance, Seri."

"I know you're right, Father. I'm just not ready yet," I replied.

There was a pause and then Father turned and asked, "What happened to your hair anyway?"

"Lice."

"Lice, huh. Well, that explains it."

When we came up to the house, Father turned the horse off the main road and down the lane right up to the front door. He tethered the reigns to the broken down fence and came around to help me from the wagon. With his assistance I climbed down, traipsing through the overgrowth to get to the door. Anticipation made my heart beat a little faster, and I could feel the blood course through my veins.

The key slid easily into the lock and turned with a smooth click. The doorknob squeaked a little as I twisted it in my hand. The hinges, which needed a good oiling, resisted with a plaintive screech as I pushed the solid door open.

Chapter 5

I swung the door wide, the sunlight from behind me streaming in to thinly illuminate a path for my feet as I ventured in, excited and scared all at once. Father held back, unloading things from the wagon bed, as though he were giving me a moment to experience it on my own for the first time. I allowed my eyes to adjust to the dim interior and then looked around with an intense curiosity.

The front entrance was small, a modest little square with the stair landing directly in front of me and an oversized doorway on either side. The doorway to the right was a sitting room with wood floors and exposed wooden beams on the ceiling. It looked as though a piano was left behind, perhaps too heavy for anyone to care to try and move it. On the far wall was a door that led to a bedroom.

There too, a bed had been left behind with rope weaving and a mattress that I could see right off would need replacing. It was stuffed with molding straw. There was enough room for the bed and perhaps a chest of drawers. The window allowed for plenty of natural light in the daytime.

The doorway to the left of the entry was a dining room, where I could fit a sizable table. Off of that room was the kitchen. A spacious fireplace occupied the outside wall, soot darkening the brick encasement above. I believed the wide planked hardwood floors to be walnut. Directly across from the fireplace and below a large window was a dry sink. Built around the window were some open shelves and a cupboard. I rubbed away some of the dirt from the window panes and peered out onto the back lawn where it was very green and very overgrown.

I went back through the dining room and into the front foyer and took the stairs quickly, wanting to see what the house held for me on the second floor. On either side of the staircase were two bedrooms, the ceiling slanted to mimic the pitch of the roof. Upon first inspection, I knew. I could feel it. This was a place I would grow to love. It would be more than a house. It would be a home. It was as though the walls were whispering to me. *You belong here. I've been waiting for you.* Welcoming me with an eager anticipation that equaled my own.

I sentimentally thought perhaps it had been lonely these many years. After all, the purpose of a house is to shelter and make warm. And here sat the two story brick cottage, empty and idle, unable to fill the measure of its creation. With no life to fill it up, it had no purpose-no occupants to give it a soul. I whispered back to it, "I am home."

When I returned to the main landing Father had begun carrying things through the front door. He dropped his load and looked around inquisitively. I don't know why but I nearly held my breath, waiting to see what he would say. For some reason his approval of the place was necessary to complete my joy in the moment. I needed him to like it too.

"Not too shabby," he said favorably. "Ought to be a right nice place for you." I felt relieved that he had praise and not dissatisfaction for the place.

"It'll need a great deal of work, but I believe it'll clean up nicely," I agreed modestly, with a proud nod of my head. "I'll begin right away, I think."

"Well, let's get the rest of it unloaded, then."

I followed him out into the yard and helped him carry everything but the fabrics I had chosen into the house. When we were finished he climbed back onto the wagon to go home. I squinted against the sun to look up at him.

"Should I come around supper to fetch you?" he asked.

"That's too much trouble. I'll walk back when I'm finished for the day."

After he had gone I went back into the house, shutting the door behind me. It was so very quiet, and I stood in the shadow of the entryway with my back pressed to the door, my eyes shut, feeling the silence wash over me. It pleased me greatly to know I belonged here, it was my home, and when Sam came back to me this would be our place. Soon people would call it the Barlow Place and forget all about the previous Derringers who once resided here.

Nothing like hard work to make you feel a kinship to a dwelling. I thought of the hut that Sam and I had shared, and how it had been so dear to me because we had built it ourselves. I could sense, with a giddy optimism, this would be no less of a challenge with an even greater reward. I took off my jacket, rolled up my sleeves, and got to work.

At the end of a very long day, I gathered up the rubbish I had accumulated and made a pile in the front yard to burn later. I decided it was about time to head home for the night. Feeling weary to the bone, I trudged along the road in the dusk, letting my feet lead the way home.

I thought perhaps if Sam were there to see all of my hard work he would have been pleased by it. The next morning, I got up early and went over to the house to begin work again. I took the moldering mattress from the bed and dragged it clumsily out the front door where I tossed it into a heap on the pile I started. The smell of mildew tickled my throat and made me cough. It was after noon when I finished cleaning out the house, all of the rooms swept out, washed down, and windows cleaned.

I went out into the yard and started the rubbish pile burning. I stood mesmerized by the flames, my eyes glazing over from the smoke and color holding my arm over my mouth and nose to try and block the smoke and odor. A movement in the distance caught my eye and I became aware of a wagon pulling off of the main road and turning down the lane. No one else knew I was here, except for my father. I wondered who it could be.

There was a moment of inspection, with squinted eyes and trained concentration, when the two of us, each in anticipation of discovering one another, curiously focused upon a face. As he pulled up, I waited. The moment of understanding dawned upon both of us nearly simultaneously. His face fell as my shoulders slumped, and I took several steps back, my eyes hastily dropping. When I recognized Sam's father it was too late to do anything but stand there like a fool. I felt a surge of sudden sickness shoot through me, my gaze darting side to side, searching for some route of escape. But there was none. My face burned, and my throat felt as though it had closed off.

In that moment of our eyes meeting, I knew that he knew.

Chapter 6

There was no doubt that he had put two and two together and the expression on his face was one of confusion and bewilderment. With my gaze firmly fixed upon the mattress, I dared not glance up to discover what his next move would be. I simply stood there dumbly waiting, a feeling of shame sweeping over my body and overcoming me completely.

After what seemed a very long pause, the springs of the wagon seat squeaked as he climbed down from the rig, his two sons following after him. He gave the impression that he was just as uncertain as I, standing with his hat in hand, shifting his weight from one foot to the other. I could see Sam in him, his dark hair, his lips, his chin, but Sam was still very much his own man. The discomfort only grew when I noted the older of the two boys, Jacob, seemed to realize too. He'd been with his father when they visited camp the winter before last.

Jacob looked at me and then to his father as though he was waiting for his father to tell him what to do next. "Father..." he began with a voice that mirrored his confusion.

"Go get started on unloading, son," he commanded.

"But-"

"The wagon, go unload the wagon," John said more sternly this time.

Jacob and Hyrum started slightly, perhaps surprised by John's sudden gruffness, and then did their father's bidding and went back to the wagon, pulling wood and shingles and buckets of tar from the bed. I was left in semi privacy with John Barlow, still without any words to explain myself. Eventually, he had mercy upon me and spoke.

"I am John Barlow, Sampson's father," he introduced, offering me his hand. I couldn't make heads or tails of it. It took me a moment to register he wanted to shake. When I realized what he was trying to do, I lurched forward to accept his hand.

"I am Serena," I stammered.

"It is good to finally meet you," he replied. I was stunned. Was he really acting as though he didn't know who I was? Was he actually going to play it off as though he didn't recognize me, as if we had never met? I felt relieved but also grateful to him. Tears came to my eyes, which I couldn't fully explain, and I did my best to keep them in check. I nodded slightly, to let him know that I understood and would play along with the game.

"It is so good to meet you too, sir."

"None of that 'sir.' You may call me father, or John, or whatever else you like," he chuckled nervously. "Sorry, Sam is the first of my children to be married, and I don't rightly know what you should call me, but don't call me 'sir.' That don't seem fitting."

"Yes," I agreed. "It doesn't."

"We were pleased to hear you came on home. I hope the trip was not too disagreeable."

His manners were impeccable, but his mannerisms revealed to me that he was very uncomfortable. His speech was halting. His eyes wavered and never truly focused on mine. He fidgeted with his hat, put his hand in his pocket, and then drew it out again several times. Yes, he was nervous and probably wanted out of the situation nearly as badly as I did. I tried to behave as though I was at ease, but I wanted nothing more than to be alone again, to have them be gone and the house to myself. I wondered what he would tell his sons once they were on their way, what he would tell his wife and the rest of the family.

"It was long but as agreeable as *could* be," I said.

"Good to hear." After too long of a pause he took a deep breath. "Well, we come to repair this roof of yours. So we'll just be getting to it."

"That was awfully good of you. I am very grateful."

"That's what family's for, helping out when needed. With you all just starting out, we'll do all we can to lend a hand. How's the inside? Need any fixing?"

"I've worked on cleaning it and getting it in good order. I'm afraid there's not too much to it right now, but you ought to come in and take a look," I offered.

He followed me into the house, and I showed him from room to room. He didn't say anything, just tagged along behind me. He went to the doors and tried them all, opened the windows, checked to make sure that the mechanics of the place were in working condition. I was proud of the fact that the house was clean and tidy, even though it was empty.

"Me and the boys'll clean up the yard, cut some firewood for the winter pile," he offered.

"Thank you. That would be very good of you."

"Well, we'll get to the roof then," he said and he went out front with Sam's brothers.

I drifted about the house, doing my best to stay busy while they worked. I didn't want to go out front with them. I was terribly uncomfortable to have them there. I could hear the sound of their footsteps and the clatter of tools and supplies overhead and felt completely unnerved by it. What must he think of me? What would he tell others? The anxiety it caused nearly made me lose my mind. I was so fretful that I didn't know what to do with myself. Thankfully Father showed up an hour or so later to pick me up.

When I came out on the porch I had to ease my way around the roofing supplies and ladders and tools to get to the yard. Father climbed down from the wagon and approached Sam's father and brothers. They had worked up quite a sweat laboring in the hot sun, the shingles and wood littering the yard proof that they had been hard at it.

John Barlow stopped what he was doing long enough to speak with father. "Hello, Matthew," he called from his perch on the roof.

"Hello," my father replied. The two of them were speaking in loud tones in order for the other to hear. "Looks as though you've been busy."

"We'll stay at it awhile longer before we stop for the night. It'll take all of tomorrow too, I should think, and then some."

"I'd be willing to pitch in if you need an extra hand," father offered.

"Oh, no. I've got the boys here. They are handy to have about, my boys."

I felt a twinge of pain for Father, who had lost his only son and was now stuck with a needy and useless daughter. But father didn't seem to react at all to John Barlow's words. Perhaps it had only been me to think of Caleb in that moment. I stood awkwardly while the two of them carried on a rather loud conversation as they shouted to one another from the yard and the roof.

"Well, I ought to be getting along. Seri wants to check the post office and we must leave now to be back home in time for supper."

"Take care then. We will see you tomorrow, Serena," he said pointedly to me.

I could appreciate what he was doing, he was trying to convey to me his intentions were good, he was friendly, and I should be at ease with him. It didn't help. I could feel nothing but the rush of shame and intense discomfort when he spoke to me.

"Tomorrow, yes," I said with a shy nod. I retreated quickly to the wagon, climbing up to the bench in short order. I tucked my hands between my knees and waited impatiently as Father took his time urging the horse on. As we pulled away, I caught one last glance of Sam's father and brothers working away on the roof.

Chapter 7

The interior of the Mayflower Post Office was cool and dark. Now that evening was coming on, there wasn't very much natural light to filter through the windows. I went to the booth where Aida Turner sat in her chair, squinting her dark eyes in order to read a novel in the twilight shadow. Aida had worked the post office as long as I could remember. There were many whispered discussions regarding Aida among the ladies of how tragic it was she had never found anyone to share her life with. These dialogs inevitably included the ugly terms *old maid* or *spinster* and nearly always ended with the phrase *it's a shame* with clicking of tongues.

Aida had to be nearly thirty now, which meant that her life was nearly over. I wondered if she was sad about that or if she didn't care. Who's to say, it may have been her own choosing that she had never married. She was a decent looking girl, and always seemed pleasant enough when I had observed her in the past, politely asking how your day was and giving everyone she encountered an agreeable smile.

Aida kept the post office much like she kept herself, neat, precise, and simple. The envelopes and papers were all immaculately organized, never a thing out of place. The floors were swept, and the ledges dusted. Each day she diligently sorted the mail into the rows of slots behind the counter, taking special care to deliver the official looking letters in person. Better to receive bad news from a sympathetic party right away, than to be handed it from a cold, unfeeling hand that lingers behind the barrier of a window at the post office.

When I approached her she hastily stuck a pink ribbon in between the pages she was reading and set the book aside to give me her full attention. She stood up from her stool, rubbing her fingers over her dark hair, pushing stray wisps away from her freckled face and back into place.

"May I help you?" she asked with what was meant to be a smile. It was more tired than cheerful. She had perhaps seen a long day, and now at the close did not have the stamina to do more than turn the corners of her lips up. Or maybe she was just preoccupied with the plot of her book, her mind on other things, and she was sorry to have to lay it down to help me. At any rate, I appreciated her attempt at the smile.

"I have a letter here to send, and I wanted to check and see if I had gotten any letters as well," I told her. I slid the letter I had written to Sam across the counter toward her.

"Name?"

"Serena Stark." Once I said it I realized I had said it wrong. "I'm sorry. I meant Serena Barlow," I corrected.

Aida became almost immediately interested, coming to attention with her shoulders perking and her head snapping up, so that she might study me closely through the window. It being a small town, I was sure that word had gotten around about Sam and me marrying. It had been two years since I had left, but I thought that she doubtless didn't remember me-Sam, maybe, but not me. I hadn't come around enough for her to be familiar with me. That same self-conscious uneasiness crept over me, and I had the strangest need to straighten my bonnet, tidy my dress, to make myself more neat and presentable. I didn't like being scrutinized.

"John Barlow said you'd come home," she said pleasantly. "I'm sure you've got a tale to tell after being a nurse for so long. I would love to hear all about your adventures. Perhaps someday you'll share them with me."

"It really wasn't as exciting as you might think."

"And it seems I owe you congratulations as well, for Mr. Barlow has also told me that you and his son were wed."

Thinking of Sam made me happy and sad at the same time. I nodded. "It is true."

"That is excellent news," she said, flashing me a smile. I noted that she had one crooked tooth, which I liked because I thought it balanced out the rest of her flawless appearance.

"Thank you." I didn't know what else to say to her. I felt as though I were standing there quite dumbly while she smiled at me. I wondered if she was expecting something, but I wasn't sure what that might be. While I thought it was very kind of her to be so friendly, I was ready to leave, and I was eager to see if Sam had sent me anything.

I cleared my throat. "Have I received any letters?"

"Oh, well, let me look," she offered. She went and rummaged around through neatly stacked piles and came back with two letters. "They arrived yesterday afternoon."

The thrill at seeing those two thin slips of paper neatly folded and addressed to me made my heart beat faster. I snatched them from her hands and inspected them quickly to make sure they were indeed mine. There I recognized Sam's poor handwriting and couldn't help but grin broadly. "Oh, thank you!" I told Aida Turner.

"You are certainly welcome." She was very happy right along with me.

I nearly stumbled over the steps as I rushed back to the wagon. "Father, he's sent word!" I cried waving the letters in the air for him to see.

Father gave me his hand, and I took it as I drew myself up the side of the wagon and back on the bench next to him. I ripped the papers open eagerly and unfolded them, checking the dates to see which I should read first. The older of the two was dated May fourth, the very day I had left on the train.

Dearest Serena,

Gone only a few hours and I feel the loss of you as if you were an arm or a leg that had been amputated. Marcus Carvey told me even after they took his leg he could still feel it there and it hurt terrible. Well, now I know how he must have felt. You have been with me since the beginning, and now that you are gone, it does not feel right. And while you aren't here in body, I feel you here in spirit. I feel you here in my heart.

I know you were upset when last we spoke, and it is a memory I try not to dwell on because it pains me to think of it. I hate to think of you being cross with me. I hope you have come to understand that I done what I done for your wellbeing and out of my love for you. I pray most fervently you were safe on the journey home, that you are now well and safe in the bosom of your family.

I have little time to write, as we are on the march and being pressed hard. You know how that is. I just wanted to assure you my thoughts are with you, and I desperately desire to see your lovely face again. We must have faith a reunion will not be long in coming and I will have you in my arms before another winter. I should like very much to be there before the baby comes.

I have written also to my father asking him to help as much as he can with getting you situated and making sure you are well cared for. I have explained to him we will be having a child, to eliminate the need for you to have such a conversation with him, as I know it would be a difficult discussion for you to have.

Your Devoted Husband,

Sampson John Barlow

It struck me as funny he should sign his full name at the conclusion of the letter. I quickly read through it again. Several things stood out to me. First of all, I'd left Sam concerned and worried about my being angry with him. I must remedy that as soon as possible. I didn't want him stewing over whether I was still upset with him. Although I was disappointed over the fact he sent me home, I hadn't been *angry* with him. I felt terrible he should think I was.

Second of all, he missed me. This made me feel redeemed somehow. I was important to him. I made a mark. As strange as it was that he should compare me to an amputated limb, it was the sweetest thing I'd ever heard. He suffered as I did. He missed me as much.

Third, he had written his father. I wondered what his letter entailed, if it gave any explanation whatsoever as to my being Frank while simultaneously being Serena. He had told his father about our expecting. That was a relief, because I wouldn't know how to begin to broach the subject. Being with child was a delicate, if not borderline taboo topic.

It wasn't so long ago that a woman of social status didn't make any public appearances once she began to show her condition. The same was not so for the country ladies from around here. Necessity kept a woman active and working up to the day of birth in these parts. But it was still a subject matter you didn't discuss. I had heard women talk of it in discreet tones amongst themselves. But it was not generally a thing brought up in mixed company. The idea of speaking to a man directly about my condition was a painful notion for me.

Feeling that I'd neglected the other letter long enough, I launched into the text of it soon after finishing the first. It was written only a day later than the first, on the 5th. That was a week and a half ago. New to me, but ancient history for Sam. Where was he now? Was he still on the march or had he reached his destination by now?

Chapter 8

Dearest Serena,

There has been much speculation on several counts. First off, the others are concerned over you and why you left so abruptly. They find it nearly incomprehensible you chose to desert after being so stalwart for so long. It is difficult to keep my mouth shut on the matter. I would like to tell them you are now my wife and I have sired a child with you. But I am sure it would seem too extraordinary to them that Frank and I took up with one another, you know. Don't want to distress them with the thought of it. So I let them gossip and have a little chuckle over their theories. Reed Haney knows and the two of us enjoy exchanging jests over it behind the rest of their backs.

Next, we all wish to know where we are headed and what our role will be in it. There will be a battle, but it remains unknown as to where and when. I am glad you are not here to suffer the march and the heat. I am not glad you are gone. It is a strange mix of emotions I experience, leading me to believe there is no black and white, there is only the gray. And I don't mean Confederate gray.

I dreamed of you last night. I dreamed you tapped me on the shoulder to wake me, like you have so many times before. I thought you smiled and laughed when I was surprised and asked what you were doing there with me, why you weren't at home. You told me not to worry, you were only visiting. And then I dreamed we spent the night together. What a pleasant dream it was. But you were not there when I awoke. Gone only a day and it seems like ages to me.

I wonder what you are doing today. You must still be on a train somewhere, tired and alone. That makes me downhearted. Wherever you are my thoughts are with you. When you get home, things will be better. I wonder what you will think of the house? Don't try to do it all on your own. I know how stubborn you are. You must let your father and my family help you. I wish I were there to help you myself.

Pray for a swift resolution to things. Pray we will be united again soon. You are in my thoughts constantly. I look at your likeness so I do not forget what you look like. I hope you bear the same fondness for me as I do for you.

Your Devoted Husband

Sampson John Barlow

When Father and I returned home, Mother had not only finished a skirt and blouse for me in record time, but she also managed to drag out my hope chest and go through it to see what I had and what I would still need. She gave me the hope chest when I was thirteen. I didn't do much towards acquiring the things I would need to start my own household, not because I didn't want to marry, but more because I thought no one would ever ask.

The chest had some linens and a few quilts that mother and I pieced. I had a crock pitcher and five mismatched tea cups sprinkled with a variety of clustered, delicately painted flowers, which had been collected from both of my grandmothers. Although I had not actually known them personally, mother gave their cups to me in remembrance. My mother's mother had already passed away before I was born, and Father's mother was from England. She passed away without my meeting her when I was seven years old. These few items were sadly all that I had to show for my poor planning.

Mother had started a collection of her own for me. She had her best seasoned cast iron skillet, two dishes, and forks and spoons and knives from her set, some bottled fruits and vegetables, a mixing bowl, and the cradle she used for Caleb and me. Stacked inside the cradle were piles of miniature dresses and flannel jackets with ribbons that had been tied and set with age, and tiny booties and caps crocheted from delicate and fuzzy wool yarn, and square little blankets made soft by repeated washings. Father must have told her about the baby. When I saw all of the things she meant to give me, I was deeply touched.

"Mother, these are your things," I protested.

"I mean for you to have them," she said with her lips in a determined thin line. She obviously didn't want to discuss it any further. She always was a very modest woman, and I supposed it bothered her to have that sort of attention upon her.

"I…" I stopped myself from saying what I was going to say. I didn't want to upset her. I felt as though I was speaking to someone I hardly knew and lacked the ability to discern how to communicate with her. "Thank you. It is much too generous of you."

"Your father and I want you to have the beds you and Caleb used and your grandmother's china cupboard and one of the rocking chairs too."

I wanted to hug her, but I thought about the other day, how I had attempted to do just that and it had turned out very badly. She was not comfortable with me and, in turn, made me ill at ease as well. Instead of embracing her, I took her hand in mine. "I am grateful, Mother. So very grateful."

"Your father and I had help too, when we were first married. All young people ought to have someone that will lend a hand and get them on their feet starting out. That is how it should be." I could tell the subject was closed as far as she was concerned. She didn't want anymore said about it.

I spent the rest of the evening sewing and pressing curtains out of the fabric of pale yellow with red flowers I had purchased in town. Mother watched me while I worked. I am sure she could have done better, but she didn't say anything about my clumsy stitches.

I wondered if she was disappointed in the fact I was her daughter and that none of her remarkable talent had seemed to rub off on me. When I had examined the blouse and skirt she had presented to me, it really was an incredible piece of work, the perfectly even stitches small and close together and done in such a short time. She must have done nothing but work on them yesterday and today. Although I had done my best with the curtains, they couldn't hold a candle to her handy work. It made me feel a deep sympathy for her. Surely she felt bad she wasn't able to pass her skills on to me despite her best efforts.

"I think I should be able to stay at the house after tomorrow," I told her and Father. Father nodded as though he agreed. Mother seemed troubled by it but didn't protest. I thought I would win her over by pointing out the positive features of the house. "I still have much to do, some painting and such, but the house is in good enough shape I should be all right there. And there is a piano, Mother. I think it will need tuning, but it is lovely still."

"We will get Mr. Sandleburg to come out and look at it," Father promised.

"Perhaps you will visit, Mother?" I asked.

She became uncomfortable again. She concentrated a bit too closely on her needlework and noncommittally shook her head both in a yes and no fashion, for a moment making me think that she was agreeing and then the next moment making me think she was refusing. I alternated between excitement and disappointment.

"I'm not sure, we'll see," she said vaguely.

I left it at that, realizing that she would likely never step foot off of the farm again. Father had warned me she was not ready to make any public appearances, but I foolishly thought that a visit to her own daughter's home was not a public appearance. It was asking too much of her. I tried not to take it personally, but there was no stopping the scorching rejection I felt.

The next morning, I was up bright and early to get to the house. Father let me have hay for a mattress for the bed, which he loaded onto the wagon with all of my other household items, my hope chest, and the furniture my parents had given me. Before I left, Mother presented me with a meal, gave me a sterile pat on the shoulder, and then I waved good-bye as I drove away. When we pulled into the yard, Sam's father and brothers were already hard at work. The roof was nearly done, and Hyrum was painting the trim around the windows white.

I began my own projects. I helped Father unload the hay, but once I began to help him unload the heavier things Hyrum rushed over and intercepted. He wedged himself between me and the wagon as though he were guarding it from me. I raised my eyebrows in amusement, experiencing male chivalry at its best. I knew that I didn't need him to move the furniture for me, but I was grateful that he was willing to help.

"Let the men get it," he said to me.

I wasn't used to being treated like a lady, and I hardly knew how to react. When I was in the army, although I was small and the general consensus was that I was a young boy, they had never cut me any slack. They'd expected me to do my fair share. Things were vastly different now. What more could I do than allow him his kindness. I stood aside while he and father hefted the china cupboard, and the beds, and the rocking chair, and the hope chest into the house. I drifted in after them, hovering about and pointing out where I would like each piece situated and in what room. I spent the rest of the morning stuffing the mattress with hay, making the bed with my linens and quilts, and arranging things on shelves so it was just as I wanted it to be.

It was late afternoon by the time I had finished. I wandered out into the yard where Sam's father and brothers were now hard at work, cutting back limbs and trimming hedges. It was a relief they had done the yard, because that is one chore I was never very fond of. I stood silently watching them for a time before I spoke.

"It is looking a sight better than it did."

"Yes, well, just needed some hard work and sweat put into it," John Barlow replied.

"I thought I might walk to town and check the post office and see if perhaps there is a letter or news in the papers today."

"I will give you a ride," John offered.

"Really that isn't necessary," I objected.

He wiped his brow with his arm. "I insist. Boys, you finish up here. I'll be back for you shortly."

Jacob and Hyrum nodded their heads as they continued to work. There was no getting out of it. To refuse him again after his insisting would have been very bad manners indeed. I didn't want to appear ungrateful for all of the work they had done on the house, or for the fact that he was willing to give me a ride. John went and got the wagon and helped me up onto the bench. And then I found myself alone with the one man I would have done anything to avoid at that moment–my father-in-law.

Chapter 9

The ride to town was mostly quiet, with a few awkward exchanges. The conversation did not flow. It seemed as though neither of us quite knew what to do with ourselves. It was that feeling you get when you want desperately to seem at ease, but everything you do only proves that you are not.

"I certainly do appreciate your help," I told him, sounding too overly pleasant. I was mentally kicking myself for the chirpy and obviously fake good will.

"We are family now. That is what family does for one another," he said modestly. "No need to thank me."

"Family or not, I am grateful."

After a moment's pause, John said, "We received a letter from Sam. He told us that congratulations were in order."

I was acutely aware of my discomfort and the absence of familiarity with him. I barely knew the man, and I didn't know how to respond to him. I nodded one little nod to acknowledge his statement. But it hardly seemed adequate. Besides the fact we lacked any kind of connection, I was also painfully aware the truth of what he knew about me lay between us, and it seemed outrageous that I should sit there and act as though I didn't know. I was dressed as a boy when he last met me, and I couldn't go on pretending it had never happened. And now to further complicate things, he wanted to discuss my pregnancy. It was all too much.

"Yes," I acknowledged vacantly, feeling a sense of dread rush through me.

"Sam's mother and I are very pleased."

"I am glad," I told him. Now it grew silent again. In my mind I had worked over what I might do if we were ever able to speak frankly with one another. Here was my opportunity. I knew what I wanted to say, and so I gathered my courage and spoke quickly to get it over with.

"Listen, I have grown accustomed to deception, but I've never been comfortable with it. I'm sure this would just linger painfully between us for the rest of our days if I didn't say something now. I know you know. I don't wish to dwell on it, but I want you to also know I am a good girl, I am a decent girl. I had my reasons for doing what I did, but I never behaved improperly. Sam and I, we…" I couldn't figure how to tell him I was not like those girls who followed after camp seeking money for their attentions. That he might think me capable of such a thing was unbearable to me. I figured there was no polite way of addressing such a topic. I ended up blurting, "What I mean is that I was raised to be a moral person with certain standards."

He seemed mildly amused. A smile tugged at the corner of his lips, but never fully formed. "Tell the truth," he said, "I figured it was none of my business."

I felt immensely foolish. I took a deep breath and let it out, my body deflating as the air left me. It had taken all of my courage to speak to him about it, and then he had simply dismissed it. I knew, at least, I had done what I thought I should. I had said something instead of just pretending it had never happened.

"Although you say it's none of your business, you must have had some curiosity over it," I accused.

He shrugged. "Still none of my business."

"Sam didn't know I was a girl," I said. "Not at first. No one did. So he has no responsibility in it. I do. But I really didn't understand the full weight of my decision, not until I had to come home and face it. Now I must live with the consequences of it, knowing what I have done. My own father doesn't even know what I was up to."

"My son has a good head on those shoulders of his. I trust that he knows what he's doing. If he approves of you, then I do too. And from what I know of your family, there's good reason for approval. You shouldn't worry about it any longer."

I swallowed hard, blinking my eyes rapidly. His reaction was a bit of a surprise to me. I expected to have to convince him of my character. Only he had accepted it on good faith without any persuasion at all. It was then, without words, the two of us came to an understanding of one another. I told myself I didn't want to ever let my father-in-law down. I would be faithful and true and prove my worth to him at all cost. His gracious acceptance of me had won my unconditional loyalty.

"Thank you," I murmured.

He seemed confused by my gratitude but replied, "You're welcome."

When we got to the post office I waited for him to help me down, as a proper lady should. I walked in to the post office, allowing my eyes to adjust before I approached Aida, the clerk.

"Hello again," I said with a smile.

"Good day to you too," Aida replied.

"I was hoping I might have a letter?"

"Nothing today," Aida said with a sympathetic smile.

"I didn't think so, but I thought I would ask anyhow. I would like a newspaper, please."

"That's three cents."

I gave her the three pennies and eagerly accepted the *Harper's Weekly* from her, quickly scanning the front page once I received it. The headlines were in a dark, bold print and alerted me right off there was news, that there must have been a substantial fight. I read it impatiently, skimming over the particulars with a growing sense of dread. I couldn't help but pick out General Sedgwick's name in the body of the article, which meant whatever had transpired, Sam was involved in it.

The Military Situation

The Grand Movement of the Army of the Potomac is in progress. The order of General Meade to march was issued on the morning of the 3rd. General Gregg's cavalry took the advance and was engaged until late at night in repairing the roads leading to Ely's Ford, on the Rapidan. About midnight another cavalry division moved to Germania Ford and both were successful in establishing crossings. The Second Corps broke camp at midnight, effected a crossing at Ely's Ford about daylight on the 4th. The Fifth Corps crossed at Germania Ford, followed by the Sixth. No serious opposition was met until the advance reached the Wilderness, General Lee not having anticipated the movement. It threatened his communications with Richmond and forced him out of his formidable entrenchments around Orange Court House, covered by Mine Run. Accordingly, on Thursday morning Lee exhibited a determination to advance with the design of cutting our line. General Warren was directed to attack, which he did at about 11 A.M. A determined musketry fight of an hour and a half ensued, in which Warren drove him from his position, with the infliction of great loss. Griffin's division of the Fifth Corps led the attack and suffered severely, its loss being nearly 1000 in killed, wounded, and missing. The enemy next attempted to interpose an overwhelming force between Warren and Hancock, the latter of whom, in accordance with orders, was marching his corps rapidly to form a junction with the former. His advance came just in time to circumvent the rebel General, who, at 2 ½ P.M. commenced a terrific onslaught on the divisions of Birney, Gibbon, and Getty. The fight raged hotly until sometime after dark and resulted in the complete repulse of the enemy at all points. Our loss in the engagement was about 1000 men.

During the night picket firing was kept up, and early on the morning of the Friday, the 6th, the battle reopened, the enemy making a desperate attempt to turn the position of the Sixth (General Sedgwick). This assault was repulsed. The enemy then attacked the left under Hancock, but were again driven back. The battle then became general along the entire line. At a quarter past eleven o'clock a desperate assault was made upon the Fifth Corps, particularly the Fourth Division, commanded by General

James S Wadsworth. While rallying his men, leading the charge, this noble soldier was shot in the forehead, and fell dead. A partial lull ensued about noon, when another desperate assault was made on General Hancock. His veteran columns temporarily yielded to the shock, but recovered their line with a most frightful slaughter. At about seven o'clock in the evening the enemy made a furious charge upon Sedgwick's right, turning his position. A stampede ensued, but the line was soon re-established. Our loss in this engagement was quite heavy, but that of the enemy was said to be greater. General Seymour and a considerable number of our troops were captured in the confusion. Later in the night another assault was gallantly repulsed, reinforcements having been sent to Sedgwick's help. The estimate of losses on the right wing are given as follows: Wounded up to six o'clock, Friday P.M., 2100; killed up to same time 500; killed, wounded and missing during the turning of the right wing, 4000; total 6600. During Friday night General Lee withdrew from the field, establishing himself on a new line. This movement was caused by a maneuver of General Grant, who had swung his left flank (Hancock's Corps) down toward Spotsylvania Courthouse, threatening Lee's communications forcing him to retreat. Dispatches received from Grant, dated Monday noon, indicated that Lee made a stand at Spotsylvania Courthouse, six miles from Wilderness, but no battle took place. General Grant replenished his army from supply trains, so as to advance without them. The same dispatches bring the sad intelligence of Sedgwick's death. He was killed in the fighting Monday by a ball from a sharpshooter. General Wright, commanding the First Division, succeeded to the command of the Corps. General Robinson, and Morris were wounded. The former commanded the Second Division of Warren's Corps, the latter the First Brigade of the Third Division of Sedgwick.

The Losses.

Among the casualties reported from the field are the following: Generals Sedgwick, Wadsworth, and Hayes killed; Generals Getty, Gregg, Webb, Owens, Robinson, and Morris wounded. A large number of Colonels and other field and line officers were killed. Our total loss is believed not to exceed 15,000. We took 3000 prisoners up to Friday night. Very many of the wounded were but slightly hurt, and walked from the field to the rear.

The rebel Generals Longstreet and Pegram were severely wounded, and several high officers of Lee's army were killed and wounded. Intercepted dispatches from General Lee acknowledge the loss of "many wounded".

Fredericksburg was occupied on the night of the 8th, and the deport of our wounded was at once established. Stores and medical help arrived promptly the following day.

As I finished reading, I was struck dumb. Sedgwick dead along with 15,000 others! I felt all of the blood drain from my face, and I became light headed. I opened my mouth as though I might cry out but no sound escaped. My legs buckled, and I fell to the ground upon my knees clutching the paper. Aida rushed from around the desk toward me at the same time that John Barlow burst through the door, both at my side nearly simultaneously.

"Sam!" I cried. My distress was overwhelming. I felt my pulse so hard and fast that it hurt. The light and air both seemed to be drawn from the room all at once, and I thought briefly I might lose consciousness.

"What is it?" John Barlow asked as he took my hand and my arm and helped me from the floor to a nearby bench.

"Sedgwick is dead!" I began to shake all over. "Sam would have been fighting with him." My voice sounded like a pathetic squeak. I thought of my own experiences in battle, and I felt a physical ache in my chest wondering what Sam had been through, if he were dead or alive. I couldn't say how I knew, but I was certain that some unlucky tragedy had befallen him.

John snatched the paper from my tremoring hands and began reading the article. I could see his face fall, as he too read about the great loss. He understood. He knew, just as I did, that Sam may be dead. For a moment he was contemplating what he should do, and then he set his mouth firmly, as though he were resolved on the matter, folding the paper and laying it aside.

"We don't know anything for a certainty yet," he said.

"Sedgwick… I just spoke to him not two weeks ago. He's gone. And Sam…"

"Sam will get word to us when he can."

I dissolved into tears. "I should have been there with him," I mumbled in a nearly imperceptible sob. "I should never have left him."

"Let's get you home," John said. He took my arm again and helped me to my feet. I leaned against him heavily for a moment, until I remembered myself. I was behaving shamefully. Sam's father must think me a spectacle. My back straightened, and I held my head up, although I still couldn't manage to control the tears. Aida rushed ahead and opened the door for the two of us. I stumbled down the steps and then let John boost me up onto the bench of the wagon where I sat limp and weak, feeling as though the world were crashing down around me. And it was. My world, my whole world was Sam. If something happened to him, there was nothing left for me, no reason to go on.

Chapter 10

William hile I journeyed home on a train and took care of the business of getting the house ready, Sam was headed deeper into enemy territory so that Grant might faceoff with the Confederates at Spotsylvania, Virginia. How did they have the heart to call it a draw after thirty-two thousand men sacrificed their lives for it?

Sam recalled the fighting, but did not recall when he was hit. He woke in the early morning hours, when it was still dark, but the stars were gone and the moon, pale and translucent, was beginning to fade in the sky. His first thought was that he was still among the living. And the terrible throbbing down the left side of his body and the skull splitting ache in his head were proof of it. There is nothing like pain to let you know that you are yet alive.

All around him were the bodies of the dead. He had fallen alongside of them but had managed to hang on to life, while they were taken home to find their peace and rest at last. He was in a great deal of discomfort yet could think of nothing more than the terrible thirst that made him desperate for water. Summoning up what little strength he had, he called out into the shadows, his voice feeble and broken at first and then growing steady as he continued. Still he was hoarse, the words gravelly and harsh in his throat.

"Please, I need water."

Dark forms, sooty and vague, similar to the players in a nightmare, floated like goblins before him, and then as they drew nearer began to solidify and take shape. Their faces were gaunt, streaked with gunpowder and dirt, and the clothing hung from their frames loose and ragged and obviously not the deep blue of the Union uniform. The group located him among the thick pile of bodies he was nested among and worked to move several bodies out of the way to get to him. At that point, Sam could do nothing to help himself, he was at their complete and total mercy. One of them took a knee and knelt down next to him, looking him over curiously.

"What have we here?" the man asked.

"Please..." Sam begged. "Might I have a drink from your canteen?"

The man seemed to think it over, his eyes taking in all of Sam, working over the situation in his head. He finally must have decided that it would be best to help, and he took his canteen, uncapped it, and put it to Sam's lips. Sam drank it as though he had gone days instead of only hours without water. The man recapped his canteen and watched Sam thoughtfully.

"Any better?"

"Yes, thank you."

"It was a fine day to die for the rest of these fellows. But God must have had other plans for you."

"I am hurt very badly. I could yet die," Sam responded.

"Not if I have anything to do with it," the man said with a laugh. "If God spared you I shall do the same." He got up from his knee, standing tall and magnificent over Sam. "I will be back."

Sam had no choice but to wait and hope that the man would return as he promised he would. True to his word the Reb came back with a chaplain and a stretcher. Sam groaned from the pain as the two lifted him on the stretcher and carried him away from the field. Now it seemed like some time later to him, he was so uncomfortable with being jostled about, that they finally brought him to an apple orchard where they took him from the stretcher and lay him on the ground beneath one of the trees.

"I expect they will be around shortly to have a look at you," the man said.

He went to leave, but Sam stopped him. "Thank you for your kindness, sir. Short time ago we were doing our best to kill one another, and then you turn around and save me from death out on that field."

"I ain't a bad sort, and I suppose you ain't either. Just doing what we must, you and I." Then he left Sam there.

Sam felt so weak and terrible that he shut his eyes and tried to settle his mind on anything but the unfortunate situation he currently found himself in. It was not long before he surrendered to his exhaustion and fell off to sleep. Throughout the day, he would wake, become aware of his terrible surroundings, the wounded pouring in from the field, the surgeons rushing about, and collecting those who needed immediate attention, and the reality began to set in. There were dreadful cries from those who were laid out upon a barn door, which was used as a makeshift surgeon's table, as limbs were being hacked off and bullets extracted.

The pile of arms and legs grew, the number of men increased, the pain in his side vexed him sorely, and the hunger in his belly only added to his distress. Now as evening set in again, Sam was approached by a familiar face. Alden Carroll rushed towards him, lost and desperate. He seemed so relieved to see Sam that he nearly wept. Alden fell to his knees at Sam's side, and he was nearly hysterical, close to tears, but excited and eager all at once. Sam thought Alden was on the verge of a breakdown.

"Sam Barlow!" he cried.

Sam tried to focus his eyes, to make sense what was happening, to identify who was speaking to him. "Brother Carroll."

"Alden," he clarified.

"Yes, Alden."

"Boy is it ever good to see someone familiar!"

"Do you have water?" Sam asked. "Or food?"

"I will see what I can find," Alden assured Sam, and then he was gone for a time.

Sam looked up at the sky from between tree limbs and thought for a moment that it was snowing. This didn't make sense to him, because he knew that it was too warm and he knew that it was May. But in the confused state he was in it took him some time to realize that the apple blossoms were being blown by the breeze and fluttering, gentle, white petals were settling upon the ground and the men beneath. He reached up to brush several of the petals away from his face, where they tickled his lip and cheek. He recognized that it would've been an immeasurably beautiful scene if not for the dying men who profaned it.

When Alden returned he had with him two ears of corn, one in each pocket, and a canteen of water. He helped Sam to a drink first, cradling Sam's head in his hand and putting the water to his lips. "This is all that I could manage," he apologized. "I will get a fire started and put the corn on."

As promised he started a fire near Sam and laid the corn close to the flames to cook. When it was done, the two of them ate one ear each. Sam had a difficult time with the steamed flesh using only one hand, but he managed to eat it all, sucking every bit of the corn from the husk so that there was nothing left to it. He lay back, happy to feel the warmth of the fire on his feet.

"I'm wondering if a surgeon will have a chance to look at me soon. I'm in a great deal of discomfort."

"In the morning I'll go and see if I can fetch one and bring him back to you," Alden replied.

"I surely am grateful you found me. I can do nothing to help myself. And it is good to see a familiar face."

"I thought the same when I saw you over here under this tree. I thought *God be thanked*. I don't think I'd have survived without you."

"How did you become separated from your brother?"

Alden dropped his eyes, the despair evident. Whatever had happened to his brother must have acutely affected him. In the moment he was a man without a tether to keep him bound to reality. Sam thought fleetingly he resembled a frightened child, wary of everything and everyone around him, his eyes darting this way and that as his mouth drooped in a frown. He was concerned that Alden would lose his ability to function if he were pushed any further. He waited patiently for the other man to speak without prodding him.

"Some gray back run him through." Alden choked out, as though he were still amazed over it. His gaze was unfocused and drifting. "I grabbed him up and thought to carry him to safety. But I didn't get far when they overtook me. I didn't have my weapon, I dropped my rifle so's I could carry Leonard. Well, there was nothing to do but do as I was told. I went with them as a prisoner, still carrying Leonard. I asked them to look after him, but it was too late, he was gone." His voice quivered and he began to cry. "He was dead. No last rites or nothing." At those words he completely lost it and wept piteously. "They'll put him in a hole for sure with all them other men out on the field." The thought of it was too much for him. He bawled like a baby, barely able to get out the words, "Oh, it will break Ma's heart."

"I know it's hard on you," Sam consoled. "But listen here, Alden…" He waited for Alden to get a hold of himself, waited to make sure he was paying attention. "Listen! You must be comforted in the knowledge that he is in a better place."

"What will I do with myself? Don't remember never having him around-Leonard. I should have done more for him. I should have…I should have looked out for him better."

"You done what you could, Alden. You can't do more than that," Sam said. "Can you?" Alden didn't answer. "Can you?"

"No," he agreed. "No." He did his best to try and get control of himself. After a moment he murmured, "Tomorrow I will go and find a surgeon."

The darkness fell as softly as a feather, gradual in degrees of light. The fire was warm and comforting. Sam was still very hungry, but he had at least gotten an ear of corn, so the pain of an empty belly was not so sharp. Alden settled in next to him, under the apple tree. The two were lulled to sleep by the calls for help, for water, for God, for mother, for home, or a dear one's name, the suffering that surrounded them somehow placating.

Chapter 11

Shortly after dawn, Alden was up and gone-determined, it seemed, to make good on his promise to find a surgeon. Sam was left alone again, feeling the ground beneath him growing harder by the minute. He hadn't moved much since they put him there the day before yesterday, and his back and legs began to ache. He tried shifting to alleviate the discomfort, but it did little good. He looked at the tree above him and contemplated his situation. He knew he must surely go to prison, for he was now a prisoner of war. This gave him cause to worry.

There was no end to the stories of brutality which transpired behind the walls of those prisons, Andersonville and Libby. The South didn't have the means of providing for their own troops, much less the enemy soldiers captured in battle. Sam knew whatever was ahead of him would test him to the limits.

He still possessed the wherewithal to know that anything he carried on his person would be considered fair game, most likely to be confiscated once he was taken to wherever it was they were taking him. He was glad then he sent his father's pistol and most of his money with me. At least they couldn't take those things away. But he was still concerned for the paper money he now carried and for the daguerreotype of the two of us after our wedding. They both were precious to him, and he didn't wish to be parted with either.

With great effort he removed his cap, carefully unpicking stitches with his fingertips in the lining of the inside of the hat to make an opening just large enough to stick the picture inside for safe keeping. He felt someone would have to inspect it very thoroughly in order to find the picture there, and perhaps they would only casually look over it and give up quickly when they didn't see anything right away, in which case the picture would be safe.

Then he took the money from his pockets and folded the bills neatly and precisely into the smallest little bundles he could force them into, making sure that the folds were crisp by running over the creases with his fingernails. Using his pen knife, he worked on his coat to pry the tops of his buttons off. The inside of the buttons were hollow. There he put the larger of the bills, filling each one and then snapping the tops of the buttons back in place again. They were nearly too bulky to fit, but Sam somehow managed to force all of the tops back on and conceal the bills within.

When he ran out of buttons, he placed the rest of the rolled up wads of money inside the hemline of the coat at intervals, so that they were not all bunched up together and made obvious. Then he put a few dollars back in his pocket, where they would be easily found. Perhaps if they searched him and found the money in his pocket, they would then think to look no further.

The exertion from completing this small task tired him out completely. After he finished he leaned his head back and breathed deeply. Sam did his best to keep his eyelids open, but they felt so heavy, and it seemed an impossible task to him. After fighting to stay awake for a short while, he dozed off to sleep again while he waited for Alden Carroll to return.

Unaware of how much time had passed, Sam was roughly awakened by the hands of strangers as he was lifted from the ground and placed on a stretcher. He started.

"Where are you taking me?" he slurred. He was alarmed. Not only did he feel disoriented after being awakened, but he didn't see Alden Carroll anywhere around, the only person he knew.

"They are moving everyone out," said one of the fellows who was helping to transport him.

"My friend, he went to try and get a surgeon to look at me. He won't know where I am. Could you wait a moment?"

"Can't be helped," the other replied, not bothering to look at Sam. He kept his eyes carefully from Sam's. It becomes harder to tell someone no when you've made eye contact with them. Sam thought the man didn't want to have any human connection with him so that it would be easier to do his work without feeling remorse or sentiment.

"He said he wouldn't be long," Sam insisted.

Without Alden, he was not entirely sure he would survive. Who would get him water? Who would make sure that he had food?

"Maybe you could let me stay a bit longer, take some of the others first, and come back for me a while later," he suggested.

"We ain't got the time to mess with you," the one who avoided eye contact said. He didn't seem angry; his voice was more of a neutral calm. Sam knew then they wouldn't be of any help to him. He stayed quiet because it would do no good to plead. He lay back and let them do their jobs without further protest.

Sam wasn't only afraid for his own welfare. He imagined Alden returning to an empty piece of ground where Sam had been and worried what might happen when he found the only familiar face he knew gone. Sam felt pangs of empathy burning in his chest. Alden was only hanging on by a thread after the death of his brother. The man had never been truly alone, always in Leonard's company from the time of birth. He thought the only thing that kept Alden from losing it completely was having Sam there to keep him from the fear and terror of being on his own. Sam was afraid that Alden Carroll wouldn't be able to cope with him gone too. But there was nothing to do for it now. Sam wasn't free to do as he wished in the matter.

Being bumped and jostled around did little to ease the discomfort that Sam was experiencing. He was in terrible pain and did his best to grit his teeth and bear it well. The two men loaded him none-too-gently into the back of a wagon with other wounded Unions. When the wagon bed was full and overflowing the driver pulled away, heading to a yet unknown location. As the wheels traveled over uneven ground and jolted the occupants of the wagon around, a collective groan went up from the men. The heat and flies did their work too, and the lot of them was a miserable assembly.

Eventually the wagon came to a stop. Sam used his good arm to leverage himself up to see over the side of the wagon bed. His depleted strength only allowed him a brief glimpse. A train pulling nothing but cattle cars sat idle upon a set of railroad tracks. He let himself fall back onto the stretcher and waited.

Two new sets of hands worked to move him and the others from the wagon to the car. The dark interior of the cattle car was crowded and smelled very similar to rotting beef, but was more likely rotting flesh of living men. The smell and all of the moving around made Sam sick to his stomach, and if he had any food in it, he might have thrown up. As it was, he just felt queasy and disoriented, as though his head were spinning and his stomach were turning all at once.

After a long delay, the train finally began to rumble, and the more pleasant smell of smoke filled the cramped car. The whistle blew, and the sound of steam and steel against steel alerted him to the fact that they would be leaving soon. To where, he did not know.

Chapter 12

By the time Sam reached Augusta, Georgia, he had been in and out of consciousness for the better part of two days. The soldiers who were well enough to walk on their own were marched from the train depot to be held in an empty warehouse under guard. The guards were all very old men who were too sickly or too old to fight properly as soldiers, but because of the shortage of southern men they were required to still do their part in whatever capacity they were able. It was their duty to watch with their rifles to ensure that there was no trouble with the prisoners.

The others who were wounded or sick and unable to walk or leave the train of their own free will, Sam being among them, were transferred to what once was a church, where a hospital had been set up. The hospital was run by the Sisters of Charity, women dressed in black crepe, somber bonnets, and veils. They were once proper nuns but now served as nurses because the need was so great. By this time Sam was feverish, dehydrated, and in a great deal of pain. They brought him in on the same stretcher he had occupied since he was loaded up and shipped out, and they sat him next to a window in a room with no furniture. The floors were stained with blood, and the place smelled strongly of vinegar.

In his weakened state, Sam was unaware of where he was or what was happening around him. He suffered from violent hallucinations which forced the nuns to tie his arms and legs to the stretcher to keep him from rolling on to the ground or from harming himself.

"Don't hurt her! Don't you hurt her! Stay away I say! Serena! You get away from her, you hear?" He was screaming.

One of the sisters attempted to sooth him. "It's all right," she was saying softly, with her hands pressed into his shoulders as she tried to keep him still.

"Don't let him hurt her," he begged. "Please, don't let him touch her!"

"We'll take care of her. Don't worry."

Two of the sisters struggled to peel away his clothing and saw that from just above his knee, in the meaty part of his outer thigh, to his already scared shoulder and down his side in between, there was shrapnel embedded in his flesh. His skin was a terrible color, sallow and swollen around each chunk of metal that peppered his body.

The wounds had gone for days without any medical attention and were now in an advanced state of infection. For the better part of the day two of the women knelt next to him and concentrated on extracting each small missile. Using a large pair of tweezers, they tugged forcefully at the twisted bits of metal, until they felt a piece give, after which it was dropped with a loud ping into a crock bowl lying on the floor next to the stretcher. When they finished their task his body looked more like wormwood than human flesh. They washed the wounds and then left him alone to see if he would make it through the night.

In the morning Sam awoke in a hazy, disoriented state, feeling the pain anew and sweating profusely. The sheet they covered him with was discolored with his dried blood, and after lifting it up and peaking under he was alarmed to discover he was completely naked beneath. He hastily pulled the sheet back down, feeling ashamed for his lack of clothing as he searched about to try and acclimate himself to his surroundings. He attempted to call out but didn't have the strength for even that. Eventually one of the sisters came around, saw he was awake, and brought him a drink.

"How are you feeling?" she asked. Her voice was soft and hushed, putting Sam at ease.

"I been better," he whispered.

"We've done what we could for you. They've told us you will be moved tomorrow. Something we advised them against, but they won't let you stay," she said gently. Sam observed she was forty years of age or more, looked as though she hadn't had a good night's sleep in many days, and her eyes were very sad and troubled, her mouth grim. He sensed she felt remorse for the fact that she could not keep him there until he healed properly.

"I'm sure you've done all you could, Sister," he consoled her. This brought tears to her eyes, and he immediately felt bad for having caused her any measure of distress.

"Are you up to having something to eat?" she asked.

"I'd be very grateful."

She went away for a time and then returned with a bowl of fried mush. Sam did his best to prop himself up on the stretcher with his good elbow, flinching from the pain his movement brought on. The woman benevolently spoon fed him the bowl of mush, which he ate ravenously, and then she gave him another drink before she stood to move on to the next man in need. Sam felt panic when he saw she was going to leave him. He was aware of his profound vulnerability, and it penetrated through to his very core. Without her, he would die. His need for her, his complete defenselessness, terrified him as he had never been terrified before. She was a kind face with sympathetic hands that had worked to save him, and seeing her going made him tremble.

"Please..." he begged.

She stopped. "What is it?"

"Where am I?"

"Augusta, Georgia. You're in a hospital, with the Sisters of Charity."

If he hadn't been in such bad shape he might have laughed. As it was, a feeble smile played at his lips. A memory came to him, a memory of the two of us bickering light-heartedly over what we should name our baby. It amused him this should be the place of his deliverance.

"Augusta?" he asked in disbelief.

"Yes," she replied, appearing confused by his reaction.

"If you have time, might you write a letter for me?" he wanted to know, with such restrained pleading the sister didn't have the heart to tell him no.

"I will be back shortly, if I can manage it," she agreed. Before she could go he stopped her again.

"May I have my hat?" he requested before she could leave. This time his voice cracked with emotion.

She must've thought his request strange. Here was a man as helpless as a baby, and as exposed as one too, and this was his one request? She stooped next to the stretcher and pulled his neatly-folded clothing from beneath it. Resting atop was the hat. She laid it on his chest, and he clutched it in his good hand as though it were his salvation.

Sam was comforted by the fact his searching fingertips could still detect the daguerreotype within the lining of the hat. He could feel the warmth of the sun through the window, could see the open space beyond, and didn't feel as claustrophobic as he did on the train. He wondered if he would last through another night but thought if not, he would at least die in the hands of the compassionate Sisters of Charity. He supposed it would be better than within the walls of an enemy prison. He calmed a bit and submitted himself to waiting patiently.

Chapter 13

I received the letter on a Thursday. I nearly gave up hope but something inside wouldn't let my faith die completely. After writing so many letters to so many people, vainly attempting to discover what had become of Sam, I was beginning to wonder if there was any point to it. I was most disappointed in Mr. Haney's response to my inquiries. Marching into battle he and Sam were together. But through the smoke and chaos and trees they were separated. Mr. Haney said his last recollection of Sam was when he saw him charging forward with a valiant yell, his bayonet fixed, as they plunged headlong into a lost cause.

Mr. Haney himself was now recuperating in a hospital just outside of Washington D.C. He was struck through three times by the bullets from enemy fire, and he considered it nothing short of a miracle that he was still alive. So many others weren't as lucky. The 121st suffered great losses, with a total of three hundred and forty-seven men killed in battle. Mr. Haney said our very own Colonel Upton, now promoted to Brigadier-General for his gallantry on the field, suffered from a serious wound. His letter ended quite sadly with an admission that things would never be the same.

When I prayed at night for Sam and his safe return to me, I included both Mr. Haney and Colonel Upton in those prayers. I implored God for so long that my knees were bruised from bowing myself to the floor. None of it seemed real to me. It felt as if I were lost in some hypnopompic daze, my mind processing but not fully understanding all that was happening around me. I felt confused and lacked the ability to remember what I was doing or saying from moment to moment, my memory failing me at random and diverse times. There was a numbness, an apathy in me that expunged my ability to experience emotions. Those first few days I did nothing but cry. Every time I felt I had cried my fill, and it wasn't possible to cry any more, I would think of Sam and my heart would rend within my breast, and it would begin all over again. But now I couldn't cry if I wanted to. I felt as if I were watching myself from afar, as though I did not possess my own body.

It became a habit of mine to rise in the morning, dress and eat my breakfast, and then after cleaning my plate, I would head into town. I enjoyed the solitary walks in the early hours of the day. I tried to focus on the birds singing, or the sound of my feet upon the dirt as it created the slightest little crunch, or the view of familiar sights I had begun to memorize. I did anything to keep my mind off of my current woes, including counting, as Sam had taught me. One, two, three, four… One, two, three, four…

When I entered the post office that morning, I expected to be given another grim shake of the head before I could even ask, as was the response I had grown accustomed to. But that morning Aida sprung from her chair waving an envelope in her hand with the most satisfied look upon her face that I ever saw her wear. "A letter!" she squealed.

I didn't waste time on pleasantries. I ripped the letter from her hand and tore it open in a heated frenzy. Aida was hovering over my shoulder, as eager to find out what the news within might be as a dear friend or relative. After so many days of having me about, we formed a bond sprung from my tragedy. It didn't seem at all odd she was hanging around to discover what the letter held.

Mrs. Sampson Barlow,

I write to you on behalf of your husband, whom I have tended here at the Church of the Penitent Saints in Augusta, Georgia. Your husband was most anxious I should get this letter out to you so you might know he is yet alive as of May 15th.

During his stay here with the Sisters of Charity he was cared for as well as our capacities allowed, with significant damage to the left side of his body. We hope and pray for his swift recovery. He will be with us only until tomorrow, after which to travel by train to Raleigh, North Carolina and then on to Richmond, Virginia where he will be received at Libby Prison.

He wished for me to tell you to be of good cheer. All is not lost. Our Father in Heaven watches over and provides. What is meant to be will surely come to pass, and your husband will be with you again at long last.

He also wished to tell you that he is not so opposed to the name Augusta any longer, as this place has provided a brief moment of refuge and endears him to the title. He also says with a smile that my name might also suffice, as I am named after the Saint who offers protection from storms, and surely this will be the most difficult storm you will be forced to weather.

He also wishes to ensure you of his affections for you, although he says that he cannot do it in the way he wishes with a third party as the scribe. It seems he has not lost his humor in the midst of his difficulties.

I will also pray that the two of you will soon be reunited.

Sincerely,
Sister Valeria

"He is alive." The emotional void I felt for nearly a month broke, and I was weeping tears of joy. "He is alive!"

"It's wonderful news," Aida said encouragingly.

"I must go tell his family," I told her, hastily wiping the tears from my face. "They will be just as eager to hear."

I rushed from the post office to the mill, where I knew Sam's father and brothers would be working. When they saw me running down the street, with no thought as to how I looked to anyone else, they must have understood that I carried news. They dropped what they were doing and hastened to meet me.

"A letter!" I yelled, before we fully reached one another. "He is alive!"

After we shared in the joy, it was then that I realized that he *was* alive as of the fifteenth of May. It now being nearly the end of June, I had no idea what his current condition was. And then I also understood he was on his way to Libby Prison. This was not a place of rest and recuperation. This was the worst sort of place there was. The letter was really nothing more than false hope. What had become of Sam between the writing of this letter and now? Should I ever see him in the flesh again?

Chapter 14

Sam suffered in the Libby Prison hospital for many weeks. He knew had it not been for the Sisters of Charity he would've most certainly died. He wished vainly he could be back there, instead of staying in prison with the unfeeling surgeon who checked on him only occasionally. He was reminded daily of his incarceration and the terrible state in which our country was now in.

When he arrived, rough hands searched his clothing, trying to discover any personal possessions he might have on him. They took his pocket knife and discovered the money he had hidden in the hem of his coat, to which one of the Confederates said, "We seen that trick before," but they overlooked the money he hid in his buttons and the picture of the two of us he concealed in his hat. This gave him a great deal of comfort. It made him feel as though he had some reason for living. They were his things, something that was his secret and his alone, something they were unsuccessful in taking from him.

Sam knew if he wasn't gravely ill they may have done a more thorough search, and he was grateful for his poor condition. Not only did it provide a means for him to keep his belongings, but he would be kept in the hospital and not the prison itself, a far better place to be. Once they searched him, they assigned him a cot which he was made to move to of his own accord and without any assistance. The room was a long narrow place with brick walls and few windows. The cots ran along the outer walls with two rows back to back down the middle of the room.

Sam drew himself up with great effort and moved himself onto the cot they provided, and then, after so much exertion, he fell into a deep sleep. He awoke to the pathetic whimpering of the man next to him. The poor fellow was missing both of his feet and his legs emitted a rank smell, as though they were infected. Sam was moved to compassion for him.

"Can I help you?" Sam asked.

It was not food, nor water, nor the comfort of a warm blanket he sought. The man very wretchedly said, "I must get word to my mother."

Sam was at a loss for what to say. This was not something he had control over. But it hardly seemed the thing to tell him. Sam asked, "What's your name?"

"Darrell," the man managed to reply.

"Well, Darrell, they've sent word to your mother. She will be here soon," Sam lied.

This seemed to calm the man, his ragged breathing became less troubled, and he lay still. "She'll be here soon," he murmured. "She'll be here soon..."

Another man who lay in a cot opposite Sam's, one of the beds that ran down the middle of the room, was sitting up and watching the exchange between Sam and Darrell. He looked about furtively to see no one was observing them and then he came to Sam's side, kneeling down close to him so they might speak without being heard.

"Where do you come from?" the man asked.

"New York."

"I come from Pennsylvania. Cooper Hardy."

"Sam Barlow."

"Where was it you got them wounds?"

"Spotsylvania."

"Heard about it some. Don't get much news in here, and what we do get is from them. We got beat pretty bad didn't we?"

"Yea, pretty bad."

"What was it happened there?"

"All my time, I've never seen anything like it," Sam told him. "Could hardly see my hand in front of my face, the fog and smoke was so thick and the cannons fired on us point-blank, steady as a drum beat. In the midst of all of this I saw General Sedgwick fall. They were picking us off right and left, and he, thinking to boost our spirits I suppose, he starts to taunt them. *Look at em*, he says, *such poor shots they couldn't hit the broad side of an elephant.* He starts to laughing, like he had really told a good one. And then a bullet hits him in the face, and he fell to the ground dead. He always was the sort of man that liked his fun, laughing to the end."

Cooper Hardy was listening intently. There was nothing as precious to a man incarcerated than news from the outside. "Go on," he prodded in quiet tones.

"Not much more to say. I've had the honor of fighting under Colonel Upton for the past few years now. I've always thought him to be a good and upright man. I clearly remember him still mounted-- only fellow in sight on a horse-although all of his staff officers were hit by enemy fire and even our General Sedgwick was gone, still he would not dismount. He would not dismount. He was cheering us, ordering double charge as we opened fire on them. He was pleading with us *Hold this point! Hold this point!*

"He'd rather die than lose ground, the Colonel. As I looked around me I saw the bodies piled up four feet deep, like logs for the wood pile, and the artillery never let up. And Upton, he fell. Don't know what become of him after that. Don't remember much else."

Sam felt a grave sadness at the thought of his beloved Upton falling. He had no way of knowing that Upton survived and was even now recuperating in a hospital in Washington, a sight better place than Libby. Nor did he know how lucky he was to come away only wounded, that he had not been one of the men to fall into the muddy waters that had collected in the trench work of the enemy, where bodies floated like bits of meat in a devilish stew. There was no taking away his feelings of keen loss for many of his fellow regiment brothers who had fallen around him that day. It would forever haunt him.

Cooper Hardy broke the silence with a rough and sympathetic pat on his shoulder.

"Well, Sam. You gone and got yourself captured. And this ain't no fine hotel, but we look after each other here. Just like you done for Darrell there."

"I am grateful," Sam replied.

The other man had been whispering all the while, but dropped his voice even further, so Sam knew he was confiding in him. "I ain't too sick really. I made it out to be worse than it was so I could stay here, but I moan and groan and they take for me being bad off and they keep me."

"How long you been here?"

"Couple of months."

"Have they treated you well?"

"Now I made friends with the surgeon, and he sees to it that I'm well cared for, but them others-they've got nothing but contempt for us, especially that tall fellow with the pretty mustache."

"I'll keep it in mind," Sam replied. "Thanks for the advice."

"Think nothing of it. We look after each other, cause they sure won't. You need anything, let me know. You hear?"

"Yes. Yes, I will."

"Keep your head about you and you may just survive this."

Chapter 15

When I first felt the baby move within me, I was laying still upon my bed, hoping that sleep would soon find me. It was very late, too dark to see the clock upon the chest of drawers. My mind would not rest, and so my body would not either. Sam was all that I could think about. I wondered where he was, whether safe or in immediate danger, and I longed to be with him again very soon. I began to think of outrageous strategies in order to get him out of prison, knowing full well none of my planning would amount to anything. But I couldn't seem to stop myself.

There was a breeze at the window that stirred the curtains, and I could see clearly in the night sky the melon slice of a nearly gray moon. While I fretted over Sam and what I should do, it happened. The smallest little thump from the inside out. I thought if it was from the outside in it could have been comparable to the flick of a gentle finger. As minor as the movement was, I was startled by it.

I rested my hand over the slight swell of my belly and waited earnestly for any other sign of life. After some time it came again. I couldn't feel it with my hand, but I felt it nonetheless. I gave a little gasp of surprise, because I knew it was not my imagination, as I suspected it may have been. It was real.

Over the next several weeks I discovered I could detect the baby's active moments when I sat motionless, or at night when I lay in bed and all was still and quiet. I marveled over every minor prod, thinking it a complete wonder. Up to then I could have been suffering from nothing more than an acute case of indigestion. But when I felt those urges in my womb it somehow felt real, something to be measured, something of substance. It was the only thing that could make me smile. Occasionally it made me break down into tears without any explanation as to why.

I was terribly confused by my mix of emotions which seemed to bound from one extreme to another without any in-betweens. I felt helpless to control them. Mother told me this was normal, but I didn't see how it possibly could be. I disliked myself immensely for my inability to master myself and the helplessness I felt when I thought of Sam in a faraway prison.

I had written countless letters to anyone and everyone I could think of who might have some influence over getting him out. I was told as kindly as possible by many of them they did not have the power to extract him from Libby. In July of last year prisoner exchanges had been suspended along with the ability to send provisions to the prisoners. Up to that point you could at least send food or much needed items to a loved one. Now it was lucky if you got a letter through to them.

I hadn't received a letter from Sam since his stay with the nuns in Augusta and the suspense of not knowing if he was all right or not was killing me. I was making myself ill over it. I felt the heavy burden of patience keenly and longed to do something, anything, to get information.

"I feel I should go to him," I told my mother one day. I had walked home to visit, because I felt so alone and so unsettled in my own little house when I woke in the morning. Mother still hadn't come to visit. I knew if I wanted her companionship I would have to come to her. She put me to work snapping green beans as we sat at the table.

"You know that you cannot do that," she mildly chided.

"Why not?" I asked stubbornly.

"You can't go running off. You have the baby to think about. You need to concentrate on your health and let what happens happen."

"I can't do that, Mother."

"You must. We don't often have a choice in what we endure in this life, we only can choose how we respond to what we are given. You must respond with grace," she replied.

I suppose she realized the advice she was giving me was advice she had not abided by when Caleb was lost. She knew I knew, and we both became uncomfortable. Instead of simply letting it go, she felt compelled to address it.

"I have been weak," she acknowledged. "When Caleb was taken from me, well, I struggled. I faltered. I have not been a good model for you. I know it. I am sorry for that, Serena. I am sorry."

"Mother, I have always been a source of disappointment to you. I know it should have been me who died and not Caleb. Things would've been better if it had been me. I do not fault you for that."

She looked at me in surprise. I kept my eyes upon my work as I snapped the ends off of the beans and then broke them into bite size pieces and dumped them into the bowl. I thought it many times, but never had the courage to voice it. Mother put her hand over mine, to stop me from continuing with my work. I looked up at her reluctantly. She was crying, and so I began to cry too.

"I could never have traded you for him," she said adamantly. "I could never have been made to choose between you two, and I was never sorry it was he and not you."

"I apologize. I didn't mean to upset you."

"If I have ever made you feel that way, I didn't mean to. I've been woefully off the mark as a mother if that's how you saw it."

"How else should I have seen it, Mother? You abandoned me. I had no one to talk to about the things I must know as a woman. Even now he is dead, he keeps you from completely loving me. It's not that I blame you. I know there's nothing remarkable about me. I must be a great disappointment. But it still hurts."

She was silent, her eyes earnestly searching my face. "I had no idea you believed such things. Serena, I love you as much as I ever loved Caleb."

I didn't know what to say. I wanted to believe her, but there was a nagging doubt that wouldn't allow for it. If she loved me as much, why hadn't she loved me enough to be there for me when I needed her so? Why was she still not there for me now? Whether she wanted to see it or not, she still kept me safely at arm's length. She hadn't even bothered to come see my new home.

I went back to snapping beans and did my best to figure out what to say next. There was nothing to say. Finally, I told her. "I received a letter from Secretary of War, Mr. Stanton, yesterday."

Mother saw I was doing my best to switch topics and obliged me. "Yes?" And between our moments of conversation was the comforting sound of green beans snapping.

"A condolence letter more than anything. He doesn't have any new information. He cannot help me. There will be no further prisoner exchanges thanks to 'the South's blatant disregard for rules of civilized warfare.' What do I care for such rules when I know my husband is rotting away in some prison somewhere? They make it sound as though their indifference for Sam's suffering is somehow noble."

"You aren't the only loved one who has petitioned them, I'm sure. There are many others who suffer in a like manner."

I was immediately peeved with her, although I couldn't clearly say why. The fact she was defending them, instead of sympathizing with me, made me feel raw. I felt she was being disloyal to me. I snapped the green beans a little more forcefully and threw them into the bowl.

"I don't care about those other people! I don't care about anyone but Sam! My Sam! And I'll do whatever it takes to get him out of that wretched place!"

She didn't say more, perhaps afraid whatever she said would be met with the same anguished rage. When Father came in from working to eat, he could sense the strain but said nothing, just looked from me to Mother and then back again, wary of the two of us. I left for home shortly after, entering the darkened rooms with relief. I was glad I was alone again so I could feel ashamed for my behavior towards my mother in private.

After the outburst with my mother, things seemed to change between us. The morning after, I got up and got myself dressed, as usual, and was about my daily routine. Now that I was over the sickness and feeling much improved, I could eat from daylight till dark and still want for more. My appetite was like a bottomless void that was difficult to fill.

I had taken to craving a particularly odd breakfast, which surely wouldn't have appealed to me before, but which made my mouth water and my stomach long for it now. I would take a can of spinach and lay it out upon my plate, soggy and stringy in a deep green mass, and on top of that I would place an over easy egg, the whites fried crisp in the skillet with a bit of salt and pepper. When I cut into the yolk it would run over the spinach, and I would eat it with a bit of bread to sop up what was left.

I'd just finished my egg and spinach and was washing my dish when there was a knock at the door. There were days when Sam's family would come to visit, his mother or father or brothers or sisters, but they never came so early. I was at a loss as to who it might be. Imagine my shock when I opened the door and there upon the threshold stood my mother.

Chapter 16

She wore an expression of wide eyed apprehension, her hands working feverishly as she twisted the cinched strings of her miser purse. My reaction could've hardly put her at ease. I stood there dumbly looking at her, feeling confused and caught off guard.

"Mother?" It had the sort of surprised quality to it you do your best to hide under normal circumstances for fear it may insult. We stared at one another for a while before I came to my senses. "I'm sorry, how rude of me... Come in! Come in!"

I stepped aside out of the doorway and she came in. The way she behaved was like an animal wary of its new surroundings. She looked this way and that, her shoulders slightly hunched and her posture alert and ready. She stood in the entry as though she were waiting for someone or something to assail her, but she wasn't sure from which direction the threat might come.

"I didn't know you were coming," I said, for lack of anything else to say.

"I can come back another time," she offered.

"No! I am glad you are here. I just didn't expect it..."

"So this is your new home," she said.

"Yes," I replied. I was able to shake myself out of my disbelief and come to attention. "Yes, it is. May I show you around?"

"Of course."

"Shall I take your bonnet?"

She worked to loosen the ribbons and handed me her bonnet and her purse, and I hung them from the banister of the stairs. We wandered through the rooms, she making comments here and there as she observed the house and how it was arranged. I watched her closely to see what her body language might say that she was not verbally saying. But it was difficult to tell anything from her behavior, because she was so tense, so nervous, it seemed to be the only thing I *could* read upon her.

"The curtains turned out quite nicely," she commented as she ran her finger and thumb over the hem. "Very cheery."

"Thank you."

I showed her to the parlor, which contained the piano and the rocking chair and nothing more. "I know there's not much to it yet, but I often use the rocking chair you gave me," I said.

"Have you had the piano tuned?"

"Yes. I peck at it now and again, but I can't play like you."

"You were becoming quite satisfactory as I recall."

She was speaking of a time nearly four years ago now. Under her tutelage I mastered the ability to read and play some of the moderately difficult pieces, but I could hardly have been considered gifted. Now as I played the piano, I was getting to know it again, becoming re-acquainted as I struggled to remember how to move my fingers in the quick, fluid way she'd tried to teach me.

"It's been a long time," I reminded her. "I am having a difficult time getting my fingers to obey. But I am getting a little better each day."

She ran her gloved fingers over the ivory keys as if she were petting them. I watched her, remembering how it was one of my great joys as a child to listen to her play, to watch her reverently hunch herself over the keys as she made love to it with her hands.

"You should play," I suggested.

"Yes?"

"Yes."

She tugged her gloves off, taking a great deal of time over it, and then stacked them neatly upon one another before she laid them on the top of the piano. Mother sat upon the stool, adjusting it so her feet could comfortably reach the peddles. There was a brief pause, as though she were preparing herself mentally for what she was about to do. I sat in the rocking chair and watched. Once she was ready she lifted her hands, hovering just above the keys and then she plunged into Chopin's *Opus Nine Number Two*.

It was always a particular favorite of mine, making me feel nostalgic and emotional. As she worked her fingers over the keys, and her body became a part of the music, I felt a warmth engulf me. Mother played it with reverence, with compassion, as opposed to some who play it with gusto. I could feel the vibration of the music roll over me, and the baby must have felt it too, because he responded to it with his own movements. I leaned back in the chair with my hands on my belly, my eyes shut, enjoying the moment. Tears coursed down my face as I felt a barrage of varying emotions. It is strange how a piece of music can illicit so many sentiments.

I remembered Caleb and me, as children, sitting next to Mother on the piano bench while she played the same piece. I realized I possessed the same fervent awe now as I did then over her talent. I wanted so very much to be like her when I was young. I thought she was beautiful and clever and good at everything. There was a conscious realization at about the age of ten I would never hold a candle to her. I would never be as she was. I would forever live in her shadow, and endlessly only wish to aspire to her greatness.

It all changed when Caleb died. I wanted more to be like my father after that. Because Mother was weak, Mother was selfish and feeble. I resented her for what she put my father and me through. All of the adoration I placed upon her as a child slowly dissolved into a bitterness that cankered my compassion for her. She had robbed me! I did my best to change my feelings to form them into something kinder, more Christian, but the struggle was like the battles of this Great War our country was fighting. Some days the fight seemed favorable, other days a terrible defeat which left me angry and frustrated.

I then thought of Sam in prison, far away and surely suffering. For the briefest moment I understood. It was revealed to me the suffering and agony Mother must have felt. I always saw it all from my own perspective, from my own unique pain. I had little sympathy for her, for what she must have experienced. Feeling my child stir within me, in response to her music, I was overcome by a terrible and penetrating fear. It gripped me with a cruel embrace. What would I do if I lost this child? A child whose face I'd never seen, whose cries I'd never heard? How would I go on?

What must my Mother have gone through? How she must have suffered when Caleb, her babe grown nearly to a man, was taken from her. She knew his particular preferences and dislikes. She knew his personality in and out. How painful it must have been to have him taken from her so. She finished the piece and we sat in the thick silence, consumed by palpable emotion. I wiped my eyes clumsily with the backs of my hands and dried them on my skirt. Eventually I heard her voice, small and timid, while her back still faced me.

"I am sorry, Serena. I am sorry. Please forgive me."

There was no choice. I must forgive her. Only an unfeeling, callous person would have ignored her suffering and hardened their heart against her apparent remorse.

Chapter 17

"What are you up to in there?" I asked. The baby was being rather active just then. My bulging stomach seemed to have a mind of its own at times, and I could actually see him moving within if I watched closely.

I played a game with him sometimes. He would kick and I would poke my belly where he had kicked, and he would kick back. When I moved to a different location to poke again, he would move to that spot and kick there, following my pokes as I teased him. Occasionally I would balance my hair brush on my belly, and he would kick it repeatedly until the brush would jiggle off and tumble to the side. I drew great amusement from our interactions.

"You are clever and strong, my sweet Luke," I told him. There were nights when he kept me up with his movement. He was so vigorous with his kicks and prods I could not sleep because of it. Perhaps it should have bothered me, but I was so grateful for the diversion, so thankful for proof I was not utterly alone, that I welcomed it.

I didn't only take up the habit of talking to the baby, I also began talking to Sam, as if he was there and I was sharing it all with him. I was sure Sam could somehow sense he was not forgotten if I included him in my daily rounds. "You should have felt that one!" I would say after the baby had really put some muscle behind it with a particularly strapping kick to my ribs.

Or "Sam, he is getting so big. If only you could feel how heavy he grows." My own voice filled the empty space when I was alone, when there was no one to keep me company.

I was not used to being alone-not like that anyway. For the past few years I was surrounded on every side, hardly able to find a moment to slip away just to take care of my privy needs. Now I could hear every creak the house made, every noise no matter how small. Mostly, I tried to keep myself busy by cooking or cleaning or reading a novel Aida had loaned me. I pecked at the piano or attempted to sew a few things for the baby. Sometimes I would sing out loud just to fill the empty spaces I was surrounded by. But there were times when I sat consumed by the stillness, and I became afraid.

At those times I would see the bodies piled up at Antietam or the graves we passed through on our way to Gettysburg, the images filling my mind with relentless ease. I would try and push them away, scrambling to think of something else, anything else. But it was as useless as stopping water through a sieve. The scenes of slaughter would not be so easily banished.

And then there was Jack Monroe and the picture of his face as we covered it with dirt. I was sitting in the rocking chair when I dozed off one afternoon. I dreamed I heard a baby cry. I was certain it was my baby. I tiptoed quietly into the bedroom where the cradle was. As I entered the room, to my astonishment there was someone already there, hunched over the cradle with his back to me rocking it to and froe, the floorboards creaking with the rhythm.

"What are you doing?" I asked, the dread rising in my breast. I didn't know why but I was alarmed. I could sense something was very wrong.

He slowly turned to me, his mouth formed in that cruel grin he so often wore. It was Jack Monroe. I was immediately on guard. I knew, with a terrible premonition, the baby in the cradle, my baby, was in danger.

"Get away from there!" I squealed.

He slowly raised his finger to his lips, pressing it firmly there. "Shhhh. You don't want to frighten him."

I awoke with a start, nearly dumping myself onto the floor in the process. I began to whimper, panic stricken, looking about to try to remember where I was. But I was in my little house. I was safe. My baby was safe. Jack was far away in a place he could never hurt me again. It was nothing more than a dream. But I had enough bad dreams to know it was not my last.

He came again, unbidden, on a terrible, stormy night. The peels of thunder sounded like cannon fire in the distance. Reason told me it was no such thing, but then I began to think perhaps the Confederates were invading.

"What would the Rebs be doing this far north?" I scolded myself. I tried to persuade myself that if the Confederates made Washington the war would be over. They would have no need to move any further north. And they most certainly would not be in New York. "It's just a storm. Nothing more!" A violent boom reverberated through the house, shaking the frame and making the timbers shift and crack. Nearly simultaneously there was a flash of lightning. When it lit up the window I thought I saw Jack Monroe peering in at me, the water running down his colorless face as the rain poured down upon him.

I rolled hastily out of the bed, grabbing my pillow as I pressed myself against the wall and slid down to the floor. I put the pillow up to my mouth to muffle my screaming. I sat in a ball with my knees drawn up, trying to talk myself out of what I'd seen. I resolved I must face my fears. I slowly unfolded myself to a standing position. On trembling legs, I inched my way to the window, holding my breath as I forced myself to look out into the dark night. There was nothing. Nothing at all. Just the steady, insistent rain. Yet I wondered, where would Old Whiskers show up next? Why would he not leave me in peace?

Chapter 18

Sam was growing better. This both pleased him and frightened him. Once he was well enough to leave the infirmary, where would he go? He knew he would not get the same kind of soft treatment he got here. Still he counted himself lucky he would be able to leave at all. Darrell died the day after Sam arrived.

Sam knew that the poor man was suffering terribly. His petitions for his mother became more fraught with emotion, more desperate and frenzied. There were moments when Sam thought he might go mad from it. There was no quiet, not a moment of peace. Even in his sleep, Darrell thrashed about. Sam did his best to console Darrell, but it seemed there was no comfort for him. Eventually he slipped into a silence that disturbed Sam more than his rantings and pleadings had.

"Darrell?" he whispered.

There was no answer. Sam felt sick to his stomach. He knew without having to be told the other man was nearing his end. He rolled off of his cot and knelt next to Darrell's bed and said, "Darrell, you must hold on, she will be here shortly."

Darrell's ragged breath seemed laborious and difficult. "I can't wait any more," he said, in nothing more than a croak of a whisper.

"You must."

"Would you tell her something for me?"

"You grow well and tell her yourself."

"You must tell her I was a good boy and did not forget God, as she told me not to."

He took his last breath, eyes grew unfocused, and a deep sigh escaped his lips as he expired. Sam went back to his cot and waited for the evening roll call so he might tell the guard Darrell had passed away. Now Sam knew he would get better, but he also knew if they put him in with the other prisoners he may end up as Darrell, and he wanted desperately to survive this ordeal.

Sam knew he had a wife and baby to return to, and he promised me he would be coming home. He promised. He took the meager portions he was given and forced them down, although the turned meat made him want to gag. He slept when he could. He did his best to conserve his energy and stay out of trouble. But always he was worried. Always he carried with him the fear of death.

Chapter 19

Cooper woke Sam in the middle of the night, rousing him from a troubled sleep. The night guard was sitting in a chair in the corner of the room, his feet propped up on a table, his chin drooping to his chest as he slumbered. Sam was at first very startled, his natural reaction was to struggle against Cooper. He pulled away from his prison mate, raising his fist as though he might assault him. He was ready to strike, until he realized who it was and dropped his arm, rubbing his face to try to clear his brain.

"Cooper?" he mumbled. "What are you doing?"

"Shhh. Keep it down," Cooper warned.

Sam obliged him, lowering his voice to a barely audible hiss. "What are you doing?"

"Me and Timothy Dyne are breaking out," he replied.

"What?"

"We got enough between us that we bribed one of the guards, and tonight we are heading out."

"Who have you bribed?" Sam wondered.

"It's better you not know," Cooper answered. "I only tell you this much because I need your help."

Sam grew perplexed. "My help?"

"If you can give us some time," Cooper began. "If you can figure out a way to keep us undetected-at least just for the morning.

That should help us on our way before they send out parties to search for us."

"What do you want me to do?" Sam asked.

"If they ask after us, well, make up an excuse, or tell them whatever you can think to keep them off of us for a while."

"I'll do it, if you promise to do something for me," Sam bargained.

"Can't take you with us in your shape," Cooper warned.

"All I ask is that you get this to my wife," Sam said, digging into his coat pocket. He withdrew a letter he had written upon a scrap of newspaper, filling the blank spaces between the type and in the margins with his own message for me. "Serena Barlow of Richfield, New York."

Cooper took the letter and put it in his pocket. "You have my word," he said.

Sam watched as Cooper Hardy and Timothy Dyne crept from the room and disappeared into the shadows beyond. There was a moment of acute disappointment that he was not going with them but also an overwhelming triumph for having got an uncensored letter out. It stands true in times of war as in times of peace, a human soul cannot be held in bondage regardless of the circumstances he finds himself in. Tyranny will ever foster rebellion, and free agency will always find a way to prevail.

In the morning the guard with the mustache-Sam since learned his name was Wheeler-strolled 'round the room counting the men to make sure all were accounted for. Sam lay still upon his bed, as though he were in a deep sleep, waiting for Wheeler to count him and then pass by. Once Wheeler walked past and his back was to Sam, Sam quickly pulled himself up from his cot, crossed the gap between his bed and an empty one across the aisle and lay down upon it, laying upon his stomach so that his face could not be seen. Another man, one of Timothy Dyne's friends, caught on to what Sam was doing and followed suit.

Wheeler made his way to the end of the row of cots pressed up against the wall, doubled back to count the next row, and seemed not to notice he counted Sam or the other fellow twice. When he finished his task he wrote the numbers down on paper and went on with his other duties, completely unaware Cooper Hardy and Timothy Dyne were missing. Sam felt a secret satisfaction to be instrumental in aiding the two men's escape.

He ate the meager rations they gave him for breakfast with a twinkle to his eye and a concealed smile upon his lips. It seemed like the sweetest sort of revenge that he should deceive Wheeler in such a simple but effective way. The day wore on, and as night set in another guard by the name of Jepson also did a head count. Sam and his partner in crime pulled the same stunt, transferring to a different cot after they were counted, with the same success. They had given Hardy and Dyne a twenty-four-hour head start. This was cause to rejoice.

The next day passed as the one previous. Sam and Timothy Dyne's friend were counted twice for the morning and evening head count. Sam lay in the dark that night, unable to sleep for the thrill he felt when he thought of Cooper Hardy posting his letter. He began to entertain thoughts of his own escape. They hadn't discovered the money he concealed in the buttons of his coat. Perhaps he too could find a guard willing to take money in exchange for looking the other way.

Shortly after dawn, on the third morning, Wheeler went about counting the men, as was his custom. He passed Sam, with a tick upon his paper, and moved along. Sam drew himself up from his cot and launched himself across the aisle to the empty cot and waited. As Wheeler came around, this time he paused and stood over Sam, taking far too long in producing his tick and moving on.

After what seemed an eternity he moved toward Sam, taking him by the shoulder and rolling him over. Sam put on an act, behaving as though he'd just been awoken and was in a state of confusion. But Wheeler was not buying it.

"What game are you at?" Wheeler barked.

"Game? What are you talking about?" Sam asked.

Wheeler, who was just beginning to suspect he'd been had, pursed his lips, his eyes narrowing, and called out, "Everyone up! Everyone up, and get yourselves in line for roll call."

Sam's heart sank. He knew he was found out. There was no fear for Hardy and Dyne, for they were most certainly far away and safe by now. It was for himself he now feared. Wheeler discovered his game, and there would most certainly be consequences.

Sam did as he was told and joined the other men in line. Even those in very poor shape were assisted to the line, leaning heavily on a fellow soldier who was in better shape than they. Once every cot was empty the roll began again, this time with names.

"Barlow?"

"Here," Sam answered.

In a like manner the rest were called and it was discovered that Cooper Hardy and Timothy Dyne were unaccounted for. Sam waited with dread for what was to come next. Wheeler came to him, jerked him up roughly by the arm and led him away. Sam was careful to keep his eyes forward and his face cautiously blank, but as he passed Timothy's friend he saw the pleading glance the man shot to him. *Don't tell on me,* he said without words. Sam gave him an ever so slight nod of the head to reassure him, otherwise betraying nothing else.

Chapter 20

The interior of the office was well lit, as there were several windows. Captain Turner sat behind his desk like a lord upon his throne. The Commandant was a middle aged man with long flowing hair and a generous beard to match. He wore his uniform with an eye for detail, everything in precise order, the buttons of his coat polished, his trousers neatly pressed. When he looked up at Wheeler and Sam as they came into the room, his stare was hard and intense. Sam thought he should be intimidated, but refused to allow it. Sam never was the sort to be cowed into insecurity. He met Captain Turner's gaze with resolute poise.

"Is this him?" Captain Turner asked Wheeler, as though he were expecting someone else.

Wheeler nodded the affirmative. "Yes, Sir."

"Have a seat, won't you?" The Captain said to Sam, indicating the chair in front of the desk. Wheeler gave him no chance to sit on his own. He roughly yanked him to the chair and then pushed him down so that Sam nearly missed the chair completely. Sam took a moment to straighten himself and then sat at attention, his palms resting on his legs. He waited to be spoken to.

"What do you know of inmates Timothy Dyne and Cooper Hardy's absence, Sir?"

Sam gave him a blank look. "I would have to say next to nothing, Sir."

"When you say next to nothing, that indicates to me you know a little something," the Captain maintained in a persuasive voice.

"I know only what you know. They are gone, Sir."

"And how is it you were the one discovered in this scheme to throw us off the numbers?" he asked.

"What scheme are you referring to, Sir?"

"You know damn well what scheme!" Wheeler yelled.

Captain Turner ignored the outburst. "Something I have learned in the course of my service is that patience produces results. And I am a patient man, Lieutenant Barlow. But those who have tried my patience often see that beyond my fortitude I am also a man of very little restraint."

He got up from his position behind the desk, moved around so he was standing before Sam, and then casually leaned himself against the desk with his ankles crossed. Wheeler moved in as well, standing next to Sam instead of behind him. Sam knew this was meant to intimidate him.

"Now, let's get to the bottom of all of this before it gets ugly."

"I have told you all I know. Hardy and Dyne are gone. I am as much surprised as you must now be."

Without warning Wheeler knocked Sam in the face with the back of his clenched fist. Sam's head snapped back, and he could taste the blood in his mouth. He straightened himself without a word and waited.

"When?"

"I'm sorry?" Sam asked.

"When did they leave?"

"I couldn't say." He looked to Wheeler and inquired. "When did you note they were gone?" To which Wheeler hit him again.

"This…this is unpleasant business," Captain Turner said between clenched teeth as he waved his hands before him. "I'm sure you can appreciate we can't have this sort of thing going on here. Not wise to have chaos and anarchy amongst the inmates. The heathens would tear each other limb for limb over a crust of bread if we weren't here to govern them."

Sam knew the captain was trying to anger him, goad him into reacting. His first thought was to rebuke the man for starving them, forcing them to live like animals. As difficult as it was, he managed to remain silent. There would be no point in giving a lecture to these two. They were beyond humanity. Was it possible to enjoy such a position as theirs? If it was, they certainly seemed to.

"You have one last chance, son. You may tell us what you know or you may suffer the consequences. Dyne and Hardy-where are they?"

"As I said before, Sir. I am unaware of their exact whereabouts. But if I were to guess at it, I should think they are safe now under the protection of the Stars and Stripes, Old Glory herself. And I'll tell you frankly I will do all I can to join them there."

At this Wheeler struck him in the back of the head, knocking Sam to the floor. He began to kick him in a most vicious manner until Captain Turner put a hand on his shoulder in a calm and slow intercession.

"Sergeant Wheeler, that isn't necessary. What this soldier needs is some fresh air, some cooling off. See to it he gets the exercise he needs out in the yard, won't you? Set him to walking. And see he walks right lively, or you have my permission to give him the bayonet."

Wheeler pulled Sam up from the ground and shoved him roughly toward the door. "Yes, Sir," he said gleefully. Then to Sam he said, "You heard him." He pushed Sam out the door, down the corridor, and out into the yard, where a dozen or more centuries stood guard. "Nothing I like better than to see a hard case like you get whipped. Start walking."

The day wore on and the sun beat down upon Sam. His head throbbed from the beating he had taken. His body ached something terrible too. Because of his wounds and his incarceration, he hadn't done anything very physical in months and his muscles rebelled against the intense strain as he walked round and round the perimeter of the yard. As if this were not cruel enough treatment, he was afforded nothing to eat or drink. His fatigue nearly overcame him and yet he forced his feet and continued his walk.

Occasionally Sergeant Wheeler would call out to him, "Pick it up, or I'll run you through!" But Sam just ignored him and persisted in limping along at the same pace he was going. Evening set in and the lights from inside the prison lit his way.

He saw Captain Turner passing by, pausing to observe from the doorway of the great brick building. This made him angry. What sort of human being would delight in another's suffering? He knew he should ignore him, but he couldn't stand for it. Taking what little strength he had left he called out to him.

"Captain Turner, do you think I've had sufficient exercise for one man?"

Wheeler was positively peeved. He got up as though he might accost Sam again and abuse him further. Captain Turner stopped him with a shake of his head, so Wheeler stood ready to do as the Captain bade.

"It would seem so, Lieutenant. Sergeant Wheeler, see to it this man is taken upstairs with the rest of them."

"Sir, I have a place in the hospital."

"You look well to me," he replied.

"I am not healed yet," Sam insisted.

Captain Turner gave his attention to Wheeler. "Take him upstairs," he said pointedly.

Sam hobbled after Wheeler back into Libby and up the stairs to where the main body of prisoners were housed. Once Wheeler left him, Sam's first order of business was to head for the bucket, draw the ladle up filled with water, and drink again and again until he made himself sick. The others watched him with nothing like surprise. It was likely a familiar scene to them, or perhaps they'd seen worse and so nothing affected them anymore. When he finished he found himself a corner on the floor, next to a wall, and lay down. There were no empty cots, no bedrolls, no blankets, only the hard floorboards to cushion his body.

Each time he moved he heard the displaced water slosh in his gut. His body ached like it never had before. The remnants of his wounds burned like so many red ants stinging his flesh, and his hips throbbed, as his muscles jerked plaintively. Out of sheer exhaustion, he managed to get into a comfortable enough position to fall into a deep sleep.

Chapter 21

Reed Haney looked vastly different from the last time I saw him. He'd lost weight-enough that his cheeks were nearly hollow, and his hair seemed somehow thicker. He looked downright fragile. I tried not to eye his pant leg that was pinned up on his left leg as we sat together in his brother's front parlor. But it was a difficult if not impossible undertaking. I found myself glancing at it when he was looking away or preoccupied by some diversion beyond the parlor window.

"I hope you like nut bread," I said enthusiastically.

"I do. Love it," he replied, clutching the loaf I made for him in his lap.

It was silent for a moment. Then I said, very honestly, "It is good to see you Mr. Haney. I have missed you."

He smiled. "I have missed you too."

"How are you, really?"

"I been better, I suppose, but I'm not bad either."

"Do you think you'll take up work with your brother again?" I inquired.

"I'll do what I can to help out, but I don't suppose I'll be much use as I am. Still, my brother's a good man and will give me a crack at it."

"I know you well enough to know a leg won't keep you from doing what needs to be done," I scolded.

"There isn't much a man can do sitting down, so I hope you are right." He laughed, but I couldn't tell if it was sincere or not.

"If smithing doesn't work out for you there are other things... Have you ever felt a fondness for any other occupation perhaps?"

"I don't know. Nothing right off the top of my head, but I'm not too concerned over it. I got other pressing things to think about."

I was amused and intrigued. "Do tell," I coaxed.

"I am of a mind to settle down. This old bachelor has intentions of finding a nice girl and starting a family of my own. Hear the pitter patter of little feet, a babe to bounce upon my knee. I still have one knee left I can devote to it, you know."

To say I was shocked was an understatement. I'm sure my jaw dropped and my eyes bulged at the notion. He was in love with a girl who died years and years ago, wasn't he? Not to mention he was a man of a certain age. He must be at least fifty, several years older than my parents. If he hadn't found his heart's desire by now shouldn't he be past thinking of courtship and settling down?

"Are you teasing me?"

He chuckled. "No. No, I mean it."

"I don't wish to be indelicate, so stop me if I become offensive, but I thought your devotions lay elsewhere."

"I suppose everyone knows my story, the one of Flora and me," he said, scratching his head and growing somewhat uncomfortable.

"Your love story is legendary, the very topic of every young girl's romantic fantasies. I never knew her, and yet I feel as though she were a very dear old friend."

"She was a beautiful woman. She had the ability to converse with ease, and with that charming humor and poise she always exhibited. At times I remember her so well, and at other times I wonder if it all was nothing more than a dream." I didn't want to admit I could relate to him. As a matter of fact it bothered me greatly because I knew exactly what he was talking about.

"Have you lost your love for her?"

He seemed to scoff at the notion. "Heavens no! I shall always hold her dear to my heart. Always."

"Then what has changed, Mr. Haney?" He seemed as though he didn't know what to say. His expression was thoughtful for a moment. He was searching his mind for the right words perhaps.

"I have. May sound stale and worn out, saying nearly dying makes a man awake to life, but it's really how I see it."

"No. It doesn't sound that way at all."

"You know, I always thought I was keeping her memory by never loving another. But what sort of tribute is it to hold myself apart, to live a life that isn't worth anything? Because I have nothing to show for all of these years now. I've no wife, no children. Would Flora have wished such a life for me? I certainly wouldn't have wished it for her. I would've wanted her to be happy, to find someone and enjoy her time. I wouldn't have wanted her to be alone."

Mr. Haney smiled sentimentally. "You young people, you think death so romantic. Where is the romance in it? I will tell you now, death effectively ends a love affair. It is all fine and good to keep a memory, but memories don't keep you warm at night. Memories don't put their arms around you to console you after a hard day. That is not a life, subsisting on something dead and gone."

It made sense, what he was saying, and yet the notion of him wanting to marry and start a family stunned me so I found it difficult to accept for a moment. "I see," I said.

"I don't blame you for not understanding. But let me pose a question to you. Was it out of love for Flora I never loved another, or was it because I was afraid to move on, because I wouldn't allow myself to be open to new prospects, to different opportunities?"

"Only you could answer that question, Mr. Haney. Only you know your own heart," I answered.

He grew sheepish. "Silly, I suppose, my philosophical ramblings. Don't know what's got into me of late. Probably shouldn't have said anything."

"No. No, I don't think finding someone to love a bad idea at all. Why not?"

"Surely an old man like myself is ready to accept, with grace, his senior years and throw away such foolishness."

The silence between us was not uncomfortable, but it dragged on. I interrupted the silence to ask, "Do you think you might be up for a walk?"

"A walk?" He was surprised by the change of subject.

"I was hoping you might accompany me to the post office. As pointless as it is, I still like to check to make sure there are no letters regarding Sam, or news in the papers. I thought it might be nice not to have to go alone, and perhaps good for you to get a breath of fresh air?"

"Hand me my crutch there," he said motioning toward the crutch leaning against the wall next to the door with a determined pucker to his lips.

"You're sure it's not too much trouble?"

"Fresh air just *might* do me good," he said with a resolute nod of his head.

Once I gave him his crutch he righted himself, hopping on his good leg a few times to balance himself. I rushed ahead of him to open the door, and then we made our way slowly down the street to the post office, he hobbling on his crutch and I waddling with my off-centered weight. When I opened the door for him again, once we got to the post office, he nodded his head and seemed somewhat embarrassed.

"Never had a lady open the door for me before. Seems unnatural."

"Yes, well, I am quite used to holding the door," I said with an ironic grin. Mr. Haney gave me a smirk. He knew to what I was referring.

"Breaking barriers is something you seem to have a knack for," he admitted.

I didn't respond, only smiled and shook my head. When we came into the lobby of the post office, Aida looked up, saw it was me, drew her eyebrows together and wordlessly mouthed a *what?* to me. Regardless of her misgivings, she ended up smiling and stood to greet us. In my mind I was begging her not to say what she was thinking, but my ability to mentally silence her was useless.

"Back so soon?" she asked.

"You know how desperate I am for news," I countered, hoping she would leave it at that.

"Well, I have nothing new to report since you last came this morning."

She had said it. Now Mr. Haney must know I was up to something. But when I chuckled nervously and smiled at him with a shrug, he didn't let on he was suspicious as to what my intentions might be, so I acted as though what Aida said was of no consequence. "I thought not but felt I should try one last time before I headed home anyway."

"I wish I were able to give you some good news, but alas I am not."

"I suppose I should have learned some patience by now. I hope I do not vex you too sorely, Aida."

"You do not vex me at all. I do so enjoy your company that I am glad you have a reason to want to come here on such a regular occasion."

"Aida is a treasure, a real support to me," I said to Mr. Haney. "Aida this is my dear friend, Mr. Reed Haney. I grew to know him during my service as a nurse." I noted Mr. Haney's subtle but questioning glance when I mentioned my service as a nurse. I chose to ignore it.

"It is very good to meet you, Mr. Haney," Aida said, extending her hand to him so he might bow over it and nearly touch the back of her hand with his lips. He did so as a dutiful gentleman ought.

"Mr. Haney, this is Miss Aida Turner. She's been an absolute blessing these many long months as I've waited to hear about Sam."

"It is good to meet you as well, Miss Turner."

"Miss Turner shares your passion for reading mysteries, Mr. Haney," I added. "Didn't you just finish one, Aida?"

"Ah, yes, I have. *The Notting Hill Mystery* by Charles Felix. It has the cleverest fellow in it."

"Perhaps you might lend it to Mr. Haney," I suggested.

"Certainly," she offered, enthusiastically. "Indeed, if you like a good mystery, you will most certainly take a liking to this one."

It only took her a moment to step behind the counter, retrieve the book and come back to the two of us waiting near the door. She held the book in her two hands with her arms extended out to Mr. Haney. He took it from her, studying the cover with interest. "You will have to tell me what you thought of it when you've finished," Aida told him.

"I will," he promised. I noted that Mr. Haney suddenly did not look well. The color seemed to drain from his skin, and he looked quite pale.

"Are you all right, Mr. Haney?" I asked.

"As good as it was to meet you, I must be getting along." Mr. Haney spoke to me now with hesitation in his voice. "I'm afraid I'm not quite up to the physical excitement of our little outing yet. I should head home."

"Oh, I do hope I didn't put you out too much, asking you to accompany me," I apologized.

"I was glad to. It isn't often I have such pleasant company," he said, shooting a smile and a nod to Aida. She returned his smile. "And thank you for the loan of your novel. I will return it as quickly as I can read it."

"I hope you enjoy it as much as I did."

"I'm sure I will."

"Well, thank you, Aida. Have a pleasant day and we shall speak soon," I said, as Mr. Haney and I left the post office.

It was nearly two days later I received Aida at my home. I was somewhat surprised when I opened the door to find her standing upon the threshold. She'd never visited me before. Therefore, I was not expecting her. Still I was pleased..

"Well, what are you doing here?" I asked.

Chapter 22

Aida looked like a mother goose, prim and proper, her neck long and graceful, her face pleasant but amused, with her gloved hands clasped at her waist, standing on my front step. She was expectant. If I were a proper lady I would have immediately let her in. Sometimes I forgot myself. Sometimes I forgot what was expected of me. I was smiling and she was smiling. I thought I knew to what I owed her visit.

"How very rude! Aren't you going to ask me in?" she teased with mock displeasure.

"Of course. You are more than welcome. I'm surprised is all. This is not our regular fashion, you seeing me at my house instead of me seeing you at the post office. Come in." I stepped away from the door and allowed her to pass.

"What a sweet little house you have," she said with genuine delight. "I've always wondered what this place was like on the inside, as I've passed it a million times over."

"What are you doing out and about? I should think you would be tending shop this time of day."

"I put a closed sign in the window and hastened to see you. I must get back quickly. You understand I don't want angry customers lining up to insult my dedication upon my return."

"You've come all this way to see me, take a moment to visit, won't you? Have a seat. I've got just enough for you," I laughed as I showed her the rocking chair in the parlor, the only seat in the room. "May I offer you some coffee?"

"Is it any good?" she asked rather bluntly. That was Aida, speaking her mind without a care as to what others might think of her. I considered this the likely reason she was a spinster, but I liked her candor immensely and wished I was more like her.

"Well, it probably isn't the best you've had, but it will do."

"Thank you. I would love to have a cup."

I drifted into the kitchen to pour her a cup from the kettle that sat near the hearth, still warm from this morning but not fresh. She raised her voice from the other room so I could hear her.

"You are a sly little minx, aren't you, Serena?" I smiled to myself, knowing full well what she was referring to, but took a moment to compose myself before I returned to the parlor with her cup. I faced her with a straight expression.

"Whatever do you mean?" I asked innocently as I handed the coffee to her.

"Bringing Mr. Haney to the post office the other day."

"He is a dear old friend, and I was merely taking him for a walk for his health."

"You don't fool me," she countered.

"I wasn't trying to."

"I should hope not. It isn't the first time someone has tried to play matchmaker with me."

"I only wish to say I think Mr. Haney one of the most noble, decent individuals I've had the privilege of knowing, and while he is a bit older, his experience would be an advantage to someone such as yourself who is learned and knows something of the world. Now I will leave it at that."

"He seemed very kind, and if you like him so, I have no doubt he's as honorable as you portray. I thank you for your concern, I do, but I have never had something like this work out before, and so I bear no great hope it will in the present case."

"But it has piqued your interest hasn't it?"

She shrugged with a small smile upon her lips, taking a dainty sip from her cup. "Perhaps."

"Enough for you to shirk your duties at the post office to come visit with me."

"I haven't shirked my responsibilities. I'm here on official business."

"You are?"

"I didn't think I could wait for you to come in. I had to bring this to you. I closed up shop just to get here as soon as I could." Aida pulled a small envelope from the pocket of her skirts and handed it to me.

I inspected it for a moment, puzzling over the return address. "Cooper Hardy, of Lititz, Pennsylvania? I don't recall knowing anyone by that name."

"Perhaps someone you met while you served as nurse?"

"I don't think so," I said.

I turned the envelope over, running my finger beneath the seal and drawing out the folded paper. A bit of newspaper fell from the folds and floated to the floor. I bent to pick it up, curious as to what it might be. It did not appear to be anything of importance. The edges were ripped in such a way that only half of the article was legible and seemed to be random, of no significance to me. I put it aside and instead focused on the letter, hoping to shed light on the meaning of it.

"What does it say?" Aida asked.

I began to read aloud,

"Mrs. Barlow, I am writing on behalf of your husband, whom I was held with at Libby Prison for several months' time in the hospital there. In exchange for his aid in escaping that place, I made a promise I would see to it you received this note from him. Sam Barlow has my sincere gratitude, as do you. When last I saw him, he was mending well from the wounds received at Spotsylvania and bid me to tell you not worry over his welfare.

Yours truly, Cooper Hardy."

I could hardly believe it. My heart pounded so, and I gasped a little in surprise. I looked at Aida with my mouth open and tears burning my eyes. After months of wishing to know what Sam's fate was it was a relief, and yet a sad and terrible thing to contemplate him in prison, at the mercy of the enemy, in the same moment. I took the scrap of newspaper and inspected it again, turning it over in my hand. On the back side of the paper I could see, in very small print, Sam's handwriting in the margins and in-between the lines of type.

Feel very clever to have figured a way to get word without prying eyes. Have been in hospital. Don't know how long luck will last. Am well for now. Pray same for you. Love you. Love you. Sam.

I gasped in surprised. "Sam, you are alive!"

Chapter 23

The air was stifling in the dungeon-like rooms. The low ceilings and the perpetual darkness, even during daylight hours, made a man feel buried alive. Because the prison was situated near the river it seemed forever damp. So many sweaty men clustered about the place did not help matters. To say it was overcrowded would have been an understatement. It was unseasonably hot for late September, and with the smell of body odor and the stench of the privy pots it was nearly unbearable. This is what drove Sam to the window one afternoon to try to get some relief. He drew near to the window and lifted it a fraction of an inch, thinking to get some fresh air, when a bullet came sailing through a window pane, shattering glass all around. The gunfire was accompanied by a string of insults and curses from the guards in the courtyard below.

Sam fell to the floor before another bullet came at him. He lay there upon his belly for a moment in shock and dismay. He only meant to try and get a breath of fresh air--why would they shoot at him? From a short distance away, a fellow prisoner who watched the whole incident began to laugh. Sam looked up from his position on the ground to see a young man, full- and thick-bearded and dark haired, observing him from his perch on a chair near the wall.

"You haven't been here long, now have you?" the man asked with an amused expression. Sam moved to get up from the ground, but the man stopped him. "I wouldn't do that if I was you. They look for someone to use as target practice. Any excuse and they'll shoot to kill. Move away from there."

"But I've done nothing," Sam defended.

"You got too close to the window. If they can see you to put a bead on you, they'll shoot you. Stay away from the windows."

Sam crawled away from the window on his hands and knees, until he felt he was a safe distance from it and then he got up and approached the man. "Thank you for the warning," Sam said.

"Likewise, you should never be found outside of doors or in the basement, or anywhere else they deem off limits. They don't ask questions, they shoot first."

"Jolly sort, aren't they?"

"Never met any jollier."

"First Lieutenant Sam Barlow of New York," Sam informed the stranger, holding his hand out to shake.

The man accepted Sam's hand. "Colonel Thomas Rose of Pennsylvania."

"How long you been here?" Sam asked.

"Too long," Colonel Rose replied, although Sam discovered later it hadn't been long at all.

"I was in the hospital for a time," Sam told him.

"You were one of the lucky ones then," the Colonel said.

"I suppose so. It wasn't nearly as crowded. And there were beds to lay on. My body aches so from sleeping on the floor. Not even a blanket afforded."

"Fine way to treat a man. But I suppose they have no blankets to give. Our blockades have done their job well."

"Whatever the reason, it doesn't console me any."

"Yes, well, I tell myself it can get no worse only to find it can. Be grateful for the small bit we are given. Any day now that could be taken away too."

"I will tell you now, and tell you true, I don't mean to stay here. I will get out if I can or die trying," Sam said. There was an edge to his voice that surprised even himself.

Colonel Rose's eyes narrowed, and he searched Sam's face for a brief moment. "I don't doubt you. However, you may want to keep that to yourself. There is speculation about whether they have spies amongst us, prisoners they've bribed in order to get information."

Sam was taken aback by this. "Surely no Union soldier would do something so low down!"

"Desperate men do desperate things," Colonel Rose said with a shrug.

"Thank you for the counsel. I will keep it in remembrance." To change the subject, Sam asked, "You say you are from Pennsylvania. What part do you hale from?"

"I come from Pittsburg."

"Is it anywhere near Gettysburg?"

Colonel Rose was amused. "Not really. Nearly two hundred miles' distance. Pittsburg is a nice quiet farming community. Is Gettysburg all you know of Pennsylvania?"

"Mostly, I suppose. My wife and I honeymooned there. A tiny little place called Carroll Valley. Do you know of it?"

"Can't say that I've ever heard of it. I trust it was a pleasant trip?"

"Very. My wife and I found it favorable in every way."

"How long have you been married now?"

"It will be a year at the end of December. We are to have a baby." Sam took the cap from his head, fishing around the inside for our likeness. He held it out proudly for Colonel Rose to see. "This is my wife."

"She is a handsome woman."

"What about you, Colonel? Are you married?"

"I am. Lydia. Her name is Lydia, my wife. And just call me Tom, won't you. No sense in formalities. Here in prison we are equals."

"Do you have children?"

"Yes. They are a blessing. Before all of this, I was principal of the South Pittsburg schools. I thoroughly enjoy children."

"You are a man of learning. That impresses me. I did nothing more than work at a saw mill before I signed up."

"Any job has its merits and is part of a greater good. Without the timbers from a saw mill there would be no school to congregate and learn in. My job was no more important than yours."

"I thought at one point to be a preacher, but I suppose my disposition is such that it would never have worked out."

"You a hell raiser?"

"No. I wouldn't say so. Just have a rebellious streak that's gotten me into trouble now and again," said Sam.

"That's not a character flaw. It's the mark of a man who understands how precious his free will is. It's the complacent I fear more."

"I like your sentiment. I will have to remember it to reference it later," Sam said with a chuckle. "I have enjoyed your company and will seek you out again if you have no objections to it."

"Please do," the Colonel agreed.

This was the first meeting Sam had with Colonel Thomas E. Rose, the man who would later involve Sam and several others in a plot to escape Libby Prison.

Chapter 24

As my middle grew larger, I wore my skirts higher to accommodate the baby. I was pleased that my hair began to grow in thick, and although it was still short, it was longer than it had been, well past my ears now. Near the middle of October Sam's father came by the house with a beautiful, handmade oak table with turned legs for the dining room. He and Sam's brothers unloaded it from the wagon and set it up for me. I could tell they'd put a great deal of work into it, and it exhibited excellent craftsmanship. I ran my fingers along the top as I admired it.

After John sent the boys off to cut wood for the wood pile and haul water in from the well for me, I sat at the table with him and served him a cup of coffee. I was now more comfortable with him after growing to know him better over the past few months. I could see where Sam got his humor and his down-to-earth sensibilities from, and it made me like John very much.

"It's beautiful!" I said reverently as we sipped from our mugs.

"I'm glad you like it," he replied.

"I *love* it! It is a work of art."

"Well, now, I don't know about that," he said modestly.

I leaned forward in my chair, my elbows resting on the table with my mug between my hands. I had something I wanted to ask John, but I wasn't sure how to broach the subject. I thought about it a great deal but couldn't seem to find an easy way of saying it. He noticed my peculiar behavior and leaned back in his chair as though he were waiting for me to speak.

"What is it?" he asked.

Ever since I saw the article in the newspaper about the injustices committed at Libby Prison, I had been thinking on it. I knew I needed to find a way to get Sam out of there. One of the quotes from a surgeon read: *We are horrified when we picture the wholesale misery and death that will come with the biting frost of winter.* Another excerpt said: *These men are starved deliberately. No other alternative is suggested.*

The thought of Sam starving to death in some stinking prison in Virginia was more than I could bear. It rendered me ill. For several days after reading the article I was confined to my bed, unable to eat anything more than broth. The only thing that relieved my distress over the suffering I imagined Sam to be enduring was the thought I must get him out of there.

I hesitated, as I tried to find the right words to say to John. "You have been so generous to me," I began.

He wouldn't allow me to beat around the bush. He came right to the point. "What is it?"

"I need you to do something for me," I admitted.

"Anything," he agreed. "Name it."

"I...I need you to build something."

His lips formed into a smile. "Well, sure."

"My father said I could use his wagon," I explained. "I need you to fix it for me."

"What is it needs fixing?"

"I know it sounds...that it's going to sound strange, but I need you to build a false bottom in the wagon bed."

John grew suspicious, his eyes narrowing. He couldn't make sense of what I was saying. "Why?"

"It's difficult to explain. I've-I've been thinking...I... well, I've decided I am going after Sam."

The silence was unbearable. I couldn't tell what he was thinking, and all I could do was wait for his response. I couldn't force myself to make eye contact. I kept my own gaze on the grain of the wood, tracing it with my fingertip as I waited. Sam's father cleared his throat.

"You can't do that," he finally said.

"Why not?"

"What do you mean why not? You're going to have a baby," he pointed out.

"I know," I said. "I plan on waiting until after the baby comes."

He was exasperated. "And then what?"

"I am going to Richmond. I plan on finding a way to bring Sam home."

"That's just crazy."

"Why?"

"You can't go to Richmond alone with a baby."

"I know that too," I said quietly. "I won't be taking the baby."

He shook his head, as if he were trying to clear it. "Serena, you aren't making any sense."

"Please, just listen," I begged.

"There isn't anything to listen to. I'm not going to let you put yourself in danger. It's bad enough that Sampson is-is... It's bad enough he's rotting in some prison somewhere, but I won't let you put yourself in danger too."

"John, I can't do this anymore. I can't sit around imagining what may be happening to him and do nothing to help him."

"What do you think *you* can do about it?"

"I am going to find a way to get him out of there. That's what I'm going to do."

"This isn't some game, girl. You can't just waltz in and ask them to give him back. That isn't how it's done."

"I never said it was," I said defensively. "But there must be some way. And I aim to find it. I was hoping you would understand."

John shifted angles. He grew calm, entreating. "This, this is my responsibility. If anyone should go, it should be me."

"That won't work!" I cried.

"Well, I won't let you go."

"Why?"

"Because you are a woman. I can't let you put yourself in harm's way."

"That's the very reason it should be me," I pointed out. "A woman can move more easily across the lines. A woman would be less likely to raise suspicion. A woman, if caught, would be treated more lenient than a man. It is completely logical if you think about it."

"I don't like it. I don't like it at all."

"I've made up my mind," I told him.

"You can't do what it is you're proposing," he insisted.

"John, I'm going. You can either help me or not, but I am going."

Chapter 25

After tightening the notch on his belt several times, Sam estimated he'd lost four or more inches around his waist. He noted too that his hair had begun to fall out in clumps when he ran his fingers through it, and he was dizzy to the point of collapse when he got up too quickly. His stomach made a cacophony of strange noises, and he felt always the desire for food.

He recalled the early days we spent in the army when there were no rations to speak of and we were constantly looking to find food, and he longed for those days. At least he was free to try and make his own way. In this hell-hole there were no greens. He managed to survive on mealy corn bread which was hard and aged, meat apparently rotted from the smell, color, and taste of it, and black bean soup with more bugs than beans. Of this detestable fare, the rations were meager and unpredictable. It was not enough to sustain a grown man.

Waking and sleeping, food was always on his mind, all he could think about; all he desired was to have a meal to fill him up. When he did eat, he swallowed as quickly as possible, and then struggled to keep it down as his belly protested. The food was not edible, and his body attempted to reject it. But he fought off the urge to vomit, knowing the slop they fed him was the only thing keeping him alive.

Sam looked upon the skeletal and ruined walking corpses surrounding him, and although he was repulsed by them, he knew he must look very much the same. It appalled him and humbled him and scared him. His mortality was an ever present threat, as he struggled to survive within the whitewashed brick walls of that prison.

No fewer than a hundred men a month were dying now. Their bodies stacked up to await disposal in a bleak reminder of how close he was to Heaven's gate himself. He thought at one point it might be a means of escaping. If he simply lay upon the floor, refusing to respond to the kicking and prodding of the guards, perhaps they would take him for dead and carry his body away. He could hold very still and take their abuse, if it meant getting out. It seemed like a good plan until he saw the guards bayonetting the bodies to make sure they were good and dead. Sam realized feigning death to get out of his sentence was not an option.

On one occasion, during a very bad storm, Sam and three other men took turns sawing the wooden bars covering the window in the kitchen on the first floor with a pocket knife one of them managed to conceal from the guards. Out of the four men, two got away. But Sam was not one of them. At the last minute one of the escapees tossed the pocket knife back to Sam. He was pleased the others found a way out, although he was also troubled he was not one of them. Still, he looked for any chance he could of escape, hoping against all hope he wouldn't have to remain there for much longer.

One day as he squatted over the meager meal they provided him, Colonel Rose approached him. The thing the Colonel had on his mind was that he wanted very much to go home and he wanted to make an alliance among those who were of a like mind. Colonel Rose was watching Sam for a time now. Suspicious of everyone and everything, he took mental notes on whom he felt he could trust. After careful deliberation, Sam finally passed his test when he was nearly caught trying to escape through the kitchen window.

Besides that, Sam was a sober sort. Many of the other young men behaved outrageously out of boredom, fighting and wrestling, conducting themselves like young boys too full of energy. Sam appreciated the musical and theatrical performances, joining in on singing and the like, but he never made a fool of himself, or drew unneeded attention. This had not gone unnoted by Colonel Rose.

"Sam," he said, by way of a greeting.

"Hello, Tom."

"When you finish there, I'd like you to meet someone."

Sam put the last of his cornbread in his mouth, licking his fingers to make sure he'd gotten every last crumb of it. The cornbread was too hard to chew, so Sam sucked on it, like a lemon drop. Only it tasted nothing like a lemon drop as it slowly dissolved into grainy lumps small enough to swallow.

"Who would you like me to meet?" Sam asked, stretching his legs until he was standing. He ignored the throbbing of his hips and the pain in his joints as he allowed his body to acclimate to this new position.

"Come with me."

Sam followed along after the Colonel, his curiosity piqued. Rose ushered him to a corner of the room, apart from the others who were eating or conversing. There stood a tall, thin man with a receding hairline, a straggly beard, and piercing eyes, with a grimly held mouth. He looked Sam up and down carefully, then turned his gaze to Colonel Rose and gave a small nod.

"Sam this is Major Andrew Hamilton."

Sam looked from the Colonel to the Major questioningly. However, he didn't say anything. He knew there was more than a friendly introduction transpiring between them. He sensed it was an interview of sorts. Sam held his hand out and the Major shook it firmly. "Good to meet you, Major Hamilton. If you are a friend of Tom's, then you are a friend of mine."

"Good to meet you as well, Lieutenant. Colonel Rose speaks highly of you. He thinks you are a decent young man. Do you think you are a decent young man?"

The question made Sam uncomfortable. "I aim to be, Sir."

The Major dropped his voice dangerously low at this point, his eyes scanning the room and not focused on Sam as he spoke. "The colonel and I are of the opinion we must do all in our power to escape this place. We are looking for others who are of a like mind."

Rose leaned in toward Sam and asked, "How do you feel about getting out of here?"

Sam paused thoughtfully. "I have a wife back home, a child that will be born soon, if not already. It isn't my wish to make her a widow nor to leave my child fatherless. If you feel there is a chance we can escape, I am all for it, but let it be in prudence, well thought out and cautiously executed. If we share the same view, then I am in."

"See, Andrew, I told you so."

"Yes, you did."

"Well, then, Sam, we are in business."

"Colonel Rose and I have been looking about, trying to find a way that would allow for concealment. After several attempts, we've discovered what we feel would be the best location for our endeavor."

"The cellar kitchen, now abandoned, seems to be the perfect setting for our next attempt," Rose said in a hushed tone.

"That room is off limits," Sam pointed out. "How do you contrive to get to it?"

"We are working on that," Hamilton replied.

"What of the rats? They've overrun the basement."

"I do not care for rats myself, but I can endure anything if it means my freedom."

"I suppose you are right," Sam agreed.

Rose grew dead sober. "The time is now, friends. I have heard talk they will be transferring a large number of us further south to a place even more abominable than this one. With such a move, our chances of survival or escape grow dimmer and dimmer. This may be the last and only chance we have at preserving our lives."

"What do you need from me?" Sam asked eagerly.

"We need tools. We need man power. We need men with smarts who will take care and not alert the guards to our doings."

"I can do all but provide tools." Sam bent down and retrieved the pocket knife from his boot, the knife he got from the men he helped escape through the kitchen window. "I have this pocket knife. I know it isn't much, but it may prove useful."

Rose and Hamilton accepted it eagerly. Rose put his back to the room, hunched his shoulders, and turned the knife over in his hand, opened it and closed it as he inspected it carefully. "This should serve some purpose. It's better than nothing."

"I may be able to help in another way as well. I managed to smuggle some money in when I came here, unknown to the guards. A Union dollar goes a long ways here. They are desperate for cash money. I've been told the Negro soldiers who are housed in one of the cellar rooms are sometimes sent to do labor in the town. We may be able to acquire needed supplies through them, give them the money, tell them what we need, and have them sneak it back in."

"Good thinking, Sam. That just may work," Thomas Rose said with approval.

Andrew Hamilton remained skeptical. "You understand if you are caught, you are on your own. You must not implicate anyone else involved in this," he warned.

"You have my word, Sir," Sam assured him.

"Good. Then we shall endeavor to orchestrate a prison break, gentlemen."

Chapter 26

I couldn't sleep. After tossing and turning for what seemed like hours, I wasn't able to grow comfortable in my bed. Despite my attempts at shifting, there seemed to be no relief, and my back ached so badly I could hardly breathe. I tried rubbing my lower back with my fingers, but it didn't ease my pain. I finally gave up on sleep and got up from bed, wandering from room to room with my robe hanging loose over my shoulders. I sat in the rocking chair and made a mental list of things I needed to get done, trying to distract myself from the pain I suffered through.

Eventually the frosted windows began to glow with the faint light of the morning sun, and I forced myself to get up and prepare for the day. I dressed myself with the slow clumsiness I was growing accustomed to, my body feeling as though gravity were magnified, and the weight of it was making the smallest of tasks a struggle. I awkwardly got to my feet after managing to get my shoes on despite my bulging belly, and I went to the kitchen, taking the wooden bucket from the shelf, heading out to the well to draw some water.

It was now the first week of November, and the frost lay in a thick cover over everything. The trees were nearly bare of their leaves, and when the sun rose it was late in the morning. I shivered in the brisk chilly temperatures, wishing I'd thought to put on my shawl. The short walk to the well took all of my energy and left me out of breath. That is how it was for me over the most nominal of tasks; everything seemed to require more energy than I had. I leaned against the stone enclosure, gulping air in puffy white clouds and gathering my strength so I could eventually draw the water. The bucket was heavy, and I strained to carry it back to the house, switching it from one hand to the other several times.

As I stood on the threshold of the kitchen and swung the door wide, I felt a sudden rush of warm liquid course down my legs and pool on the ground beneath my feet. I stood dumbly for a moment, trying to register what had just happened. Strangely enough I thought I had somehow dumped the bucket of water on myself. But the handle was still firmly grasped in my hand and the water full to the brim. I realized my water must have broken, but still did my best to tell myself it couldn't be so. I was not ready for it, not today.

I walked across the floor, leaving a trail of water behind me as I went, which unsettled me terribly. I took the mop and worked to clean it up, making more of a mess in the process because everywhere I moved I left more fluid in my wake. I grabbed a pile of towels and made my way to the bedroom, taking off my soiled clothing and toweling myself dry as best I could. Eventually, I got into some clean, dry undergarments and sat perched on the edge of my bed wondering what I should do next.

The baby was coming, my water breaking being an unmistakable sign. I should go to my parents' house. I should go to my mother. She would know what to do. The thought of the seven-mile trek overwhelmed me, made me shudder. I wasn't at all sure I could make it. Did I really want to give birth to my baby alone, in a ditch by the roadside? I was closer to town. Perhaps I should try to make it there to get help.

I got up, thinking I should get dressed, but in that moment I experienced my first birthing pain and nearly fell to the floor with the shock of it. It gripped my belly and stretched with cruel fingers around my sides and into my back, leaving my womb as tight as a drum. I stumbled backward, resting on the bed again, my hands spread wide and gripping my abdomen as I gasped in pain. When it passed I sat dazed and unable to move for a moment.

If I was not afraid before, I surely was now. I fleetingly speculated whether I would live through the birth or not. I knew I couldn't make it the seven miles to my parents or the four miles to town all the while experiencing pain like this. I simply couldn't chance it. I would stay here. At least I would have a bed to give birth in, which seemed an infinitely better option than squatting in the road.

With this determination, I forced myself to get up and do what I must to prepare. I wrapped my robe over my underclothing and shuffled barefooted to the kitchen. My trembling fingers worked to build a fire, and once it was steady, I put a large pot of water on to boil. When a pain came upon me I stopped what I was doing until it passed, and then I continued in my task. In the meantime, I took a knife and set it over the flames, making sure it was good and hot, before I wrapped it in a towel to be used later.

There was a pile of clean sheets in the linen cupboard, which I took and sat on the chest of drawers in the bedroom. I then got the baby's things ready - a cloth diaper, a dress, booties and a cap, a blanket - and lay them out on the bedside table, within easy reach. Then I sat in the rocking chair and waited.

By this time, the pains were coming at regular intervals, more insistent and fiercer with each one. In the silent walls of my home I struggled loudly, knowing there was no one there to hear it. As one began, I would breathe rapidly and as it grew in strength, I concluded with a noisy and distressed groan. The sweat formed upon my brow, wetted the fabric of my chemise, making me feel damp and uncomfortable.

I realized, at one point, I was gritting my teeth and tried to relax my jaw, with little effect. My fingers frantically pulled at my skirt, twisting the cotton this way and that in desperation. In my fear and pain I cried out.

"Oh God, please…Oh, please! I cannot do it alone!" With each pain I cried out anew. "Oh, God, please… Please, help me!" I thought it must be soon--it *had* to be soon. I could not go on like this much longer.

About midmorning I heard a knock at the front door. Now, I wasn't sure at all if it was real or imagined. Perhaps I was only hearing it because I wanted to. But then it came again, firm, resolute. I struggled to pull myself up from the chair, my knees shaking, hardly able to hold my weight. I moved tediously to the door, dragging my feet and gasping for air. Once I got there I flung the door wide, and there stood my mother cradling a loaf of bread in one arm and holding a milk pail in the other.

She took one look at me and her face fell, her eyes growing alarmed. I was so relieved to see her I began to cry, tears streaming down my face.

"Mother!" I whimpered.

She rushed through the door, putting the milk and bread on the table, before she came to my side and helped me make it back to the bedroom. I leaned on her heavily, feeling as though all my strength had left me. Once she assisted me to the bed, I laid back upon my pillow and moaned as another pain hit me.

"How long has it been?" Mother asked.

"I can't do this!" I howled. "Please, please don't make me do this!"

"Serena, how long has it been?"

"Hours! Hours!"

"Shh. Calm down," she coaxed. "Calm down."

"I will die! I will surely die!"

"Serena, calm down!"

I began to cry again. "Please, Mother, please…don't make me do this. I can't do it…"

Mother was rolling up her sleeves, washing her hands in the wash basin. "You can do it, and you must."

She came to me and rolled my petticoat up to my thighs. "I'm just going to check to see how far along you are." Her voice was gentle, meant to calm me, but I felt far from calm. "It will be soon," she informed me. "Very soon. Do you feel as though you want to push yet?"

"No," I murmured. Another pain began, and I writhed in agony. "Please…no, no, no, no!"

Mother waited for me to become calm again and then arranged my pillows and pulled me to a nearly sitting position, my back supported by the cushioned nest she had just built. As she worked, I pleaded with her. "Mother, I can't do this!"

She grew stern. "That's enough. You can do this, and you will. There's no going back now, my girl." She dipped a cloth in the wash basin and swabbed my brow with it. "Try to relax," she told me.

"How can I relax? The pain is so great!" I was incredulous.

"Let the pain work for you. Let it work on your behalf. Breathe," she said.

I took in a deep cleansing breath. I attempted to unclench my body. "I didn't know…" I said as I breathed out.

"What?"

"That it would be so bad."

"I suppose if we did know the human race would have been extinct a long time ago."

I began to laugh, but the laugh somehow ended up being a desperate sob. "Yes, yes, I suppose so. And yet you had five. What would possess you to have five?"

"God has given women the magnificent gift of forgetting."

"I will never forget this," I replied incredulously.

"So you say," she said with a knowing smile.

As I began to experience another pain I sucked all of my air in and held it. I could feel the thrumming of my pulse in my eyeballs and the pounding in my temples.

"Keep breathing," she ordered. "Think of something that will take your mind from it."

"Sam…Sam said I should count."

"If that helps, then do it," she said.

I took a breath and held it counting, "One, two, three, four…" I let my breath out and counted again. "One, two, three, four…"

When the contractions came upon me, I bared my teeth and counted through them, as my mother whispered, "Nearly over. Nearly over."

"Stop saying that!" I fumed. "You keep saying it, but it's not true! You're lying to me! You lie!"

"Pull yourself together," Mother replied calmly. Her unruffled demeanor made me all the more angry. It took everything I had within me not to assault her with a string of profane words I had heard many times in camp, all of which a decent lady would never say. To be safe, I said nothing. I clamped my mouth shut and counted in my head.

After a while I said to her, "I think I need to push now!"

Chapter 27

"Show me how strong you are! Show me how brave you are!" she was yelling.

I was irritated beyond all measure. I couldn't say why, but I felt like yelling back at her. I wanted to scream in her face, *Leave me alone! Just leave me alone! I'm not strong! I'm not brave!* But I was too weak and too beaten to do much more than push when she told me to. I grunted loudly with each push and then spent the time in between trying to catch my breath. It seemed to go on forever. After a time I began to think I was never going to have that baby.

"Here we go," she told me. "Here we go. Push your legs further apart."

"I can't, Mama! I can't!"

She put her hands on my knees and pressed them back and apart, and I cried out in agony. "It hurts!"

"Push!" she hollered back.

I did what she told me to. I would have done anything--anything at all--if it meant it would end. I pressed down with all of my might, moaning loudly.

"There it is!" she exclaimed. "There is the head! Just a little more, Serena! Come on!"

I leaned forward against my drawn up legs and pushed again until I felt a flood of relief as the head broke through and popped out with a gush of fluid. Mother let go of my legs and used her hands to guide the shoulders out one at a time. The rest of the body seemed to glide out with no trouble at all. I let my head sag backward against the pillows and sighed with relief.

I watched through the slits of my eyelids as Mother stuck her finger into the baby's mouth and down its throat. And then the baby began to choke and cry all at the same time. Its puffy little red face became indignant, and it let out a loud yell with trembling lips and quaking chin.

"A girl!" she informed me.

I lay there with such a sense of release that my body felt as though it were tingling all over, and I felt as if I were no longer connected to the bed or confined by the walls of the room. Every muscle in my body became loose and languid, for a moment I experienced no pain at all, and I reveled in the crying. Mother wrapped my daughter's little body in a blanket and sat the bundle on my chest, where I steadied her with my hand.

"We aren't done yet, Serena. I need you to push a little more."

"But I'm so tired," I complained.

"It's easier now," she assured me.

I pushed as she asked, until I had delivered the placenta. Strangely enough, I was hardly aware of it or of Mother cutting the umbilical cord with the knife I had prepared. I was studying the baby that squirmed against me. She continued to cry, and I did my best to soothe her.

"She's so beautiful," I murmured.

"Yes, she is," Mother agreed.

"So beautiful…" Then I burst into tears.

"It's all over now. What's the matter?"

"She will have to go through this," I said through tears.

"That's a long ways off, don't worry about that now," Mother admonished. "Here, let me help you." She began unbuttoning my chemise.

"What are you doing?" I asked.

"You must feed her."

"Oh," I said. But really it was like I was in a dream; I felt so weary and so spent I simply allowed her to pull my breast out, as if it were an everyday commonality. I had no dignity, no modesty left, no control over my own body. I didn't even think to be embarrassed in front of her.

"Here, prop her up." Mother helped me move the baby to the crook of my arm. The little mouth searched like a baby bird with its eyes still sealed shut, bobbing her head with no control over her neck yet, as she sought her dinner. Finally her probing lips found my nipple, and she latched on and began to suck feverishly.

"This one knows what she is doing," Mother said, very pleased. "Look at that, didn't need any coaxing at all. Some of them have to be taught."

When she finished nursing, Mother took her from me, holding her against her shoulder and patting her gently on the back. "May I have a drink of water?" I requested. "I'm so very thirsty."

"Rightfully so," Mother said. She left the room and returned with a glass of water, which I drank all at once. It tasted so good upon my dry tongue, until it hit my stomach and then came right back up.

"I feel sick," I said. Mother rushed to grab the wash basin with her free hand and thrust it in front of me just as I vomited. I was ashamed my mother should have to wait upon me when I was in such a condition, but I was at her mercy without the ability to do anything for myself. She put the baby in the cradle and cleaned me up, helping me move from the bed so she could put fresh bed linens on. Once it was done, she helped me back into the bed, covering me with a quilt.

"Try again, only drink slowly," she said, offering me a drink. I did as she bade me, managing to get half a glass of water down before I grew too tired to hold the cup in my hand.

I leaned back against the pillow again and promptly fell asleep. A dreamless and dark slumber consumed me. Occasionally I came awake, feeling as though I could not move my body. My limbs were so heavy and my brain simply refused to function. I was only vaguely aware of it for a brief moment and then I would doze off again. The shadows of evening were expanding across the room when Mother shook me awake and I, at last, managed to keep my eyes open.

"She's wanting to be fed again," Mother whispered.

With great effort I drew myself upright and pulled my other breast out. Again she latched on with no trouble at all and began to eat. Mother had bathed her and dressed her in the flannel dress and knitted cap I laid out, swaddling her in a tight bundle with her blanket. I held her close and smelled her skin. What a sweet smell. As she fed a strange feeling spread through me, as though her lips tugged at a string that ran through my body and pulled at my womb. Although not nearly as painful as the birthing contractions, it was still uncomfortable.

"It feels strange," I said, rubbing my hand over my belly.

"That's just your body righting itself, drawing your womb back to where it should be."

"I thought this would be gone," I admitted forlornly as I felt the sizeable mound that was still left behind.

"It will be soon enough. It takes some time," Mother informed me. "It took nine months to change you, and it will take several months to put you back."

"I feel so tired."

"You've done a day's work."

"I wish Sam was here." Again I felt the tears welling up. I didn't want to be any more pathetic than I already was, but I also didn't want to be alone. I was afraid. I had this tiny little creature nestled in my arms and it was up to me and me alone to care for her and see to her every need. The prospect was nearly overwhelming. Everything about that day was overwhelming. What if I should make a mistake? What if I should mess it up?

"I know," she said, sympathetically, giving me a reticent little pat on the shoulder.

"He was so thrilled with the idea of this child. If he were here I have no doubt he would be strutting about the place like a proud papa ought to."

"He will hold her soon enough, Serena."

"I hope so," I said softly. "At least I wasn't alone. I am certainly lucky you came when you did. I don't think I could have done it without you." It struck me as peculiar she had come at all. The only time she had been to my home was when she visited for the first time several months ago and played the piano for me.

"I woke this morning, and I thought I must come to see you," she said. "I didn't know why, but I knew I must come. I felt foolish about it. I thought perhaps I was being irrational, you know. But then again it came to me: *You must go and visit Serena.*"

"It was an answer to my prayers," I told her.

Chapter 28

When the baby finished feeding, I gave her back to Mother and promptly fell asleep again. Sometime in the late evening Father came round. After waiting for Mother to return home, he grew worried and came by with the horse and wagon to make sure all was well. I heard him and Mother whispering in the other room, probably trying to keep from disturbing my sleep.

"I'm awake," I called out.

Father came to the bedroom door, looking uncertain and nervous. It must have been strange for him, his only living child having a child of her own. I smiled weakly to try to reassure him. For some reason, seeing him standing there nearly made me cry again. He seemed older, more worn around the edges. I thought fleetingly I had done that to him; I had caused some of those gray hairs and worry lines.

"How are you, girl?" he asked.

"Better now."

"Mother says you have a daughter."

"Yes. She's in the cradle," I said, indicating with a nod of my head where he could find her.

He tiptoed toward the cradle and stood over the baby in solemn amazement. "Look at that, Seri," he said.

"Would you like to hold her?"

"Should I?"

"If you want to."

He bent down and picked the baby up, holding her out along the length of his arm so he could get a good look at her. "She looks like you," he observed.

"Does she?"

"Yes."

"I hope she looks more like Sam. I noticed she has his ears. I thought that was good at least."

"What's the matter with your ears?"

"They stick out. It's my least favorite thing about myself."

"Oh, now, your ears are fine."

"If you say so," I said skeptically.

"What have you named her?"

"I don't know yet."

"No name?"

"Sam wanted Luke for a boy. I liked that fine. But he didn't like Augusta, which is what I would have chosen for a girl. He's not here to consult with. I'm almost afraid to pick it by myself. What if he doesn't care for it?"

"I'm sure it will come to you," he assured me.

Mother came in with a bowl of broth and a sizeable chunk of bread slathered in apple butter. "Are you hungry?"

"Yes, please," I said, realizing I was indeed hungry, possibly hungrier than I'd ever been. I didn't bother with the spoon. I drank the broth from the bowl until it was gone and then I ate the bread, licking my fingers clean when I finished.

"I have never tasted anything so good," I commented.

"Would you like anything else?" Mother asked.

"No thank you. Only, Father, could you get word to Sam's family the baby's come?"

"I will go on over there once I leave here," Father promised.

"I don't wish for them to see me in such a state," I admitted. "But I'm sure they are eager to know. Perhaps they could come to see her tomorrow afternoon, after I've had a chance to prepare for them."

"Don't worry about that now, Serena. Just rest and grow strong. Give no thought for the morrow for the morrow shall take thought for the things of itself."

"So the Bible says," I replied with a yawn. "But it was written by men, Mother."

She seemed surprised by my observation, but then allowed a chuckle. "You have learned to speak your mind," she observed. "You always did have a quick wit about you, but you were too shy to say much when you were younger. Our girl has grown up, Matthew."

"Certainly has," Father said as he looked down on the baby he held in his arms. He handed the baby back to Mother, taking great care, as though she were a precious and breakable parcel. One very plump little leg broke free from the dress and blanket and dangled on display. "I should be heading out, if I am going to stop in town." Then Father moved to my side, giving me a kiss atop my head, as he had when I was just a little child. "Take care now, and let Mother spoil you some," he said.

"I will."

Then he drifted over to Mother, gave her an affectionate pat on the back. "I will be back tomorrow. Would you like me to bring anything?"

"I didn't expect to be staying. I haven't got a thing. Could you bring a clean dress and apron?"

"I will." He looked as though he felt badly over leaving, gave us each a nod, and then headed out.

Chapter 29

It was growing so very cold. After the intense heat of summer, the fall was happily welcomed. The cool temperatures were much more tolerable than the sweltering days Sam had thus far seen. But it passed far too quickly, and with the winter coming on and no blankets or a fireplace to huddle around, the men of Libby Prison experienced a new discomfort in a place where discomforts were the only constant, the only thing to be counted on.

There was no feast on Christmas day. In fact, the men were lucky to get a cut of blackening beef, smelling so badly they breathed through their mouths to avoid the stench of it as they devoured it. If you swallowed fast enough, the sour taste did not linger as long.

While I was safe and sound at home, eating a goose my mother roasted all the day long, holding our baby daughter in my arms before the warm fire, Sam squatted near the cooking stove to try to make himself warm as he ate his overly ripe meat. As terrible as it tasted, he savored each bite, so desperately hungry it produced the effect of making his meal desirable. He didn't speak to anyone when he ate. No one else spoke either. The only sounds were the men's collective grunts, loud chewing, and audible swallowing, as they postured with their shoulders stooped forward eyeing everyone around them, in the fear that what little they had might be taken from them. They were hungry. So desperately hungry they were consumed with the very short task of eating what was given.

Once Sam finished he brushed his hands against his trousers and then picked himself up and began to mingle. As the day progressed into evening, he wandered about the rooms, finally discovering an empty chair. He sat down wearily, questioning how he could be so tired after doing so little. For a time he dozed in the chair but was shortly awakened by the sound of music. Some of the Union soldiers had formed a group and were now singing Christmas hymns. The voices of the choir complemented one another in a way most pleasing to hear. Although he was surrounded by ugliness on all sides, desperate and hopeless after having lived in such squalid and hostile conditions for so long, the music was so lovely Sam was overcome by a wave of altruism, making him feel warm inside, and he was so moved by it he had to stop himself from shedding tears.

His mouth formed the words of the songs, although his voice remained silent, as he enjoyed their serenade. It was now nearly eight months since he had come to this place. And this was the first time he could remember feeling any sort of peace during that period. Sam's mind began to reflect upon home and family. He knew he was probably a father by now, that I must have had our baby, and yet the lack of official news would not allow him to feel any sort of joy over it.

He felt as though he were trapped in time, with no progression of hours or days or weeks. It would go on forever this way. There would be no end. He began to wonder if he would ever see home or family again. He wondered if they'd all forgotten about him and moved on with their lives, figuring him to be a lost cause. But in that brief moment of truth, with the men singing Christmas hymns and the inner concord of stillness, he allowed himself to experience hope. It gave him a burning feeling in his chest, a sense of well-being he sorely missed.

Eventually the night came on, and he found a spot on the floor to settle into and sleep. It was several hours before dawn when he was stirred awake by Thomas Rose. Sam struggled against him at first, but then grew still when he saw Colonel Rose hold his finger to his lips, telling him without words to quiet down. Sam grew still as he looked at his friend in confusion.

"Tom," Sam said in surprise. "What are you doing? Has something happened?"

"I have a Christmas present for you," the Colonel replied.

"You have?" Sam wasn't sure if he could trust his faculties, what with his hunger and being woke from a deep sleep.

"Come with me," Tom Rose whispered. He wore a look upon his face which could only be described as intense satisfaction.

Sam got up quietly and moved noiselessly through the men who still slept, moving his feet with careful precision over the squealing floorboards. Each noise made him shudder inside, made him listen in alarm for approaching guards. The colonel led the way and together they went to the kitchen. As bizarre as the circumstances were it grew even more so when Andrew Hamilton appeared from the shadows of the room, looking like a cat who'd just eaten the canary. He had known the Major for several months now and had gleaned no real information on his private life. Likewise, the Major seemed to keep his emotions carefully guarded, never betraying his state of sentiments. So when Sam saw him looking as he did, a little thrill ran through him making the goose pimples form.

Something was up.

For a moment he wasn't sure what to think. He wasn't sure if he should turn the other way and run, or if the alarm he was experiencing was unfounded. "What's going on?" he asked in a hiss.

"We have something to show you," Thomas Rose said. He then prodded the Major. "Show him Andrew."

The two men worked strenuously to move the cooking stove aside as quietly as was possible, then gently pulled the bricks from the back wall one at a time. When they'd finished there before them was a gaping hole, black and portentous in the dark room. They stood back so Sam could inspect it. He took a tentative step forward, standing upon the precipice and peering down into the hole.

Sam didn't know at the time that it took the men the better part of two weeks to achieve their goal of creating this new passageway.

Working with the pocket knife Sam had given them, and a chisel they managed to acquire with some of the money he kept in his brass buttons, Rose and Hamilton carefully and painstakingly worked on the project each night while everyone else slept, until they accomplished what they'd set out to do. They now waited eagerly for Sam's reaction.

"I don't understand," Sam said.

"It's a tunnel," the colonel explained enthusiastically.

"To where?" Sam asked. After all, they were on the second floor, so it couldn't be a tunnel leading outside. He didn't grasp the full implications of what the portal meant. He didn't understand why he should feel as pleased as they seemed to be over it.

Hamilton answered with a smile, "To the east cellar."

Chapter 30

Thomas Rose was the first to go through, his body hovering above the floor before he disappeared into the abyss. Then Andrew Hamilton followed, telling Sam to trust the rope. Sam felt a sick excitement in the pit of his stomach as he went down. Or perhaps it was just the lack of food in his belly. He slipped down into the hole, his hands wrapped tightly around the rope.

It was a short distance, in an *S* shape from the kitchen hearth through the wall and down into the ceiling of the cellar, where Sam landed lightly on his feet into the darkest of rooms. He could smell the rot and decay, making him feel as though he couldn't expand his lungs completely to breathe, and he could hear the rats squealing and scratching loudly, could feel them running over his boots. He kicked them away as he put his hands out seeking to orient himself, afraid of what might be in the room with him.

Eventually his eyes began to adjust, and the small half window that was just above ground shed barely enough light from the street lamp above that he could make out the inky outlines of the other two men who led the way. The smell was overwhelming. Sam choked, coughed a few times, and then remembered to breathe through his mouth and not his nose. The men took him by the arm and slipped wordlessly through the room until they came to the outside wall on the south east corner. Rose worked to move a bit of straw out of the way, rats scurrying over his hand as he displaced them from their hiding places.

"We have done some digging, and have come to the conclusion that this will be the best place to begin," he whispered.

"The dirt is more tightly packed here. Less likely to have a cave in," Hamilton added.

"You mean to tunnel your way out?" Sam asked. His voice was replete with misgivings. His immediate reaction was to balk at the prospect of such an undertaking. How long would it take to dig a tunnel? Where would the tunnel end? How realistic was it to believe that such a task could be accomplished? The anticipation he felt when they showed him the hole in the bricks on the floor above came abruptly crashing down. He was immensely disappointed.

Hamilton spoke first, allowing his annoyance with Sam to show. "No one is going to force you to go along with it," he said.

Rose interceded. "Now, Sam. We tried everything else we could think to, and not one of them has worked…"

"You got a better idea?" Andrew cut in. He seemed somewhat insulted by Sam's hesitation.

"Andrew, he doesn't see it yet. Give him some time to see it." Thomas Rose turned to Sam. "The way we figure it, we dig until we reach the sewer line. We hit that and it will take us to Kanawha Canal which would then empty into the river. Once we intercept the Canal, we follow it on out to the water and we're home free."

"That will take some doing," Sam pointed out.

"Yes, we've thought of that. We are considering bringing others in on it. We could take shifts, working through the night, until it is done."

"The more people we bring in on this, the more likely we are to be found out."

"We agree there, Sam. Which is why we would only include those we know to be completely trustworthy. Now, you're in or you're out, but either way we need you to promise you won't disclose any of this to anyone else."

Sam pursed his lips, thinking it over in his head. If they got caught it meant being put in front of a firing squad, or being hanged.

Both produced the same result. But with the lack of food, and the cold coming on, and the threat of a transfer to Andersonville, Sam did not doubt that was where he was headed anyhow. He had one foot in the grave, and he knew there really was no choice. He must do what he could to get out while he still was able.

"You have my word," Sam pledged. "I won't tell anyone, and you can count me in. I'll help any way I can."

"See I told you. Didn't I tell you?" Thomas Rose asked Andrew Hamilton as he shook Sam's hand.

"We'll start tomorrow. The sooner we get this thing underway the better."

Chapter 31

Given the joyful event I was attending, I should have been in a better mood, but I found it difficult to force a smiling face. I, of course, was very happy for my friends, and yet their good fortune made me reflect upon my own current hardships. I sat with little Lucia in my arms, holding her close, smelling her hair, pressing my lips again and again to her forehead, and doing my best to suppress my tears. I felt as though I should be able to be more in control of myself, and yet when the tears came, I was helpless to stop them.

It was not so long ago Sam and I were married in a small white church in Pennsylvania. I recalled how eager he was, how happy it made me that he wanted me for his wife. It was like a dream now. Almost as if it never happened at all. I longed to see him again. To hear him speak. And I imagined whatever he might say, even if it was something as commonplace as a simple hello, it would be the most profound of messages coming from the sweetest of lips.

The terrible truth was, I had begun to forget what he looked like. In those moments when I could not form his face, the mole on his jawbone, his hands, thick fingers and boney knuckles, his hair, dark and unruly, I would begin to panic. I would hastily pull out our likeness together, and I would study the details in a frenzied need to memorize every small feature, until I was satisfied I wouldn't forget again, only to repeat the process several times a day. It frightened me that if I could forget so easily, it would all disappear and there would be nothing left of him, or of the two of us.

Several weeks before, I hit an all-time low. The papers came out with yet another article on the wretched conditions of Libby Prison. It painted a terrible picture of starvation, sickness, crowded conditions, and squalor, coupled with abuse and ill treatment from prison guards and staff. For days I couldn't make myself get out of bed. I cried and cried and was unable to be consoled. Mother sent for the doctor, who said that it was sometimes normal for a woman to be melancholy after having a baby. He gave Mother herbs for a tea for me.

When I finally got up out of bed, my joints ached, and I didn't feel up to doing much. I didn't see the point in doing anything anyhow. Why do the wash, cook a meal, keep up the house? What good did it do? Lucia was fussy and irritable, and Mother said it was because she could sense my unhappiness. I felt very guilty for my bad attitude and meant to repent and change my ways, but it seemed as though I had no ability to govern my emotions.

The turning point for me was when I realized I was becoming my mother. The very things I resented and held a grudge over, her grief, her darkness, her inability to see the beyond, to have faith, these were the same crimes I was guilty of now. As much as I wanted to be like my father, it was my mother I saw looking back at me in the mirror. Whether I felt like it or not, I got up each morning, dressed myself, tended to my household duties and my little daughter's needs.

One day Father said to me, "I can see you are suffering. And were it within my power I would take all of the heartache and loss away, Seri. I bet you would be ten feet tall with all of those burdens removed from off your back. But I can't. Someday you will look back on all this and know that you are stronger because of it. That's who you've always been. You've always been the one who said *it's hard, but I can do it, I will figure a way.*

You would always get that look in your eye, that determined look, and your jaw would set. I knew when I saw that look nothing was going to stop you. I want to see that look again. I want you to overcome this. But I figure the only thing can help you now is turning to the Lord in prayer."

"He doesn't hear me, Father," I told him with a heart-wrenching groan.

"He always hears. It's just his answer isn't always yes. He sometimes answers maybe, but not now, or he sometimes answers no. It is not for us to counsel him. It is for us to accept whatever his answer may be, always knowing his way is the best way."

"You don't know what it's like. You'll never know!" I cried bitterly. He gave me a kind but reproachful look, as if to say I should know better.

"I've had my share of trials, daughter. And the one thing I have learned the hard way is this, what is to be will be. But always the Lord's will be done. No matter what is to be, he will give you comfort if you will let him. Pray for comfort. Pray for the grace to accept what is to be."

There was a part of me that was angry at him for saying it. How dare he speak to me that way? He didn't know my heartache, he didn't know the pain I was experiencing. Yet, I knew that no matter how I fought against it, what he said was truth. My pride would not allow me to acknowledge he was right. But I was listening and thereafter prayed all the day long. I fell asleep praying, I woke realizing I hadn't finished my prayer and began praying where I'd left off. It seemed all I could do was pray and express the agony I felt in knowing that Sam was far off and suffering terribly. I begged the Lord to preserve him, to keep him for me, until I could be with him again.

Now it was with gladness and sorrow I attended Reed Haney and Aida Turner's wedding the day after Christmas in the old church Sam and I had gone to since our christenings. Others had expressed the opinion that these two were an odd couple. But I could see that there was something very appealing about their pairing. Mother told me Reed was two years older than she was, which put him at forty-six. And Aida was thirty-two. I suppose most people presumed that she was past her prime and would never marry. And then the age difference between he and she was a bit unconventional, but with so many men not coming home from the war there were more and more couples with unusual circumstances, such as extreme age differences, that it certainly wasn't unheard of.

Seeing them together might make anyone wonder why they had to wait so long to find each other. I couldn't help but admire Aida's pale rose colored dress, which she told me she kept for many years in her hope chest for such an occasion, wrapped in tissue paper with sachets of lavender, spearmint, thyme, rosemary, cloves, and cinnamon to keep the moths from it. It was an old fashioned dress, yes, but with the shortage of cloth and the lack of funds for such attire, she was lucky to have planned ahead. No such dress could be found for miles around. She would have to travel all the way to New York to find such finery, and then pay a pretty penny to acquire it. Besides, I thought the out-of-date styling lended to its appeal. She was certainly smarter than I'd been. I thought of my meager trousseau and how unprepared I was and felt it was a credit to her that she had such foresight.

Mr. Haney wore his uniform, the leg pinned up so it didn't drag the floor as he walked about on his crutch, shaking people's hands. Again and again he was patted on the back and congratulated by all who knew him. Everyone was pleased he had finally found someone to share his life with, I expect. After so long at being a bachelor it was a fine surprise he managed to pull it off and in short order. It was not much more than a few months of courting and now they were married.

He appeared much younger than I'd ever seen him look, as though his good fortune were a youth elixir which reversed the effects of time. He stayed close to Aida's side, often putting his free hand around her waist or to rest against her back. The fact that he was immensely happy was obvious, not only to me, but to anyone who laid eyes upon him. After many congratulations, it was time for the food and the dancing which Mr. Haney undertook with great zeal. It was a funny thing to watch him hop around on his one leg.

Eventually my father came to stand next to me. "Let me take Lucia and you can go and get yourself some pie or visit with your friends."

"No need," I said. Lucia was the one small bit of security I had in that room full of people. I was not about to let her go.

"I want to hold my granddaughter," he said, as he gently took her from me. I didn't know what to do with my empty arms, so I let them dangle awkwardly at my sides, my shoulders slumping and my eyes roaming uncomfortably over the room full of wedding guests. No wonder Mother didn't attend such functions.

"You must feel very pleased with all of this," Father commented. I thought perhaps he was pointing out that I *should* feel pleased rather than asking me if I really was.

"I am very happy for Mr. Haney and Miss Turner."

"You ought to show it with a smile."

"I don't mean to be a sour puss, Father, but isn't it enough that I am here?"

"Your dark mood casts a shadow over it. Put aside your personal feelings and be gracious enough to think of these two people who mean so much to you. It is their day, not yours."

"Indeed it is. I am sorry for displaying such poor manners."

"There, that's an attempt at a smile," he said, and his odd expression, as though he were trying to appease a pouting toddler, made me smile all the more.

"You see, it didn't hurt so bad after all," he chuckled. Lucia's pudgy hand bobbed up and her fingers wrapped around his bottom lip and pulled, exposing yellowing teeth and fine red veins in his peach gums. He didn't seem to notice.

"I must ask you something, Father," I said, growing serious again.

He didn't lose the look of amusement he wore. I could see his curiosity was piqued. "What is it?"

"May I rely upon you in all things?"

"Of course you may. I'm your father. I'd do anything within my power to help you in any way you need."

"And Mother?"

"I can't speak for her, but I believe she is of the same mind."

"I need you to take Lucia for a time."

"Not getting any sleep at nights, I'm sure. A rest would do you good. We would be glad to take her for a few days."

"That isn't what I meant. I'm going away, Father."

Immediately his countenance changed. "What are you talking about?" he asked slowly.

"I'll be gone for a month or more. I can't say for certain how long, and I need someone I can trust, someone I know will love Lucia as I would. Aida has given me the name of a woman who has a babe of her own. I have spoken to her and she has agreed to suckle Lucia, but someone must otherwise care for her."

"And where were you thinking you would be going?" he wondered, his voice growing thin and edgy.

"I am going to Virginia. I am going to go get my Sam." Before he could say anything, I rushed on. "I know you don't understand, Father. But this is what I must do." I didn't look at him. I dare not. I knew what he must be thinking, but I was not about to acknowledge how crazy he must consider me.

After a long pause he slowly closed his eyes. "There is nothing I can say to dissuade you?"

"Nothing."

"For a moment there I saw that jaw set and I thought it was good. You were coming around."

"This is something I've been planning on for a while now. For months I have thought of little else. But I know it is finally time."

His eyes opened again and he was calm, although I was sure he was very upset by my intentions. "What am I to do with you, Seri? You no sooner come back to us, and then you are running off into harm's way again. What of your responsibility as a mother? If anything should happen to you, your child will be motherless. It's bad enough that she's fatherless but motherless too?"

"She isn't fatherless. She has a father. And he needs me just as surely as she does," I said.

Father shrugged, dropping his head in defeat. "You're right, daughter. I don't understand. But I'll help you."

"I am grateful, Father. More than you could ever know. But before you agree to help me, I have to tell you something. You may very well refuse to help me once I've told you what I must."

He grew very still, his eyes narrowing as he tried to surmise what it was I would disclose. What could be worse than what I'd already just told him? Running off and leaving my baby was not the worst of it? Finally he said, "What?" and I could sense a quaking in his voice, as though he were anxious or afraid for what I was about to say.

"I lied to you."

Chapter 32

My father froze, gripping Lucia to him as if she were protection from whatever it was I was going to say. I allowed him a moment, not only to give him time to prepare, but also that I might have a moment to gain the courage to speak the words I knew I must. He stared carefully straight ahead, watching the couples in their bright finery swirl by as they danced to a lively tune. They were all laughing, enjoying the music, the hard times momentarily forgotten for them.

"Tell me, daughter."

I could see him from the corner of my eye, but I pretended to be watching the dancers too. It was easier than facing him. If I didn't have to look at him perhaps it would come less painfully. He was pale and visibly shaken, his expression sober, with his eyebrows drawn together. Did he seem hurt? I could not be certain.

"I lied to you about being a nurse."

He turned his neck slowly to look at me, although he didn't face me full on. He was still positioned so he was pointed toward the crowd. His lips were formed as if to say *what?* but no words escaped. Eventually he asked, "What do you mean you lied about being a nurse?"

"I only told you that so you wouldn't worry. And I knew if I told you the truth, you wouldn't stand for it. You would come and get me and bring me home."

Was he going to cry? His eyes teared up and he seemed speechless. He staggered backward a step or two, his grip on Lucia growing tighter still. "What have you done?" he murmured. "What were you up to those many months?"

"I didn't cut my hair because of lice, although there was plenty of it where I was," I said.

"Why did you cut your hair? Why?" and his voice was filled with such confusion and dread that I pitied him. There is nothing worse than wanting to know and yet, desperately not wanting to know. I thought of Sam. How I would do anything to know what he was doing, how he was being treated, and then dreading the truth with my whole heart and soul. What if they were treating him badly? What if he was suffering so terribly it would hurt too deeply to know? The tug of war between knowing and remaining ignorant raged within. I was sure Father must be having similar feelings right now.

"Father, I was a soldier." Despite my beating heart and plunging stomach I managed to press on. "I…I dressed like a boy and fought alongside the men."

This really baffled him. I could see his mind working to understand what I said. He pursed his lips, and his eyes narrowed upon me. "A soldier?"

I nodded wordlessly. "I cut my hair, I wore a uniform, and I went by the name of Frank."

"And you got away with it? But…you look nothing like a boy!"

"You only say that because I am your daughter. If you had no preconceived notions about me, you might well have been tricked too," I offered by way of an explanation.

"I don't know what to say." His face was filled with betrayal, with confusion, and disbelief.

I braced myself for the worst. I grew emotional, trying in vain to keep my sentiments under control. My lips quivered as I fought the tears. "I understand if you hate me. If you don't wish to speak to me ever again. But, Father, I love you too much to go on deceiving you. It has been such a hard thing to keep it from you all this time."

His brow was still wrinkled, and yet he managed a sad half smile. "I could never hate you." He paused and then said, "I love you. No matter what you do, you are still my daughter."

Well, I couldn't keep from crying then. I ignored Lucia and drew near to him and hugged him fiercely. He put his arm around me, and I sat close to him like that for a time. "I don't know how you can feel that way after what I've done," I whispered.

"There are worse things," he said. "I thought… For a moment… Well, there are worse things."

"What did you think?" I asked, pulling away to look at him.

He shook his head, did what he could to change the subject. "You always did what you wanted. I knew never to tell you you couldn't do something. For surely you would find a way if you were told no. But this…this is a shock."

"I'm sorry. I never wished to cause you any pain. I thought if I kept it from you it would be better for you. It's just that I couldn't keep lying to you anymore. I couldn't look you in the eyes and keep lying to you. You are the dearest, kindest man I know, and I have often asked myself what sort of person I must be to have done what I did. I have regretted it a million times over, leaving you the way I did. What daughter could be so heartless and cruel to a father who does nothing but love and care for her? Only someone as cold and unfeeling as me, and for what it's worth, I'm ashamed."

"It explains a lot. How I couldn't get mail to you. I never really knew where you were, couldn't get any news. I thought that was strange, but I never would have imagined what you were up to." He paused and then thought to ask, "Who else knows?"

"No one knew for a very long time. Not until near the end. Sam found out. He was just as surprised as you are. He was honorable in his intentions. Made sure that no one found out and protected my reputation. Mr. Haney knows. He discovered it too, shortly before Sam and I were married. Sam's father, he came to visit at camp. He brought a letter from you. Do you remember?"

"Yes."

"He didn't know then, what I had done. He didn't know until I came home. When he saw me…when he saw me for the first time, when he came out to the house to call on me, he knew then too."

Father nodded his head. "I expect I knew deep down something wasn't right," he admitted. "But I never would have guessed this. Not in a million years."

"I suppose I should tell Mother as well."

"No, Seri. No. She doesn't need to know."

I thought of how he told me the truth was always better. He knew as well as I did that wasn't always the case. What would Mother do if I told her? Would she lose her place again? Would she slip away as she had before? I was relieved he'd given me permission not to tell, because I didn't want to find out what would happen.

"Go on now. Go tell Miss Turner you are pleased for her," he said.

I wept in relief. Somehow telling him made my whole body feel lighter. I started to walk away, but I stopped. I turned back, looking my father square in the eyes. "I love you, Father. You are the dearest, kindliest father a girl could ever hope for. I want to say thank you, but it isn't enough. I will never be enough. But I will try. I will try to make it all up to you somehow."

I gave him a quick kiss on the cheek and left him there to go and find Aida. The rest of the evening I tried desperately to enjoy myself, knowing I would soon be gone. I wanted to leave with good memories to carry with me.

With Father's promise that he and Mother would look after Lucia, I felt released. I knew Libby was drawing me in, pulling me away from my daughter. I could sense a change, as though I were standing on the precipice of something deep and sprawling that threatened to swallow me up and change everything in my world. I hated the thought of it, because I didn't know if it would be a good or bad change. But I had made up my mind, and it didn't take long for me to get the details worked out.

Just two days later, after making arrangements for Lucia and the farm, I set out with Father's horse and wagon on my way to Richmond, Virginia, the capital of the Confederacy. I was to again be in the bosom of my enemy, to venture into Rebel territory.

Chapter 33

Every third night Sam was scheduled to work on the tunnel. He served in different capacities, sometimes keeping watch as a sentinel, sometimes a digger, sometimes emptying the spittoon used to carry the displaced dirt. He by far preferred acting as the sentinel. He didn't have to go down into the dreaded cellar with the sour smells and rats and dark. On those nights he kept watch upstairs so he might alert the men in the basement if anything was amiss.

Sam never considered himself claustrophobic up to this point, but now in the confined and wretched conditions of the cellar and in the worm hole they were digging to get out, he had to talk himself out of panicking. He told himself this meant his freedom, meant getting back to his home and to his wife and child. These thoughts gave him courage to continue his work, and he somehow managed to talk himself out of the terrors which filled his mind.

Shortly after everyone settled in for the evening and all were sleeping, he and his other crew members got up silently and picked their way through the bodies littering the floor. Like ghosts they moved wordlessly to the kitchen and began the process of moving the stove, removing the bricks, and climbing down the rope ladder put in place for their descent.

The old familiar smells accosted him at once. He put his sleeve over his mouth and nose, breathing shallowly until he grew accustomed to it. The work was done in relative silence, faint whispers only when necessary. Sam took the fan from Thomas Rose, standing near the tunnel, and waited. The tunnel was progressed enough that the threat of suffocation became very real. In order to overcome this obstacle, Andrew Hamilton devised a rather clever way to get air into the tunnel. He lashed some pieces of wood together to form a frame, and then he stretched a rubber blanket over the frame to make a fan.

"We're making good progress. Keep it up and we may very shortly find ourselves free men," Rose murmured gleefully.

He tied a long rope to his boot, took up his spoon and the spittoon, and a nearly burned up candle before crawling on his belly to enter the tunnel. Sam stood close to the mouth of the tunnel, pumping air into the shaft by fanning it with the rubber blanket. He stood there, pushing the air to and fro with the movement of his arms for an hour or more, his shoulders aching from the work. The other fellow, who was discarding dirt, waited with his hand on his hip until he would be needed again. Occasionally he would draw the spittoon from the tunnel by a rope to empty it. The dirt from the spittoon was taken and distributed along the wall, where piles of moldering straw masked the freshly displaced soil so no one would be the wiser.

Time dragged on in a slow and tedious manner. Sam shifted slightly, trying to make himself more comfortable. Strangely enough his boots sloshed. He lifted his foot up and tried to get a look at it, but because of the dark, he set his foot down again without seeing anything. Again there was the sound of displaced water. He crouched down, cautiously putting his fingers out to touch the ground. It was wet. And then from the mouth of the tunnel a gush of water rolled out over his feet and hand.

Sam sprang up. "Pull him out!" he cried in a desperate hiss. He and the other man took hold of the rope and began pulling frantically, their hands working in fast unison, one over the other as they reeled Thomas Rose from the hole. At one point Sam lost his footing, but did not let go of the rope as he fell backward, his hands still working at pulling his friend from the tunnel.

Finally, Tom, feet first, was dragged out of the shaft with a rush of water close behind. The colonel crawled, sputtering and coughing along the floor, then collapsed onto his stomach in exhaustion. Sam scuttled over to him, putting his hand on his back.

"Tom, what happened? Are you all right?"

Still coughing and gagging Tom managed to sit up. "Think I hit the canal," he managed to get out.

Sam looked over to his fellow worker, the man who was emptying the dirt. "Go get the major," Sam ordered.

Word was sent up the rope ladder to the sentinel above. In turn the sentinel got word to Hamilton, who shortly appeared. He fumbled to the center of the room and knelt down next to Sam and Thomas Rose.

"What's the matter?"

"We got a problem," Sam told him. "Tom says we've hit the canal. The tunnel is flooded. Lucky he got out in time."

Andrew Hamilton's face fell. He put the palm of his hand to his forehead and then pulled it down over his eyes and mouth. They waited for him to speak. He shook his head back and forth.

"Ah, dammit!" Andrew Hamilton fumed, smacking his fist to the ground. "This puts us back. We'll have to start all over again."

"I think our course must have been too deep, if we hit the canal…" Tom speculated.

"Well, we'll have to close it up," he finally said.

"It's not over, Andrew. We've got time on our hands. We'll figure it out."

"Do we have time? I've heard them saying they are about to transfer the lot of us. If we end up in Andersonville, well, the chances of us getting out of there are slim to none."

"The tunnel needs to be closed up. It will be light soon. Best get to it," Thomas Rose suggested.

"I think you've done your share for tonight, Tom," Sam said. "We'll take care of it. You go get some rest."

Possibly sensing Sam's downhearted state, Tom clamped his hand on Sam's shoulder. "We aren't giving up, right, boys? We got this far. Tomorrow we will re-evaluate things and we'll start over."

Sam pursed his lips. "Yes, tomorrow. We done it once. We can do it again."

Chapter 34

After climbing the grand staircase to the covered veranda and filled with a certain amount of trepidation, I knocked at the door of the Church Hill Mansion, a breathtakingly grand four-story home with a fine view of the city. This could go very badly for me, if the information I'd been given was incorrect. Eventually the door opened a crack and a young Negro woman, a house maid from the looks of her dress, greeted me. After looking me over, she glanced this way and that down the street. I knew it was not my imagination. She was wary.

"May I help you?" she asked.

"I am here to speak with Miss Van Lew," I said. "Miss Elizabeth Van Lew." I pulled a calling card from my pocket with my name written neatly on it and offered it to her.

The maid allowed me to enter, and I stood in the front hall while she disappeared into some other part of the house. I waited self-consciously, inspecting the beautiful carpet and the lovely art pieces adorning the wall. For a moment I wondered if it was a mistake coming here. After all, I had only the whisperings of unreliable sources to go on.

Miss Van Lew appeared, small and fragile looking, on the staircase and floated down in a cloud of black taffeta. She was summing me up, I could see, by the look on her face. My first impression was that she was not a beautiful woman. I thought amusingly, if she cut her hair she may very well be able to pass for a man just as I. Her brows were thick, her lips were thin, her chin and nose prominently featured, the whole of it being framed by her very dark curled hair. However, once I grew to know her well, I thought she was much more attractive than my initial impression of her.

She offered a small boney hand to me, and I gave it a gentle shake, fearing I might crush it if I held too tightly. "I am Miss Van Lew," she informed me.

"Miss Van Lew, thank you so much for seeing me without any notice," I replied. "I am Serena Barlow."

"I feel I am at a loss. You know of me, but I, dear lady, do not know you."

"Is there a place we might speak privately?" I asked.

"That can be arranged," she said with a smile.

I thought it was strange she didn't take me to the parlor, but instead to the dining room, where we sat and drank tea as we spoke. The long mahogany table was impressive, as were the carpets and tapestries. It was much too large a room for a private and most intimate conversation, but I did my best not to notice. She sat at the head of the table, as the hostess, and I sat to her left as she poured the tea and slid the cup and saucer toward me.

"You must understand," she told me. "There is a shortage of everything but dogs here in Richmond. I normally would be serving you something a sight better than this, but we are lucky to have tea at all."

"Thank you, it is very good," I replied. Really I was not a tea drinker, and so it was all the same to me.

"I'm sure you didn't come here for the tea," she observed. "Perhaps you would like to explain to me what you *have* come for."

I hesitated, unsure of what to say now that I was given the chance. I believe this was because my only thought was to try and figure out how to arrange a meeting with her, thinking it would not be so easy. It proved much easier than I anticipated. So much so I was at a loss for words. She stared at me with those shadowy, penetrating eyes, and it felt as though they were a spotlight and I was experiencing stage fright. I shifted uneasily in my chair, cleared my throat, and then looked about to make sure we were completely alone.

"There is talk, Miss Van Lew, of you…" It was difficult for me to know how to proceed. I didn't wish to say too much, but I also wanted to make clear my intentions. "In certain circles, they say you are a sympathetic ear, a woman with a taste for your northern roots who has some influence here in Richmond as well as abroad."

Elizabeth Van Lew grew careful. I could see her expression change perceptively, although ever so slightly. Her eyes became hooded by her lids, her polite smile relaxed faintly. "I am not sure who you've been speaking with, Miss Barlow-"

"Missus," I corrected

"Excuse me…Missus Barlow. But I am a southern lady. My interests lie here in Virginia." Miss Van Lew gave her small teaspoon a gentle stir with a look of demure amusement. "And even if they did not, what makes you so bold as to speak to me of such things? I'm sure you wouldn't expect me to simply open up on such matters to a perfect stranger who I cannot trust absolutely and implicitly. That would be most foolish of me, wouldn't you say?"

"I was mistaken then, in my assumption that you are in regular correspondence with General Grant?"

Miss Van Lew slowly smiled. "Little old me? That is certainly an amusing anecdote. What should someone such as myself have to say to the man who controls the whole of the Army of the Potomac?"

"I don't presume to know. I don't care to know. I care only for my husband, who currently resides down the street in that building they call Libby Prison. You must understand. I have little else to do these days but write letters. I have written anyone I could think to that may be able to help me, and it was your name…I was given your name."

Elizabeth Van Lew stopped drinking her tea, setting the delicate cup down carefully with a tiny clatter, and then she looked at me with thoughtful consideration. The two of us remained silent until I grew desperate and whispered pleadingly, "Please!"

"What did you expect of me exactly?"

"I need your help. I will not leave without him, and I need your help in getting him out."

"Well, dear, as pure as your intentions are, there are several thousand men rotting over in that prison. What makes yours so special?"

I looked her in the eyes defiantly, thinking *how dare she ask me what made Sam so special?* Scathing retorts sprung to my lips, but I knew I needed her and I dared not be offensive. However, I'd come too far and sacrificed too much to let her discourage me from my objective.

I said simply, "Because he is the one man out of several thousand I love, who means something to *me*. He is the father of my child, and without him my life would be nothing. If you won't help me, I plan on finding someone else that will. With or without you, I mean to get him out of there. I mean to take him home with me. I haven't come this far to be stopped."

She grew very still as she met my gaze, as though she were thinking things through, weighing out the pros and cons. I was sure she was a shrewd woman, knowing she had gotten this far without being arrested by using her wits. She was wondering if one man was worth possibly getting caught. I was there to assure her Sam *was* worth the risk. I didn't take my eyes from hers.

"I cannot promise anything. I will make some inquires and let you know." She stood up to indicate our meeting was over. "Until then you don't speak a word of this to anyone. Should you fall under suspicion, I can't say what may happen to you. And I certainly couldn't help you then. Do you understand?"

"Yes," I answered. I followed her down the hall, stopping when she stopped before the front door. She turned to me.

"What you are asking for may be entirely impossible, Missus Barlow. Do you really feel it is worth the risk?"

"I will do whatever it takes. Anything!"

"Where are you staying, and I'll send word?"

I hesitated. Truth was I had no place to stay. I'd looked into every boarding house and hotel in Richmond and came up empty. There seemed to be not a single bed left in the city. I was sleeping in the wagon at night, which was both uncomfortable and frightening. Elizabeth Van Lew was right about one thing, there was no shortage of dogs in Richmond. They howled piteously all night long, starving to death no doubt. I'd feared on several occasions I might become one of their meals.

"I'm still trying to find a place. So far I've been turned away from every establishment I've inquired at."

She took in a deep breath and then let it out slowly. I was proving to be more trouble than I was worth. As I waited for her response a strange thing happened. I heard the faint sounds of a horse coming from behind the closed parlor doors. I looked from the parlor to her in confusion. She didn't acknowledge it or me. She was thinking.

"Not surprising. Many have come here thinking they're safe. The city is overrun. But there's a washer woman who lives out by the canal. If you give her my name, I believe she'll accommodate you," Miss Van Lew told me.

She was interrupted by a startling sound, again seeming to come from the direction of the parlor doors. I looked at her in alarm. "What was that?" I asked.

Miss Van Lew walked over to the doors and opened them wide. There, standing in the front room of her fine home, was a horse. He regarded us with casual candor for a moment before returning his attention to the oats he was eating. I was astounded. I looked at her in complete surprise.

"What in heaven's name have you got a horse in your parlor for?"

Miss Van Lew seemed infinitely amused by my question. I think she liked that I was shocked by it. "The army has commandeered every horse, nag, mule, and donkey for miles around to use in the war effort. But they shall not have mine. No not mine. How can they take a horse they cannot find?" she asked.

"You keep him in your parlor?"

"I move him around. Today he is in the parlor, tomorrow he may be in one of the empty slave quarters. Whatever it takes to keep them from getting him."

I smiled despite myself. There was something so very honest, so very real about her that I decided then and there I liked her. She had my loyalties. "You are a force to be reckoned with, Miss Van Lew. I can see that right now."

"Don't smile too quickly. I have agreed to help you, but you may be called upon to help me in exchange. You understand?"

I nodded my head slowly. "Nothing is without a price," I acknowledged.

Chapter 35

The cold penetrated every inch of him. There was no escape from the discomfort of it. The night before all of the men were up late formed into rows four abreast, marching double-quick to try and keep their blood flowing, to keep themselves warm. Finally, they were told to cease their racket and threatened with bodily harm if they all didn't settle down.

In the morning they were ordered to stand at attention for roll call. As the heads were counted, one man remained unaccounted for. The guard in charge went about looking for the missing man while all the others remained standing, waiting to be dismissed. The guard found him curled up on the floor, his thin blanket drawn tightly around his head and shoulders.

"Get up, you!" he yelled giving the man a prod with his boot to wake him. There was no response from the prisoner so the guard kicked him again. "Get up I say!" The man slept on. This time the guard really let him have it. He gave him another good generous kick and hollered out, "You deaf? I said get up!"

After all attempts to rouse him failed, the guard squatted down and pulled the blanket away. The man lay frozen on his side, his eyes staring blankly into space, his skin a sickly gray color. The guard was visible upset. He backed away quickly, dropping the threadbare blanket from his hand as though it were scalding him.

"Ah, mercy me," he said with a plaintive grumble. "I been kicking a dead man." He motioned for two of the prisoners to come to him. "Get 'im out of here," he told them. "Wish I could be rid of the whole lot of you. There ain't no food to feed you, and if there was I'd eat it myself. Nothing but trouble, all of you."

Once he turned away and walked off, two of the prisoners descended upon the blanket as though they were vultures picking at the carnage of a ruined carcass. Two sets of hands grasped at the thin material, gripping and re-gripping to get a better hold on it, struggling to get the advantage. They squabbled over it briefly before the stronger of the two won out and walked away with an assurance that his night would be slightly warmer, just a bit more comfortable.

Every time Sam thought it couldn't get any worse it did. The cold, the hunger, the abuse, they were all terrible things to endure, but the thing that really got to him was the fading hope he might escape this place. Several nights before, the new tunnel they'd been attempting to dig had filled with sewer, making everyone in the cellar terribly sick. The smell filled the room and brought them to vomiting and even caused a few to faint.

They hastily plugged the hole with dirt and abandoned their labors for the night, unable to continue. Now, as Sam watched the body of the unfortunate dead man being taken away, he felt a certain sense of foreboding engulf him. He and several others stood as close to the window as they dared with their backs pressed against the wall so they could look out at an angle, and they watched as the body was added to a pile of others on the dead cart. Then the mule pulled away from the prison and sauntered slowly down the road.

Once the cart was out of sight, their attention was drawn to the construction transpiring below them with such a loud racket it was impossible to ignore. The old wooden bars reinforcing all of the windows at Libby Prison were being replaced by more resilient iron bars which would not be so easy to saw through. Gradually all hope was being taken away, as surely and steadily as was their food.

"I must find a way out of here, or I fear I will be among them," Sam said with an absent and far away expression.

Thomas Rose nodded gravely. "Digging to the canal has proved to be no good. And I have been thinking…"

"Yes?" Sam asked. It was not with eagerness or relish he inquired, it was with the last vestiges of his dying faith.

"We dig through the yard out toward the road instead."

Sam's eyes traveled over the course of the yard, taking note of the guards stationed there and the long stretch of faded brown blades of grass progressively failing in the winter's cold. Thomas Rose's idea was ambitious to say the least.

"The yard?"

"Do you see that shed there?" Tom asked.

"I see it," another man complained. "That's where they keep all of the parcels sent to us from home. If we could get to those boxes there would be food a plenty."

"I hear them at night, rifling through our things, breaking the boxes open and eating what they can find. Them boxes were intended for us not for them," another fellow bitterly complained.

"If we could only access them. So close. Right there where we can see it. We are dying by inches."

"There's more people to detect us, catch us at what we're doing," Sam pointed out. "We're more likely to get caught tunneling out that direction."

"And more likely to be successful at escaping," Thomas Rose added.

"I suppose it's true. We're all headed for the grave anyhow. If they caught us at least it would be mercifully quick instead of the slow death they're subjecting us to now."

"I for one am done with all of this. I say we pick up the pace and get it finished."

"Sounds great, sure, but how do you propose we do that?" Sam wanted to know.

"We dig round the clock. Morning, noon, and night," Tom said with a determination that evoked a thrill in Sam. But then he thought of the logistics of it and quickly scolded himself for his excitement. He didn't want to be bitterly disappointed as he'd been the three previous times the tunneling failed.

One of the other men looked skeptical. "What of the roll call?"

He had a point. Every morning and evening the whole lot of them was rounded up to stand at attention as they counted out each man. If someone went unaccounted for, a search ensued until the man was found. If role call was missed there would certainly be a red flag. And if the guards went about looking they might discover the tunnel in the dark cellar below. This was the reason they dug in the night, when no one would be missed.

"We'll find a way round that. We're running out of time, and I don't aim on sitting about welcoming whatever comes with a courteous greeting. We could get it done right quick if we had someone working on it at all times," Thomas Rose pointed out. "I think we ought to get a few more men we can trust in on it. More hands to make the digging go faster."

Sam smiled in a small and cynical way. "We'll need better tools. Spoon and pocket knife won't do."

"That's right, Sam. Now we're talking," Thomas Rose encouraged him.

"That's all we do is talk. I am weary of talk." Sam pushed away from the wall and walked brazenly up to one of the guards. In that moment he could see the confusion on Thomas Rose's face, on the guard Lyle Phipps's face, and several other men who were now at attention and waiting to see what might transpire.

"Stand down, Barlow," Phipps told Sam.

Sam felt the slightest thrill when he realized the guard was afraid. To have that power, the power of influencing a man's sentiments, of making a man cower, in the moment it gave Sam courage. He didn't stand down. Instead he stepped in closer, too close, disregarding the rules of personal space and making the guard all the more uncomfortable. The guard took a hasty step backward.

"Sam!" one of the other prisoners started. I suppose he wanted to save Sam, but was afraid to get involved, because he remained with the watching crowd. His only attempt to help was to call out Sam's name in a timid warning.

"I have to say there's nothing more rotten than the meat in this place, Phipps…except for maybe you. Is it you I smell or the lingering odor of the dead man they just took away?"

Chapter 36

Lyle Phipps was utterly taken aback by the events unfolding. He never knew Sam Barlow to be a trouble maker. On the contrary. He was a model inmate who kept his head down and did what he was told. When Sam so abruptly and without warning insulted Lyle Phipps his mouth fell slightly open in shock, and then he grew angry and, in an instant, his mouth snapped shut in a firm, grim line.

"Now see here-" he sputtered.

"Oh, I see all right. I see a worthless, spineless fellow of no apparent solid constitution before me. It's a wonder you're able to stand upright."

Well this got the whole group roaring with laughter, which only incited Phipps to further anger. He looked over the jeering group in a rage. What was he to do? There was no way to take back his dignity. The only thing he could do was make an example of the trouble maker who'd started all of this to begin with.

"You think you're smart, do you?" he said to Sam, grabbing him by his arm and roughly leading him from the room.

"I would say yes, but I don't want to use big words you'd find difficult to understand."

Sam got a rifle butt to his mouth for his insurrection. He could immediately taste blood as he ran his tongue along the gaping cut on his gum line. His teeth felt loose and his jaw was shooting pain to his ear and eye socket and temple. This should have squelched his rebellious outburst, but it only made him angrier. He wiped the blood and saliva from his mouth with his jacket sleeve and attempted a smile.

"Didn't know you had it in you, Phipps," he chuckled.

"Shut it! We shall see how smart you are after walking the yard."

Now it was bitter cold and Sam had no coat to speak of, just his very worn officer's jacket riddled with holes from the shrapnel they removed from his body in Georgia. He crossed his arms and hunched his head and shoulders and started walking.

Chapter 37

Sam tried tucking his hands into his armpits to keep them warm, but truly there was no warmth for his body to offer after several hours in the cold. It was late afternoon when he saw the guard Lyle Phipps walking past the doorway, checking to see if Sam was still walking. Through chattering teeth and stiff and frozen lips Sam called out to him.

"Phipps! Phipps, I'm sorry."

Phipps hesitated, lingering at the door as though he were torn. He wasn't such a bad sort really. He'd always been soft spoken and some-what tolerant of the inmates at Libby. His disposition was not such that he enjoyed making them suffer, or finding joy in their misery like most of the others. That was one of the reasons Sam chose him.

"Phipps, please," Sam continued.

Phipps motioned for Sam to come to him, which Sam eagerly did. "What have you got to say for yourself, Barlow?" he asked, trying to sound stern.

"I don't know what got into me. I'm so hungry, so cold, and tired, so dog-tired. I just snapped. I know what I done was wrong. I just felt like I couldn't take it anymore, you know?"

He could see Lyle Phipps wavering. Should he let Sam come in? If he did what would people say about him? How would it make him look? He didn't want to appear soft to the others. That could make his life very difficult if all those men were questioning his authority, making his life miserable. He should make an example of Sam.

"I ought to make you keep walking, that's what I ought to do."

"I know I deserve it, Phipps. But if you leave me out here, I'll surely die. I am awful sorry. I mean that. You never done a thing to me to make me talk to you that way. I'm just so cold. I'm so very hungry…"

"Well, all right, Barlow. But you better tell the others not to mess with me. You better tell them I won't stand for it," Phipps said sternly.

"Oh, I will, Sir. I will," Sam agreed eagerly.

"Look, you better go to the hospital and have your mouth taken care of," Phipps said with a guilty drop of his eye as he motioned in the direction of the hospital with a jerk of his head.

"It's nothing I didn't deserve. And I know it."

"Go on, Barlow. But don't tell nobody I let you."

"Oh, I won't, Phipps. It's between you and me," Sam assured him. "No one else has to know."

Sam didn't wait for Lyle Phipps to change his mind. He headed to the hospital with all haste. The surgeon there stitched up his lip and then did the best he could, stitching up the inside of his mouth where his gums had turned black from the bruising. Sam didn't feel any of it. His face was so cold and his mind so focused on other things he sat quite still while the needle went in and out. The surgeon finished his work, tying off the thread, and then he told Sam he was free to go.

"Thank you, Sir, for fixing me up."

"Don't know it will make much of a difference. You don't look long for this world, boy."

Sam shrugged. "Maybe not, but it don't hurt to look your best for the pearly gates. Least my face will be presentable for the angels there. I'll be sure and tell 'em it was your work."

The surgeon looked at him with a mix between a grunt and a laugh. "You have a sense of humor about it. Shame I can't do more for you."

"You got any food?" Sam said it as though he were joking, but he wasn't. He was desperate. So desperate he figured it couldn't hurt to try.

The surgeon's expression was one of confusion and surprise. "You know if I did I couldn't give it to you."

"Never hurts to try, now does it?"

The surgeon was troubled. He studied Sam's face and then without a word, got up and left the room briefly. He returned with a corn pone and a very bruised, very ripe apple in his pocket. He held them out to Sam.

Sam looked at the food and then looked at the surgeon, not sure if it was real, or if the man was provoking him, being cruel. Perhaps he would wait for Sam to reach out to take it and then snatch it away from him. Laugh in his face. Finally, Sam grabbed the food from the surgeon's hands and began eating with a desperate sort of relish, ignoring the pain in his teeth. He ate it all, every last crumb, including the entire core of the apple. When he was finished he looked up to the surgeon with tears in his eyes.

"Thank you," he simply said.

The surgeon was reluctant to acknowledge Sam's gratitude. "Go on before there's trouble," he advised.

Sam nodded his head. He got up to leave, but lingered at the door for a moment, a line from *Julius Caesar* springing to his lips. "*Thou art the best 'o the cutthroats.*"

The surgeon seemed genuinely affected by the line from Shakespeare. He looked away in remorse and shame, grimacing and unable to meet Sam's gaze. Sam didn't wish to make the man feel any sorrier. He left.

When he came back to the other men they looked at him with suspicious eyes, perhaps thinking he'd lost it, he had cracked and finally gone mad. And who could blame him if he had? No one wanted to be involved with a nutter. He could cause trouble for them too. Sam staggered over to the corner where Tom Rose sat against the wall and dropped down next to him.

Tom looked about to see if any of the guards were watching. Likely he didn't want to be seen with Sam either. After all, it was Sam's even temperament and his ability to stay out of trouble that drew Thomas Rose to Sam in the first place. Now Sam would be pegged as a trouble maker and a liability to their tunneling plot.

"They served the evening meal yet?"

"No."

"So I didn't miss anything?" Sam was attempting humor, but Tom wouldn't play along.

"You look like hell."

"You don't look so great yourself," Sam observed wryly.

"What were you thinking? They're going to keep a close eye on you now," Tom said with a disappointed shake of his head.

"Fifty-three yards." Sam murmured.

"What?"

"Fifty-three yards give or take a few from the cellar wall out to the tobacco shed."

"How do you know?"

"I counted."

"You crafty son of a gun," Thomas Rose muttered, rubbing his fingers over his grinning lips.

Then Sam began turning out his pockets. First a chisel, then a nail remover, and a finally a trowel shaped like a pie server clattered to the floor. Tom gasped, frantically grabbing them, attempting to hide the tools before anyone else caught sight of them. He furtively tucked them behind his back, watching to make sure no one was looking their way.

"Where'd you get these from?"

"The construction. They're putting the metal bars in over the windows. The carpenters left their tools out in the yard."

"Genius."

"We've got tools, we know how far to dig. Let's get to it, Tom."

Chapter 38

Zora Vandyke was a hard woman, calloused like her hands, made rough from over exposer to lye soap. In many ways she reminded me of a man. Mostly, I suppose, it was her rationale that led me to this comparison. She didn't think like a woman. She wasn't tender or nurturing like most women. While I admired her intellect, I was put off by her inability to temper it with sympathy or compassion.

She wore her graying hair in a severe bun, her clothing practical, and her expression weary resignation. She didn't tell me her story, but Elizabeth Van Lew did. Born to money, Zora married a man beneath her social standing and suffered greatly for it. Now her husband was dead and gone, and she was forced to take in laundry to sustain herself. I felt badly for her, until I grew to know her, and then I didn't like her very much at all, and it was hard to remember I felt sorry for her to begin with.

When I first met her, I was offended by the blunt nature in which she spoke to me. She told me, rather scornfully, to attempt to talk with less of a northern accent or we would all be in the stocks by nightfall. But after a time, I grew used to it and determined not to be upset by it.

She put me to work immediately. My days were spent in back breaking service, stirring the pots over the heat of the fire, wringing clothing until I felt as though my hands would fall off from the ache, hanging things from the makeshift lines she strung up throughout the house. It was winter and too cold to hang them outside, so inside they came. Always she wore a look of displeasure when I caught her watching me.

I didn't understand it. When patrons came by to drop off their laundry she smiled, she made pleasant conversation, she knew everyone's name. There was a camaraderie, a familiarity with her customers, leaving the impression she was a most agreeable person. It made me long to be a part of it, to be included and feel as though I belonged. But when a customer left and it was only the two of us again, she would shift into the cynical, discontented woman I was becoming accustomed to. It was as though she were two separate persons.

"What was Miss Van Lew thinking?" she asked one evening as we sat over a simple meal of beans and cornbread. Zora studied me over her bowl. She closed her eyes, shaking her head as though she were dispelling the disbelief she felt over Elizabeth Van Lew being willing to help me at all.

Mostly I let her angry comments go without acknowledging them. Best not to antagonize my sponsor. But for some reason I didn't this time. I pursed my lips and drew my eyebrows together and spoke to her. "What do you have against me exactly? Do I not do the work well? Do I not earn my keep?"

She was surprised I stuck up for myself. I could see it in the way she seemed taken aback and then tried to think quickly of what to say. "Well, Miss Sass, if you must know, I don't think you've got what it takes," she replied defiantly. "Why would she send me some little milk sop who, I doubt, has any real world experience?"

"I don't think you know me well enough to make such an assumption," I said coolly.

"I know your type. You likely never been off the farm. If faced with any real danger or dilemma you'd probably turn tail and run. You haven't got it in you to do the hard things," she said. Her words had a harsh undertone to them, almost as if she were daring me to prove her wrong.

"Oh, I think I may surprise you," I said with an all-knowing smile. It gave me great satisfaction she so grossly underestimated me.

"That remains to be seen," she said, narrowing her eyes and taking a ferocious bite from her cornbread.

I was intimidated by her, but didn't wish for her to know it. I had plenty of practice with persecutors, enough to know you should never let them see the effect they have on you. I continued to keep eye contact with her as I said, "Yes, time will tell."

She was challenging me, goading me into proving my resolve, my strength, my worth to their cause. I don't know why I cared so much, why I felt such a desire to prove her wrong. But I was determined to make her eat her words. I would show her!

The first time she sent me to run an errand, I didn't realize what it was I was doing. She precisely folded a pile of linens and white shirts, cloth diapers, and underclothing, tied them in neat bundles with twine, and put them in a birch basket for me to carry. She sent me with the directive I stick to my job and not deviate in any way. This I did. To my astonishment the address in the Shockoe Hill neighborhood she'd jotted down on a scrap of paper ended up being the presidential home of Jefferson Davis.

The mansion was three stories high, in a classical Greek architecture, with eight massive columns as sentinels to the front door. I didn't go to the front door however; I went to the back. There a Negro woman answered my knock and ushered me into the servant's entrance.

"Good day," she said, taking the basket from me with a wary look, no doubt curious as to why Zora sent a stranger instead of coming herself. When you are doing things you shouldn't be doing, anyone and everyone becomes suspect. "Zora sent you?"

"Yes, ma'am." I replied uncertainly.

She gave me an outraged laugh, shaking her head and rolling her eyes. "Oh, no. You must never call me ma'am," she said with a displeased grunt. "What are you trying to do? Get us caught?"

"Well, no!" I said, feeling very foolish.

"I am your lesser. Always remember to deal with me as such. Understand?" I nodded dumbly. She didn't seem to notice as she busied herself with sorting through the bundles, paying particular attention to the shirts, searching through the pockets of each until she found a small bit of paper which she quickly slid into her bodice. And then she acted as if it never happened, going over to another basket filled with soiled clothing, picking it up, and bringing it back to me.

"Next time act as if you know what you're doing. You're supposed to be here. You have laundry to deliver. Y'hear?"

"Yes." I took the basket and left, my knees quaking, my heart beating. This was just as trying on my nerves as pretending to be a boy was. I didn't think it possible, but I was just as uncomfortable being a woman in Richmond as I was being a man in the army.

I took the basket back to Zora, who did just what the woman at the president's home did. She rifled through the shirt pockets until she came across what I was certain was a message and left the room at once to decode it in the privacy of her bedroom. I learned, as I went, that everything in written correspondence was all done in code, so if it were discovered it couldn't be read without a cipher.

I continued in Zora's service in this manner until I met Hetty Carr Cary just a week after I came to work for Zora. Now this is an unfortunate piece of the story. For Hetty, I would be one of the worst acquaintances she could have made. A thing which I was sorry for ever after. I will say, in my defense, I was not aware at the time what heartache I would bring to her. I wish I had never met her.

Chapter 39

I wouldn't be overstating it by saying Hetty Cary was one of the most stunningly beautiful women I'd ever seen. But that was not all, she was a proper lady, graced with the pedigree and noteworthy education I could never dream of aspiring to. Everything about her was genteel. She was wearing a deep blue frock which complemented her milky pale complexion, making her cheeks glow in a deep pink blush and her eyes shine dark and liquid behind very thick, very curled black lashes. She had the loveliest hair, nearly ebony it was such a dark brown, like straight coffee with no cream, pulled back in a bun, short tendrils curled at her temples. If I were a man I would have been smitten.

As it was I just felt the familiar pangs of classic jealousy. I was right away self-conscious and couldn't seem to make myself look her in the eyes. I thought it was lucky Zora was there and would speak for both of us. One moment she was cursing me for leaving a bundle of laundry too long in the soap and then Hetty came through the door and she was full of gracious kindness for her.

"Miss Cary, good to see you, ma'am," Zora said, dropping the paddle she was stirring the large cauldron over the fire with. She approached Hetty with a smile.

"It is good to see you too, Mrs. Vandyke. I do hope you have been well?"

"Yes, thank you," Zora replied.

"Have you taken on an apprentice?" Hetty asked, eyeing me over Zora's shoulder.

"Oh, no, Ma'am. This is my cousin. Well, a second cousin really. But I'm all she's got by way of family now," Zora said with a sigh. "Serena, come along now. Come meet Miss Cary."

I came reluctantly to them, my eyes cast down to the ground. "Serena, this is Miss Cary, a truer defender of the cause you'll never meet."

"How do you do, Miss?" I said with a small curtsy.

Hetty seemed somewhat embarrassed by Zora's praise, waving her hand to Zora as if to say *Oh, stop!* "I only do what any decent southern woman would do," she told me with a modest smile.

"Miss Cary, this is my second cousin Serena Barlow, up from Georgia."

"It is good to meet you, Miss Barlow," she said.

"It's Missus," I corrected.

"Oh, excuse me. Missus," she said with a little twitter of a laugh.

Zora looked at me with a hint of displeasure. How dare I correct the woman? What was I trying to do? I knew she was right. Being disagreeable doesn't exactly inspire sympathy.

"Serena, dear, you ought to go tend to the batch we've got going," she said, trying to dismiss me. And then to Hetty, "You must forgive my cousin, she's fallen on hard times and forgets her manners."

"Oh, no, Zora, I took no disrespect from it." Before I could go back to the wash, Hetty asked eagerly. "What brings you to Richmond, Missus Barlow?"

"I had no place else to go," I lied, doing my best to lay on as much of a southern accent as I thought I might get away with. I dropped my eyes in a pathetic down cast manner and frowned subtlety.

"That's terrible. Tell me what has happened."

Zora was watching me closely. I could feel it. She was willing me not to mess up, not to say something wrong. I looked down at my hands uncomfortably. Then, rather pathetically, I blurted, "My husband is in prison. And my baby-" genuine tears of sorrow sprung to my eyes when I spoke of Lucia. "She is gone now too," I said, my voice rising with emotion.

Hetty's striking features twisted in sympathy, her heart-shaped mouth forming a pout. She rested a hand on my arm, as if to comfort me. "You poor darling," she tutted. "It's too much, really."

"I wondered what would become of me when I lost the farm. But Zora was kind enough to take me in for a time. Although, my Sam's great-aunt Maurine says I may come and stay with her in Alabama if I've a mind to."

"She ought not to make a decision on it just yet," Zora added. "After all the girl has been through so much. I think it best she allows herself time to heal before she makes a decision. But for now, I am pleased to have a work companion."

"I'm sure you are," Hetty said with a pleasant nod of her head. "If not for my aunt and cousin, I too would have been without a home. They took me and my sister in when we were forced to flee Maryland." She was relating to me in a way that surprised me. I didn't know her history, but the story Zora had fashioned for me was one that Hetty understood, and therefore it was an excellent alibi for me.

"Yes, well, your aunt is nothing short of a saint," Zora flattered her.

"Upon that we agree," Hetty told Zora with a pleasant nod of her head. "Actually, I came on her suggestion, dear Zora."

"And what brings you to us today, Miss Cary? How can I help you?"

"I am in a bit of a bind, you see."

"What is it?" Zora asked with the most concerned tone of voice. Seeing her behave this way toward Hetty made me slightly resentful. She surely had never spoken to me with such sympathy. I reminded myself it was all part of an act--she was so good at deception.

"My mother managed to procure a travel pass from Maryland. Well, it's nothing short of a miracle..."

"A miracle indeed," Zora agreed.

"What's more, John finds himself in Petersburg. So very close. It feels as though the stars are aligning just for me!"

"It really is a bit of good luck, Miss Cary," Zora said.

"John feels it presents us with the perfect opportunity to finally move our status from betrothed to married," Hetty said, unable to keep the excitement and pleasure from her voice. "That gives us only one week to make all of the arrangements necessary."

"Oh, my! But it certainly is exciting."

"Well, I hardly know where to begin! I don't know if it's even possible. Just think of it, John and I have been engaged for three years now, and suddenly I am required to toss everything together and be ready in one week! I have a dress to fit, a reception to plan, and guests to invite, and it needs to be done, all of it, all at once."

"It can be done," I said with eager zeal. Hetty looked at me with a mixture of pity and gratitude. She was glad to hear words of encouragement, but no doubt kept my sad and pathetic story at the back of her mind as well.

"You really think so?" she asked a little breathlessly.

"Of course. You know none of the details really matter. What matters is at long last you will be the wife to your John," I continued on. I was speaking to her with some experience in the matter. I may not have had all of the preparations she was responsible for, after all it was just me and Sam when I was wed, but I understood the emotions she must be going through right now.

"I know it's true," she acknowledged. "But I still can't help but panic when I start to think of the lists and lists of things needing to be done."

"Of course, Miss Cary! Of course!" Zora sympathized.

"Which is what brings me here to you today. My aunt says I may use her Negro woman for all of my preparations if I wish. But I feel it will require more than just us two. I was wondering if you might have time to help too, Zora."

"I'd be glad to give you what time I have available," Zora said with a smile. "Only trouble is, I will still have to keep up with my work."

"Yes, I know you're a busy woman. I don't wish to impose, but any help would be greatly appreciated. And I can pay."

"I could help," I said, sounding timid and silly.

Zora's eyebrows came together just slightly, and she looked at me with careful displeasure. It was one thing for me to deliver a load of wash with a coded message folded within, but it was an entirely different matter for me to be working closely with a prominent socialite such as Hetty Carr Cary. I might make an error and mess the whole thing up, expose myself and everyone associated with me.

"I don't know if you're up to it, Serena. After all you've been through, it might be too taxing for you."

"I don't want to be a bother," Hetty began.

"It wouldn't be a bother. It might help take my mind off of things," I insisted.

"You are too wonderful for words," Hetty gushed.

"How very brave of you," Zora said, but her tone was unconvincing. "You're sure?"

"Absolutely," I asserted.

When Hetty finally left, after making arrangements, Zora turned on me with a sour face, greatly displeased. "I hope you know what you're doing," she said.

"I do too."

"Well, if you can manage it, and I say if, because I feel somewhat certain you cannot, but if you do, you will have inserted yourself into the life of someone who could be very useful. You reeled in a big one this time, Serena Barlow."

Chapter 40

I was called to Elizabeth Van Lew's home in the dark of night the day after I made arrangements to assist Hetty. When she summonsed me, I came immediately. After all, my whole purpose in being in Richmond was to save Sam, and she was the only one who could help me. When I came to the back door, as stealthily and secretive as I could, Elizabeth was meeting with someone else. I could hear their low voices as I stood outside the door on the step, but was unable to make out anything they were saying.

I knocked quietly, startled by the noise the small tap produced. I knew it was barely audible, but I was paranoid to the point it seemed loud enough to be detected by the whole of Richmond. The quiet tones within ceased. Elizabeth herself came to the door, her gaze darting this way and that before she let me in. As I slipped in, another person whom Elizabeth Van Lew was meeting with was readying herself to leave.

I recognized her right away. It was the servant at the Jefferson Davis home. The very woman who told me not to treat her as an equal. I was sure I wore the dumbest expression of shock on my face. She smiled as though this pleased her. Elizabeth followed her to the door to see her off.

"I will speak to you again soon, Mary Jane. Take care," she told the woman.

Mary Jane nodded. "If anything should arise, I will be in contact." And then she was gone into the night.

"You look surprised," Elizabeth said, a hint of defiance in her voice.

"I met her the other day at Jefferson Davis's home. She is a servant there."

"Yes, she is. Well placed, my Mary Jane."

"How do you know her?"

"I've known her since she was a child. Like the daughter I never had. I sent her up north, where she would be given a fair chance, paid for her college education. Mary Jane has traveled the world, seen Africa, the origins of her people. But she came back to me."

"How did she manage getting a job at the Confederate White House?" I stammered in disbelief.

"We have our ways. There are more sympathizers than you might imagine. Connections all over the city, as you are just now beginning to understand."

While I found all of this interesting, I was more concerned with my personal business. Particularly I wanted to know if she had gotten any information about Sam. I didn't wish to be rude, but I was eager to move on. "You sent for me?"

"I did," Elizabeth gestured for me to sit at the small table in her kitchen. When I did so she offered me a pastry. I gratefully accepted, wondering how she managed to get the flour and sugar to make such an indulgence.

"Thank you," I said, taking a bite. "Where ever did you get it from?"

"Jefferson Davis's table."

"It appears as though he has excellent taste."

"Yes, it would seems so." She waited a brief moment before getting down to business. "Zora tells me you've managed to insert yourself into the Cary household," Elizabeth said with a shrewd narrowing of her eyes.

"Hetty Cary needs help in preparing for her wedding."

"You maybe don't realize how fine a line you must walk with her," she said with an indulgent smile.

"What do you mean?" I asked, taking another bite of the almond flavored filling.

"Hetty is the darling of the south, endeared by all who know her."

"Yes, Zora said as much. And I can see why. She is very beautiful and has a very sweet disposition."

"Did Zora also tell you that Hetty is related to Jefferson Davis? That her betrothed, John Pegram is a General in the Confederate army? This is the girl who sewed the first Confederate flag, who ran the blockade to deliver medical supplies to injured soldiers. She has been the object of much ardor, written about in the papers, the subject of poetry and talk alike. Something of a Southern legend, Missus Barlow."

"I believe I understand what you are trying to convey to me, Miss Van Lew. I will do my best not to become a liability to you."

"That's what I wanted to hear. You could prove very useful so close to her when she is so close to very powerful people in the Confederacy. We need any information you can come by, particularly related to the supply routes they are using to transport goods and arms, and anything on movement and number of troops of course."

"I'll do what I can." I finished the pastry and scattered the crumbs from the table in front of me so the table appeared clean. "I'm keeping my part of the bargain. Now I want to know if you have any news for me. What of Sam?"

She smiled shrewdly. "I've had word."

I grew eager, my attention focused wholly on her. "Yes?"

"Your husband is alive."

My heart leaped within my breast. "You know this for certain? There is no doubt?"

She gave a little nod, my good humor contagious as she gave me a humored smile. "What's more, my sources tell me there will be an attempt at a prison break within a month's time, if all goes as planned."

"How did you come by this information? You don't think it could be a trick of some sort?" Her answer was vital to me, which I was sure she knew. We locked eyes, both looking grim, or perhaps that was an overstatement. We were solemn, both understanding lives hung in the balance, both able to appreciate the weight of the words we were passing between us.

She gave a small shrug, dropped her eyes until the tense moment passed and said simply, "I only know what I'm told. The information given to me is from someone I trust who's been given word from the inside. Now, how would you like to have your Sam back before February's end?"

Chapter 41

Digging round the clock proved a wise choice. Sam began to see some real headway in the tunnel. The only unfortunate part of it was once the men were in the cellar, they were forced to stay there until they could switch shifts with another crew after dark. No one must know about the secret passageway behind the hearth. So, for twelve hours two to four men would labor away at the tunnel, waiting for night to come before they were relieved by another crew. To be down in the cellar that long, in such wretched conditions, was a terrible thing to tolerate.

Either Rose or Hamilton was present for nearly every shift. It was their idea after all, and they were too eager to leave the work to others. Sam could see the conviction burning within them. They wanted out and they would do whatever it took to make it happen. With the tools acquired it seemed to be going more quickly than it had in the past. Things were smooth as silk until one night when Sam was in the hole digging.

Sam developed a particular routine to his digging. He used the nail remover, piercing the dirt several times to loosen it, before taking the trowel and removing large segments of it. He put the displaced dirt into the spittoon, which was taken by rope out the back way, dumped and then sent back to him ready to be filled again. He was moving at a good pace when the trowel came back with grass on it.

Nearly simultaneously the tunnel began to give way. Dirt and rock and grass came crumbling and rushing in on the hole, filling it at an alarmingly fast rate.

Panic and dread filled him. He clutched his tools in his hand and hastily backed out, doing his best not to breathe in the cloud of dust pursuing him. When he reached the safety of the cellar he coughed and spit, wiping the dirt from his face and beard with his trembling fingers. And then he began to tell the others the disappointing news of what happened. A real fear, cold and deliberate, spread through them. They all understood they could very well soon be discovered.

"The tunnel caved," Sam told Andrew Hamilton.

"What?"

"I was digging and I think we must have been angling upward too much. I hit above ground and the whole thing just started giving way, dirt pouring in and filling it up. What should we do?"

"Nothing to do. We all get back up there, wait and see if they notice," Hamilton replied.

The men hurriedly cleaned up, blocking the opening of the tunnel with hay and debris so it wouldn't be easily spotted, and then they one by one ascended up the rope and found a place on the floor to sleep. The next morning Hamilton and Sam explained to Tom Rose what happened. Sam felt terrible when he saw the expression of disillusionment on Tom's face.

After roll call the three approached the window carefully. Kneeling below it and taking turns, the men peered over the window frame to look out into the yard. When Sam looked out he saw a yawning hole with an old iron cooking stove turned onto its side engulfed in the loose dirt.

"Must have been the weight of that stove there that caved the tunnel," Rose observed.

They watched for a time, until they noted they weren't the only ones interested in the collapsed tunnel and the old stove. Several of the guards came to inspect it. They milled about the stove, examining it in confusion. Sam nearly held his breath as they looked over the mess, knowing their attempt at escape was soon to be revealed.

Sam expected any moment the group of guards would have a look of understanding pass over their faces. He thought they would turn toward the prison, look up to the window and see him there and immediately know it was him. He was guilty. It wouldn't take much for them to figure out the tunnel originated from the cellar. They would storm through the doors and head down the stairs to find the opening and it would all be over. His hopes would be dashed again.

The only thing he could think to do was to pray. He began to mumble to himself, "Please, Lord. Please. Don't let them find it."

"What are they saying?" Hamilton hissed.

Sam rose up on his knees and began to open the window.

"What are you doing? Get down before they kill you!" Rose cautioned, tugging at Sam's jacket. Sam pushed the window open a thin crack, then stooped down again.

"Just trying to hear," Sam told them.

Through the open window they strained to listen to the guards' faint conversation. "Something funny going on here," one of them said, squatting down to get a better look at the cave in.

"Looks like the ground gave way."

"Where did the hole come from?" the other asked, a hint incredulously, as he scratched his head.

The third man was shaking his head knowingly. "Well I think we all know where this hole come from," he replied. Sam, Tom, and Andrew were waiting, holding their breaths, eager to hear the guards' theory. "Rats!" the man said, shaking his head with a disgusted look on his face.

"Yep, that explains it."

"Explains what?" The guard that was stooping stood up and looked at the two others skeptically.

"The hole. They been tunneling in from the canal and the weight from the stove crushed in where they been digging."

"Maybe," the doubtful one replied.

"Cursed rats," the third complained.

Finally satisfied by the explanation the guards moved away from the hole and from the half consumed stove. Tom began to chuckle. The other two men looked at him as if he were raving mad.

"They think it was rats," he said in amusement.

Sam and Andrew began to laugh too, until they were nearly hysterical. "Rats!" they said through their howling laughter. "Rats!" Sam didn't know why he was so entertained by this, but once he started laughing he couldn't seem to stop. He couldn't recall the last time he had smiled, much less laughed. He felt light, borderline reckless. Perhaps there was hope.

Maybe the guards really did believe it was the work of rats, although the canal was on the other side of the building, and so their reasoning was not exactly logical. But there was an air of suspicion which prevailed from that time on. Sam noted that the guards seemed more on edge, watching more closely, their eyes narrowed and distrustful. They weren't as passive or casual in their duties or about keeping watch over the men.

The work would continue, but he and the others would have to be more careful. They couldn't risk making a mistake like the last one. Beginning a new tunnel didn't seem as daunting. After all, they made significant headway on the last tunnel, getting close to half way across the yard before the cave in. It was shortly after the day shift had begun on a Tuesday morning that they were found out.

Chapter 42

Sam worked the night shift, occupied with emptying the spittoon and sending it back. They labored for close to an hour when Bill Haggerty yawned, his efforts at fanning the tunnel growing slower, his arms becoming tired from the drudgery. He shifted his feet, changing his stance to get a different position in hopes it might help alleviate his discomfort. Now, as a rule they worked in relative silence, speaking in hushed whispers only when necessary. So when Bill grew still and completely stopped fanning the hole, Sam knew something was wrong.

Bill murmured, "Did you hear that?"

They both listened, striving to pick up on even the smallest of sounds. Did he detect something? Maybe he had. Or was he just being paranoid? He figured he'd rather be safe than sorry. Sam crouched down, tugging fiercely at the rope tied around Andrew Hamilton's ankle to give him warning. "Put out the candle," he urgently directed Bill.

Bill tossed the makeshift fan aside, dove over to the candle, and blew it out. The room was consumed in utter darkness, so black, so thick with gloom, Sam could see absolutely nothing. He put his hands out with his arms stretched before him probing until his fingers brushed the wall. With his heart hammering in his breast he crouched down, laying on the ground, and pressed himself against the wall as he madly tried to cover himself with fists of straw, burrowing deeper and deeper, and then he grew still and waited.

His ears strained to hear, as he attempted to force his breath into a calm tempo. He was not alone. Bill was somewhere in the room, and Andrew Hamilton was still in the tunnel. He was concerned over this. What if Andrew was stuck in the hole without the much needed oxygen pumped in by the fan? He could easily suffocate in there. What then? Sam certainly didn't want to be responsible for Hamilton's death, but he also didn't want to get caught, so he remained where he was, hoping Hamilton would be all right.

As he lay there, still and silent, his heart beating hard in his chest, the rats crawled over him, making him shudder in contempt of them. But he could do nothing to fight them off; he was forced to wait motionless and let them do what they might. Sam didn't have to wait long. Soon he heard the soft shuffle of footsteps and the faintest glow of candlelight broke through the heaviness of the dark room. Two prison guards came through the door, quietly cautious as they stumbled about the small space.

"I don't like it down here," one of them murmured, nearly inaudible.

The other held the candle up high, trying to get a good look at the room, panning the flame from one side of the chamber to the other. They walked the length, intermittently kicking at the straw and garbage littering the floor. One of them stepped on a rat, which made a terrible squeal and then skittered away. At one point Sam was certain one of the guards stood over him. He waited for the command to get up, his muscles aching from the tension, but none came. Finally, the guard moved away from him.

"Nothing. Now can we get out of here?"

"Yeah, let's go."

The light grew faint, receded out the door and up the staircase, and they were left in the pitch black once again. No one moved, no one said a thing for several minutes. After what seemed forever, Sam emerged from his hiding place and crawled, in a panic, across the dirt floor to the tunnel entrance.

"Hamilton?" he whispered. "Hamilton?"

From the depths of the black hole he heard Andrew Hamilton's almost imperceptible, "Yes."

Sam reached out, his fingertips brushing Hamilton's hair. The other man's head was halfway sticking out of the tunnel. Sam hastened to help him out. Now the three men stood in the utter darkness, afraid to move, afraid to talk. They dare not light the candle again.

"What should we do?" Bill finally whispered.

"We go back up and wait…" Major Hamilton replied.

Once they were back upstairs they huddled together next to the stove, puzzling over what'd just happened. "They've never come down to the cellar before," Sam said.

"They must have gotten wind of what we was up to," Bill groaned.

"Let's not jump to conclusions. They may have just been curious."

"One of them stood right on my hand. It was all I could do to keep from yelling," Bill told them.

"Real lucky they didn't find us," Andrew Hamilton said.

The next morning, before the others had stirred. Two more men went down into the cellar to begin their shift. After the scare Sam experienced the night before, he felt a sense of foreboding he couldn't seem to dispel as he watched them go.

Leaning in toward Major Hamilton, Sam asked confidentially, "Do you think we should send anyone down today after what happened last night?"

Hamilton shrugged. "They won't go to the cellar again. They didn't find anything. Why should they?"

So Sam did his best not to think about the unease he was experiencing, until the guards assembled everyone to roll call. Normally the guards did a head count and called it good. It was easy to fix the numbers. A few of the men just rearranged themselves so they were counted twice. But today was not like what they came to expect. The guards called out the names of the prisoners one at a time. Sam knew, not only had they grown suspicious of the men's activities, but also the two men down in the cellar, Captain I. N. Johnson and Major B. B. McDonald, would be missed during role call and a search would ensue.

Chapter 43

It was quite a show. Even the commandant, Captain Turner was present for it. Sam hadn't seen him since the day he reported to his office after being caught aiding the escapees from the hospital. Captain Turner's expression was grim, betraying his ill mood. The Rebel guards fanned out over the prison in search of the two missing men, calling their names, turning over the sparse furnishings, and going from room to room. During the commotion and disorder Sam, Tom, and Andrew Hamilton loitered in a corner watching the proceedings with a sense of horror welling in their chests. They recognized their complete inability to do anything to help those men, and it made them downright sick.

"What should we do?" Sam asked.

"We must wait. There is nothing else to do," Tom said miserably.

"If they search the cellar, we are finished!" Andrew added.

But they didn't search the cellar. Who knows if it was the good Lord looking out for them, or just dumb luck. Thomas Rose was right in one thing. He told Sam once it would be an ideal place to stage an escape from because it was such an appalling place. No one would ever disturb them because no one wanted to go down there. So while the hunt for the missing men raged on, they were quietly digging a hole to freedom, oblivious to the chaos they had created above.

As night set in, and the prison grew quiet, Sam and Tom went down to the cellar to inform the men what transpired while they were at work on the tunnel. They were waiting eagerly in the dark to be relieved of duty, knowing they would finally have a moment of rest from their labors and respite from the conditions of the cellar. When Thomas Rose told them about the roll call, Sam could feel the tension like a gloomy cloud hanging over them.

"I'm sorry, boys, but you can't go back up."

"Why not?" Sam could sense the apprehension, the fear in Isaac Johnson's voice.

"It will draw suspicion. I believe they already must have some idea of what's going on here. The visit to the cellar the other night and now this."

"What'll we do if we can't go back up?" Benjamin McDonald asked, although the answer to his question was obvious. They would have to remain in the cellar, in hiding until an escape could be made. The question was, how long would that be?

"You would have to stay down here, unless you can think of a way to explain why you weren't at roll call," Tom told them.

"This can't be happening," McDonald murmured. He turned away from the other men and ran his fist into the wall.

"Obviously this isn't the ideal situation, Ben, but not much can be done about it now," Sam reasoned.

"Easy for you to say. You think you could stand to stay down here in this mess? How long are we talking?" he asked turning to Rose.

"At least a few more weeks' worth of digging, if we've calculated correctly. I ain't saying it's going to be easy. I know it won't be. But if the two of you suddenly show up, well, they're going to want to know where you been."

Isaac Johnson, who had been somewhat quiet until now, said, "If it must be, then I will stay here as you've asked. If it means I'll get out of this place, I will do it."

Ben McDonald was incredulous. "You'll die down here. That's what they're asking us to do, die so they don't get caught!"

"You seem to forget that it wouldn't just mean exposing the tunnel, it would mean possibly being put in front of the firing squad. Is that what you want? You want a death sentence?" Johnson asked McDonald.

"I can't stay down here. I won't."

"Look, we'll do what we can for you. We'll bring you food and stand by you, if that's what you're worried about," Sam offered.

"I'm worried I'll go raving mad! That's what I'm worried about!"

"You think you can talk you're way out of it?" Tom asked.

"Well, I'd sure as hell like to try!" McDonald barked.

"What about you, Isaac?" Tom turned to Isaac and waited for him to speak. Isaac Johnson grew thoughtful.

"I sure don't want to be stuck down here either. But I see no way around it. If Ben here wants to go back up and take his chances, I can't blame him. But it would be much easier to explain away one man missing rather than two. I'll stay down here and see it through."

"Then, it's settled. Ben you go on back up and try and talk your way out of it. Isaac, you stay hidden down here until we can break out," Tom said.

Sam was intensely sober when he told Ben, "Keep in mind we're all counting on you. Whatever you say or do affects all of us equally. You understand?"

"I'm no fool," Ben replied.

Chapter 44

January brought in a new year. The country waited, and I waited along with it to see what 1865 held in store. We waited for the war to end and peace to prevail, for the slaughter to finally be over so our dear fathers, sons, husbands, brothers could trudge back to the lives they left behind, broken and scarred and unable to do the thing they wanted most of all--to have it be the same as it was before. Everyone said it couldn't go on much longer, and yet those stubborn Southern states held on with the tenacity of a vengeful, scorned lover, unwilling to give up or give in.

Everyone suffered in some manner, it is true, but in all of Richmond there was no such brilliance as what I witnessed among the elite there. The average southerner was without proper clothing, food, and provisions during the cold winter, dragging along at a dismal pace, just managing to survive. The only thing that seemed to keep them going was their hatred for the North, their zeal in wanting to win the war. But Jefferson Davis and his family didn't want for warmth or comfort in their stuccoed white home on Clay Street.

Hetty Carr Cary was among those whom province smiled upon as well. Not that she wasn't affected by it in her own way. I'm sure she was used to a great deal better. But her poor circumstances paled in comparison to the rest who thought it great fortune to have a crust of bread to sustain them through the long day. If prison were Hell, then she most surely was living in Paradise.

You may think my saying so is a sign I was jealous of her good fortune. On the contrary, I didn't feel resentment or anger over her abundance. In some bizarre way, I was glad for her. There was something so terribly enthralling about her. She was beautiful, yes, but so much more. She was smart and funny and everyone in her company was drawn to her. She went out of her way to make sure all were at ease in her presence and did not act as if she were superior or above those around her. In some ways I thought of Hetty as Caleb's female counterpart.

It was as though I was watching a fairytale unfold before my very eyes. Somehow watching her have her heart's desire allowed me to live through her and experience what she was experiencing. I can admit now it was something of a sick fascination that made me devoted to her happiness. I wanted her to have the fine clothing and the dashing fiancé and the splendid reception. I observed it all with detached awe, captivated by her life, by her splendor. I felt lucky to play even the smallest of parts in it.

It also helped me keep my mind off of other things. I tried not to think of Lucia, because when I did I felt an overwhelming sadness consume me, and I would begin to think nothing would be right with the world ever again. It was difficult to keep from crying, or to keep from berating myself for having left her. After all, what kind of mother would leave her baby, her own dear sweet child?

And there was Sam. Always on my mind, always driving me forward. I would think of him and I would become afraid. What if I never saw him again? What if he died and me so close to him but still unable to reach him? There was so very little restraining me from storming the walls of Libby Prison and demanding they return him to me immediately. I felt the tangible passing of time. And it felt as though time was running out, like watching the last grains of sand slipping through the narrow neck of an hour glass. Focusing on Hetty made me able to forget some of the troubles that haunted me so.

To begin with I helped Hetty out for several hours a day, doing her bidding as she prepared for her wedding that was to take place the third week of January. If it was a time of peace, oh I could only imagine the grand decadence it would have presented. As it was Hetty made do with what was available to her as a war bride.

From the moment I entered her aunt's beautiful brick home each morning until I left in the late afternoon, there was a flurry of movement and noise and excitement. Her sister and mother were nearly always present. They spoke often of their cousin Constance, who was sick in bed during the time I was with them in Richmond. The three young ladies: Hetty, Jennie her sister, and Constance her cousin, were affectionately referred to as "The Cary Invincibles."

I did my best to make myself useful, doing what I was asked in the most satisfactory way I was capable. But I was also quiet and observed much of the time, playing the part of a tragic and damaged, pale and suffering figure. It was an easy part to play, with my true feelings of grief and anguish wrenching at my heart almost constantly. I was seen, but rarely heard. And in my silent separateness I was able at times to be forgotten and listen. Any small bits of information I could glean from their conversations I would mentally make note of, thus able to tell Zora everything I learned in the Cary household when I returned to her in the evenings.

No one seemed to suspect my treachery. Quite the opposite. At times I would catch Hetty staring at me with the most affectionate and piteous expression upon her brow, as though she were suffering for me. To which I would attempt a small, humble smile to reassure her all was well. She was overly thoughtful and quite vocal in her praise for me.

She must have spoken to Zora when I wasn't present because I overheard her telling her mother I was forced to sell my hair to a wigmaker to try and save the family farm. Well, it was as good an explanation as any for my short locks. But the way she told it, as if she might cry, her voice so filled with emotion, it made my conscious smart. Her kindness made it difficult to regard her as an enemy. Yet, I had a job to do. So I told myself the bits and pieces of information I was giving to Zora didn't directly affect Hetty, and it really didn't hurt her personally.

The truth was I was like a vulture, circling overhead, waiting for death to come so I might descend upon the unfortunate victim. I was a creature of the shadows, always listening, always watching. Poor Hetty had no idea what company she was keeping, or that a malicious and destructive force had crossed her threshold. It only made the fact she trusted me more difficult to bear.

Hetty was presently going over the seating arrangements for the reception. She looked over the paper with intense concentration, working it through in her head. Finally, she gazed over at her mother who sat in thoughtful repose sewing the fragile layers of tulle Hetty would wear as a veil. I was sitting at the desk, penning the names of guests onto the ivory envelopes that would carry wedding invitations to a lucky few.

"Mother, should I seat President Davis here by General Lee?"

"Not by the General, dear. We don't want professional talk to cloud the festivities," her mother replied.

"Yes, I'm sure you're right," Hetty said, moving President Davis carefully away from General Lee on her paper. "Although there will no doubt be talk of war regardless of where I seat him."

Hetty's fiancé, General John Pegram, chose that moment to breeze in, looking quite fine in his freshly laundered uniform. I had helped Zora clean it just yesterday. He was a good looking man with thick, dark hair perfectly styled. He had a mustache and goatee surrounding his full lips. His eyes were dark, somewhat shrouded by his lids and eyebrows. He was easy to look at. I could see why she thought him so dashing.

He went to her, and her face lit up. "John, darling," she said, almost as a sigh while he bent down and kissed her chastely upon the top of her head.

"Good day, Missus Cary, Missus Barlow," he said with a polite nod to Hetty's mother and myself. I acknowledged his greeting with a smile and then turned back to my work, keeping my hands busy while they proceeded to talk. He sat down next to Hetty, leaning back and crossing his leg as she scooted closer to him, resting her hand against his.

"Let me get you some tea," Hetty offered. She called for July, the maid, and asked for some tea to be brought in. July disappeared toward the kitchen on Hetty's errand, and Hetty gave her full attention back to her fiancé.

"I hope you've had a productive day," Hetty said to John.

"Yes, very. I've just come from the church. Reverend Minnigerode has assured me all is in place and ready for the nuptials."

"Wonderful. I'm just now going over the seating arrangements for the reception. Mother and I thought it best if we seat President Davis with your mother and brothers. What do you think?"

"Oh, Mother ought to enjoy that. His wife will prove excellent company for her I should think. Very agreeable."

"Verina has advised me that she and President Davis wish to offer their private carriage so we might ride to the church in comfort. Can you believe it? The president's very own carriage."

"Very generous."

"I thought so too," Hetty agreed pleasantly.

"This is something else that should make you happy. I've been given permission to have a week off for our honeymoon. A whole week before I report back."

"Oh, John, that's wonderful!" He smiled, pleased with her reaction.

"Nearly done here, Hetty. And then you'll have to try it on to see it fits properly," Mrs. Cary said, straightening out the layers of tulle so they lay evenly.

The bell at the front door sounded, and we all looked up expectantly. After a brief pause, the butler came through the parlor doorway, stopping and waiting to be acknowledged. Hetty was pleasant to him, something else I found endearing. She always treated the slaves like they were people and not possessions.

"What is it, Scipio?"

"There's a courier here to see Mister John, ma'am."

John got up and hastily headed for the hallway, to the front door. We were all close enough we could hear everything being said. The courier asked him, "You are General John Pegram?"

"Yes, sir. That is me."

"Could you sign here?"

The courier handed the letter to John. John said, "Thank you." The courier left and John tore the envelope open. It was quiet for a moment as he no doubt read the contents. He was putting the folded paper in his jacket pocket when he returned.

"Everything all right, darling?" Hetty asked as he took his seat next to her again.

"Yes. All is well."

I was just finishing up the envelopes, but could think of nothing more than that letter in the pocket of his jacket. It was probably something of an official nature. I wondered if there was any way to get a look at it. I couldn't think of anything. I was too simple for this sort of business.

"Finished," I said quietly from my corner. I began to collect the envelopes up and put them in a neat pile.

"Wonderful. We'll get these out right away," Hetty said.

"Too bad the courier just left," her mother commented.

I got up and went to the front hall where I stacked my pile on the narrow table there. It seemed as if providence were smiling on me, for just then July came around the corner with a tray of tea cups and a steaming teapot.

"Let me take that for you, July," I offered.

She smiled at me, but I could see from the expression on her face she was slightly mistrustful. Why was I offering? I could guess no one ever offered to help her before. She reluctantly gave me the tray. "That's awful good of you. Thank you."

I went back into the parlor with the tray. "July brought tea," I said, stating the obvious. I began filling the cups with the soft brown liquid. When I filled them all I began passing them out. Now when I got to John I inhaled sharply and then acted as if I tripped on the carpet. I staggered forward and made a show at trying to save the cup from spilling, but got just enough over the side that a little spilled onto John Pegram's jacket.

His face was confusion and shock as he tried to steady me. I set the cup down on the short table in front of the sofa, my mouth open wide in horror. "General Pegram, I'm so sorry," I gasped.

He stood up, inspecting his jacket with a good natured smile. "It's all right."

"It was so clumsy of me."

"It was nothing, Serena," Hetty assured me. She was up now too, hovering about John, trying to be helpful.

"You'd think I had no practice in serving tea," I lamented.

"It was nothing," Hetty said again.

"I should have just let July do it. She couldn't have done any worse. Your jacket, General Pegram…and just laundered too!"

John began to unbutton his jacket. I rushed toward him and took hold of the collar to help him remove it. "Here, let me take it and put sodium bicarbonate on it before the stain sets!"

"Good idea," he said. His tone was good natured. He only wished to put me at ease, to take away my remorse I suppose.

"I'll have it back directly," I told him as I backed out of the parlor and headed for the kitchen. The jacket was in my hands, and the letter with it.

Chapter 45

I rushed to the kitchen with the jacket clutched to my chest. I entered the room in such a fluster, I startled one of the kitchen maids making dinner. I didn't know her name, but it didn't matter. I only needed her gone for a few minutes. "I need some sodium bicarbonate," I informed her, my voice authoritative and urgent. I remembered what Mary Ann told me when I delivered laundry to the Jefferson Davis home. I must act superior. I did my best, although I felt a bit guilty for treating the poor woman so.

Her eyes were wary. She looked me over briefly, still standing at the table with the paring knife and potato in her hands. My heart was pounding right out of my chest. I thought for a moment she might tell me no.

"Be quick about it before this tea sets into General Pegram's coat," I scolded her mildly.

She sat the knife on the table, wiped her hands on her apron and headed for the pantry. I quickly drew the letter from the jacket pocket and skimmed over it before slipping it back. When the kitchen maid returned, I was dabbing at the tea stain with a wet cloth. She brought the tin to me and handed it over.

"Thank you," I said, accepting it. I prised the lid off and sprinkled the white powder over the stain, continuing to dab at it with the cloth. She watched me for a moment and then went back to cutting potatoes.

When I was able to get the small spot of tea out of the fabric, I took it back to the parlor. Hetty had a sympathetic look upon her brow as I apologized again. I held the jacket out for John Pegram as he shrugged his arms and shoulders into it.

"Crisis averted," he said with a chuckle.

When I returned to Zora's house she was waiting up by the fire, mending clothing, as she always was. It was her habit to pump me for information when I came back from being with Hetty. I dreaded it. It would be so much easier to avoid her altogether, but that was not a possibility.

"You're late," she accused without looking up from her darning.

"No, I'm not," I retorted.

"It's nearly seven."

"But not yet seven."

She scowled at me. "Any news?"

"I need to send a message to Miss Van Lew," I told her.

Her eyes narrowed. "What about?"

"I have information regarding John Pegram."

She got up and rushed to her secretary where she kept paper, quill, and ink. She sat down with her cipher and the paper and quill and waited expectantly. "What shall I write?"

"I'd like to write my own message." I knew it would cause a stir, but I was tired of the woman. I was tired of her meanness, her harassment, her air of superiority. I finally had something that might be of worth to Miss Van Lew and I didn't want her interfering or taking credit for it.

She pursed her lips, and frowned. "You don't know how."

"If I have the cipher I will be able to figure it out," I assured her.

She grudgingly gave the cipher to me, her face full of contempt. "There is laundry needing folding. See it is done before you go to bed. Part of the agreement was you'd help out around here."

"I'll see to it." My words were defiant. She thought she could boss me around. She thought she could tell me what to do. I was growing to dislike her more and more. Why was she so cold-hearted to me? I hadn't done anything to her. I hadn't done anything to deserve this kind of treatment. She stormed from the room.

I first wrote the message I wanted to send to Elizabeth Van Lew in script. Then I took the cipher code and translated it into numbers. The cipher was like a grid with a letter of the alphabet in each box. Next to the grid there were numbers running down the side and across the bottom. By taking the number from the side and the bottom of the grid one could discover which letter was being represented.

I labored over the note with deliberation. Finally, when I was finished, I folded the thin bit of paper and put it into the laundry that I would deliver in the morning. I took the note I'd written in plain English and destroyed it, throwing it into the waning fire and watching it curl and crumble. Then I began folding the piles of clothing Zora left for me. It took quite some time to complete all of the work, but eventually I did as she asked and wearily fell into bed to sleep.

Early the next morning I took a load of laundry to the Davis home with my message safely shrouded in one of the shirts. I went around the back to the servants' entrance and knocked briefly upon the door. Shortly one of the servants answered. She was large and imposing and looked to be the sort of no nonsense person that got things done and didn't mess around with formalities.

I tried for a smile, but was rebuffed by her intense stare. "Where is Mary Jane?" I asked, trying to look past her.

She intentionally blocked the doorway from me, as if she were protecting the contents of the home by baring me out. I took a small step back, intimidated by her, as I believe she intended me to be.

"She isn't around," the woman told me. My mind began to race. Why wasn't she around? Had she been caught, found out? Or was she merely busy? "What business you got with her?"

"I am delivering laundry," I replied, holding up the basket for her to see, although it must have been apparent from the beginning. "I'll wait for Mary Jane."

"I done told you, she's busy."

"I don't mind waiting." If it were at all possible her expression became gruffer.

"I'll get it," she insisted. Before I knew what was happening the woman stepped forward and took hold of the basket as if she would take it from me. I hastily jerked it back. The two of us regarded one another for a moment before she pursed her lips in a determined scowl and then again tried to take the basket from me.

Now I was in a full on panic. I wrenched the basket back toward me, pulling so forcefully I stumbled backward, lost my balance and nearly fell. If there hadn't been a bush next to the door on which I caught myself I would have fallen to the ground. The basket heaved to one side and a good portion of the laundry went over the edge, scattering across the ground.

The woman's stern expression was gone when I looked at her again. She was downright shocked. "What in heaven's name-" she began.

Chapter 46

I didn't know what to say. I opened my mouth and then closed it again in a daze. I was on my hands and knees scrambling to collect the laundry, searching frantically for the shirt I had slipped my note into. "Oh, dear, I've soiled it. I'm so sorry," I mumbled dumbly.

"What'd you go and do that for?" the woman huffed in indignant disbelief. She started to squat down to help me, but I waved her away.

"I'll do it!" I frantically pulled the clothing toward me and threw it into a messy pile back in the basket. "I'll have to take all of it back and rewash it."

I got back to my feet, hefted the basket up, and headed back down the walkway, leaving the servant woman to watch me go. If I had sprouted a tail and grown mule ears I don't think her expression would have been any different. I turned back once, to make sure no one was following me. She was muttering under her breath, shaking her head, and rolling her eyes to the heavens as she turned to go back into the house.

Well, that couldn't have gone any worse. I was shaken and felt sick to my stomach. I determined I wasn't about to tell Zora what happened. I didn't want to hear her condescending lecture. I would rewash the clothing myself. But the message hadn't been delivered.

It was still early in the morning and I had to hurry as I was expected by Hetty. I went straight to Miss Van Lew's place and to the back door.

When I knocked, the same girl who served us tea when I first came to visit opened the door. She was distraught when she saw me.

"Wait here." She shut the door, and I stood idly on the back steps looking about in suspicion. Finally, Miss Van Lew showed up. I could see by her pinched expression she was not so happy to see me.

She opened the door, scanning the yard and streets around as she let me in. I ducked through the door and put my back to the wall, taking a deep breath of relief. I tried to calm myself as she faced me with her arms crossed and a stern expression.

"Miss Van Lew, I know it's early but I must be at Hetty's very shortly and couldn't wait."

"You shouldn't have come here, Mrs. Barlow."

My stomach plunged to my gut. She was upset with me; I could tell by the tone of her voice and her crossed arms. If I made her angry, perhaps she wouldn't help Sam. I blinked hard a few times and swallowed, trying to regain my composure. But I could feel my shoulders sagging and a sense of defeat swell in my chest. Perhaps she could see how badly I felt, because her features softened a bit.

"They are watching, Mrs. Barlow. I am under suspicion. And as the war continues to go badly for them, their distrust of me grows. If they see you here, they could connect me to Zora, and then to Mary Jane, and a host of other resistance workers. You being here has put a large number of people at risk, you see."

Why hadn't I thought of that? But I was too foolish and inexpert to realize what I was doing by coming here. I couldn't think of a thing to say. I just stood there dumbly miserable as my inner voice tore me to shreds. *What an imbecile you are, Serena! What a disgrace!* I berated myself.

"Never mind," Miss Van Lew said, shaking her head. "Why did you come?"

"I…I have information regarding General Pegram," I mumbled.

"What is it?"

"I've learned from one of his correspondences that he and Hetty will be headquartered at a farmhouse in Petersburg near the railroad. His objective will be to defend the area if need be."

Miss Van Lew's eyes narrowed. "Interesting."

She motioned for me to follow her as she headed for the study. There she pulled out several worn maps, rifling through them until she found the one she wanted. Her fingers traced over rivers and roads and then circled a spot, which I studied over her shoulder.

"This railroad? There was fighting here last summer at Ream's Station. You see these roads here, Boydton and Vaughan, these *could* be potential supply routes."

"If what you say is true, and General Pegram is being sent there to fortify it, they will be well prepared for a defense."

"You sound like you know something of stratagem, Mrs. Barlow," she said with her eyebrow raised in amusement.

I chose to ignore her comment. "So the information was useful."

"Yes. Very. Only next time go through the proper channels. We don't want to get caught, now do we?"

"Yes, ma'am."

"Get a note to Mary Jane and she will take care of it. Don't come here unless you are summonsed."

"I understand." I realized if I didn't leave then I would be late and have to make excuses to Hetty. I prepared to go but hesitated. "Have you heard anything?"

She didn't need to be told what I was referring to. She looked sympathetic as she shook her head. "No. Nothing."

I must have appeared down hearted, because then she added. "No news is good news. There would have been word if a prison break had been uncovered."

I suppressed a sob. "I'm sure you're right."

"Be patient."

"That is something I've never been very good at."

Hetty was in fine spirits when I arrived. For now, things were going as planned. She was just days away from finally becoming Mrs. John Pegram. Her mother finished the bridal veil, and we had collectively been working on alterations to her dress, which was now close to being done too. Today she wished to show the veil to her cousin, who was sick in bed and missing out on much of the preparations for the wedding, a thing that was very sore for her. Hetty thought to cheer her by coming to her and showing her what was ready and what was also planned.

I watched from a corner of the room as Hetty's mother carefully placed the veil upon Hetty's nest of dark curls. I was immediately struck by the contrast between the white gauzy veil and the brown of her hair. To add to her beauty was the sweet glow of her skin as she grew excited. She was facing the full length, oval mirror when the veil was placed, and her lips drew upward in an eager smile.

"Oh, Mother, it is breathtaking!" she squealed.

It was true. Her mother had outdone herself on it. The fragile layers of material cascaded down to the floor and trailed off behind her, framing her face and shoulders like a lovely cloud of snowy mist. Everyone in the room was entranced by Hetty. Even she couldn't be modest enough to hide her pleasure.

"Hetty, darling, you're breathtaking," her cousin Constance fawned.

She knew her mother and cousin approved, but she looked through the mirror, her gaze wandering past herself until her eyes fell on me. She wanted *my* approval. How very strange. After all, I was nobody compared to her. What did she care what I thought? Nevertheless I smiled, gave her a little nod of approval and said, "Hetty, you will be the most beautiful of brides."

Was it my imagination that Constance seemed a bit peeved? She displayed a sweet little pout on her lips as she tried to draw Hetty's attention back to herself. "I'm so very cross I had to be sick now, Hetty! I wanted so to be of service to you."

Hetty turned away from the mirror and said to Constance, "Don't be silly, cousin. You can't control when you get sick. Besides, I'm hoping you'll be up and around for the day of the wedding. I'll need all the help you can give then."

"Of course! I'd do anything for you, darling."

Suddenly, from out of nowhere, the glass in the mirror fell from its frame and shattered all over the floor. We all collectively jumped, startled by the unexpected clatter. There Hetty stood in her gorgeous veil surrounded by a thousand shards of broken mirror, a hundred little fragmented Hettys looking right back at her from an upward angle. She gave a little shriek, planting her hand to her chest.

"Oh, dear me! What in Heaven's name?" her mother gasped.

I scrambled over to gather up the layers of tulle, so that her veil was in a balled up mass in my arms, afraid it would be damaged. I passed the mass of fabric to Hetty and fell to my knees, scrambling to pick up the mess. Constance began calling out for one of the servants of the house. Eventually the house girl came running through the door and after surmising the situation left to get a broom and bag to help with the cleanup.

Hetty was watching in shocked surprise. It seemed strange to me how she could be so beautiful regardless of the situation. I felt envious that she could so effortlessly pull off playing the part of damsel in distress. Why would such a thing occur to me? I couldn't say. Only I had wished my whole life to be like her. I secretly wondered, without really even acknowledging it to myself, what Sam would think of her. If he would feel he had gotten a raw deal after meeting with her, beholding her face, hearing her feminine, fragile voice. But what a pointless notion.

"Serena, look what you've done, you've cut yourself!" she screeched. I stopped at my efforts of stacking my glass tower. When I looked up at Hetty she wore horror on her face as eloquently as she wore the veil. I'm sure my expression was more like dumbly oblivious. When her warning to me sunk in, I held my hands up to inspect them, rotating my wrist until my palms were pointing upward. To my amazement she was right. Small but deep, a dozen or more cuts crisscrossed my fingertips. Hetty groaned, "You have blood on your hands!"

Chapter 47

Zora was very cross when I left the morning of January 19th for Hetty's wedding. If I'd kept my mouth shut and not meddled in her affairs the day Hetty came in asking for help, it would be she going to the wedding and not me. I could see it was practically eating her up. I felt sorry, because really I wouldn't mind if it was her and not me, but it was too late now to change any of it.

Hetty was in full preparation mode when I arrived at the house. It was exciting to be part of it, rushing here and there to get everything ready and to help in any way I could. She hadn't fully dressed yet and was in her underclothing and a robe before the dressing table when she motioned for me to come to her. I stepped from the frantic melee of the other women as they fetched the shoes and the dress and the veil, and I came as she bid. I stood next to her for a moment, but she patted a stool that was to her right, and I took a seat, waiting expectantly.

"What is it, Hetty?" I asked.

"Nothing really," she said with a bashful smile, her eyes dropping to her hand that held a brush.

"You want to say something. I can see. You don't have to be concerned with me," I said with a persuasive smile. What a terrible lie. She would be smart to be very concerned. I wasn't trustworthy. I didn't have her best interest at heart. I'll tell you now, I wasn't thinking any of those things at the time. In that moment, I simply wanted to please her, to have the honor of having her confide in me.

"I don't feel at liberty to discuss this with my sister or cousin. They wouldn't understand. And Mother… Well, I'm having a hard enough time coming to you, but I don't have anyone else you see."

"I'll do anything you ask, Hetty."

"It's only, I don't know what to expect. I feel all nerves, and I think I must be a real goose for even bringing it up."

It dawned on me she was probably feeling many of the same things I felt the day I was married. Yet I couldn't bring myself to broach the subject. I couldn't chance being wrong about her intentions and then look like a fool for saying something that would cause embarrassment.

"You are married," she began. "Perhaps you know what I am trying to say?"

Finally, I made it easy for her. "I understand what you must be feeling, Hetty. It is only natural. But you needn't worry. You love your John and he loves you, and it will all work out as it should. Do not be afraid."

Tears came to her eyes. "What a dear friend you have become. I knew you'd understand!"

"Things we do not know, we do not understand, frighten us until we have a knowledge of it, and then we wonder why we were so frightened to begin with. Rest assured, it will be all right."

She appeared to be somewhat relieved by what I said. "Thank you. I know I must seem ungrateful. You mustn't think that. I am grateful. I love John. He means everything to me. And I'm proud of him. So proud. You know, they've asked him to safeguard Boydton Road. Once his furlough is ended we'll be stationed in Petersburg. It's an important job. An honor. I just want very much to make him proud too, so that he is glad to call me his wife."

Right away my heart began to hammer in my breast. It was no longer speculation. I knew. *I knew.* It was Boydton Road. Boydton was the supply route! I acted as though what she said was of no consequence, completely ignoring the part about Boydton Road, although that was the only thing my mind seemed to be focused on. "You worry too much. He is a lucky man to have you for a wife, and anyone would tell him so. Besides, if you could only see how he looks at you, you would know he holds you dear above all else. General Pegram adores you!"

Constance chose that moment to insert herself into our private conversation. "Hetty, you must wear these ear bobs. They will look stunning with the dress," she said, displaying a pair of dangling sapphire earrings in her cupped hand.

"Yes, I think you are quite right," Hetty agreed, accepting them from her and putting them to her earlobes.

"You ought to check and see if the iron is hot yet, Mrs. Barlow, so that we can curl her hair." I got up from the stool, nodding politely to Constance as I went to do as she asked. Hetty reached out and grabbed my hand, looking at me over her shoulder.

"Thank you," she said.

"Be of good cheer, Hetty. It is your day, and you shall finally have your heart's desire." I moved away and went in search of the curling iron.

When she was dressed in the palest blue silk, her hair done up and her veil in place, I thought she looked stunning. Her sister and cousin playfully bantered back and forth over how jealous they were, how positively miserable to not have her beauty, her style. I remained silently watching.

John Pegram stood in the front hallway as she came down the stairs. What I said to her about the way he looked at her was true. His eyes shone as he rushed forward to take her hand and help her down the last few stairs. No words passed between them, but there was much being said by the expressions on their faces. They were beyond happy, eager to at last belong to one another. There was communication with their eyes and the tender expressions they gave one another. It was poetic and beautiful, and I nearly cried because I missed that deep, encompassing intimacy.

To be loved, to be wholly accepted, to be cherished so completely. *Oh, Sam, where are you? What are you doing right now? Do you miss me as terribly as I miss you?*

"We'll see you at the church, darling," her sister Jennie said. And we hurried past them to put on our cloaks and pile into the carriage waiting for us in the front. The carriage headed down the street and pulled up in front of St. Paul's Church right in the heart of Richmond. The church was most impressive, with a massive bell tower that loomed above the town in a tall and narrow dome shape. Ten pillars held up the generous front portico. There were oversized double doors at the front entrance. It was a beautiful building.

The church was pleasantly filled with strangers I had no acquaintance with. The only way I knew who was who was to listen to Constance and Jennie whispering to one another. We sat in a pew cushioned with red velvet in the middle and to the left side of the nave. Facing forward, the front of the sanctuary was all marble, with a short set of marble stairs leading up to the chancel. The back wall of the chancel was curved in a semicircular shape with three gorgeous stained glass windows and columns etched in gold filigree equally spaced all along. Just below the ceiling, carved and painted in gold, were the words *Peace I leave with you, my peace I give unto you.*

I would have given anything for peace. Sweet blessed calm. That thought played through my mind as I sat among my enemies in the house of the Lord, mentally plotting against them.

"Oh, look, there is President Davis and his family," Constance murmured in awe.

"And General Lee," Jennie gushed.

Indeed, it seemed that all of the southern aristocracy had showed. I could only imagine what their reaction would be if they knew who I really was and my purpose in being there. I was terribly uncomfortable but did my best to conceal it. After all, I was an invited guest. Hetty wanted me there. I had just as much right as the rest of them, didn't I? Even though I told myself these things, it did little to help, because I could lie to everyone else, and they might believe me, but I knew what was true and what was not for myself. And I knew God knew too.

The appointed time came for the ceremony, and the Reverend stood at the front expectantly, wearing collar and vestments, freshly pressed. He was aglow with the significance of his calling, feeling elevated no doubt by the important people filling his pews today. Several minutes passed, and there was still no bride and groom. Eventually the Reverend wandered down the aisle and out the door toward the front of the building, and everyone else grew fidgety and began to talk amongst themselves.

"It's not like Hetty to be late," her sister said with a frown.

"When we left them they were ready to follow," Constance added.

"I can't imagine what's keeping them," the two fretted as a few of the guests pulled out their pocket watches to consult the time. Still no couple. Where were they?

Chapter 48

Constance became agitated. "I'm going to go see if I can find any-thing out," she said. She scooted past Jennie and me and exited the pew, heading off in the direction of the narthex where the Rever-end had gone.

Jennie was always kind to me, but didn't seem to have anything to say when we were alone. We sat awkwardly waiting with the rest. Perhaps fifteen minutes or more went by when Constance returned in a ruffled flurry. She squeezed through the thin space between our knees and the pew in front and took her seat.

"They've finally arrived!" she hissed to Jennie.

"What happened?"

"Oh, poor, Hetty. What a terrible order of events," Constance lamented.

"Is she all right?"

"Yes. Only the carriage that President Davis sent round for them could not be used. She says there was some sort of trouble with the horses. Can you imagine? John had to call for a hired carriage and that took some time. When they finally got here, she was in a terrible state."

"They've arrived now though?"

"Yes. But as she crossed the threshold of the church she dropped her handkerchief. Just as she bent down to pick it up her veil was caught on something. A nail perhaps? And it split her veil right in two, nearly all the way up to the crown of her head!"

Jennie sucked her breath in sharply. "My dear sister. What a terrible ordeal!" she cried.

Just then the Reverend returned, hastening up the aisle and back to his position in front of the congregation of wedding guests, taking a moment to calm himself. Next Hetty and John came through the door, Hetty holding tight to John's arm. She seemed shaken and her face had lost its rosy blush. She was pale. Her eyes briefly connected with mine, and she attempted a smile. As she passed us, I could see the tear right up the middle of the veil her mother had so earnestly worked on. I figured it wouldn't be as obvious to everyone else if they weren't aware of what happened. But poor Hetty knew.

The wedding itself went off without a hitch. The Reverend Minnigerode pronounced them husband and wife. Hetty let out a deep sigh, as thought to say, *Finally!* And then the audience cheered happily. I cheered with them. I was happy for her.

Following the ceremony, we attended the wedding dinner, which was fit for a king. The tables were spread with linen table clothes, candles, fine china, and crystal ware. In place of fresh flowers, for it was winter and none could be had, there were bows of greenery and winter berries, which were quite festive. Wine was poured. Food was served. I hadn't eaten like this since leaving home.

Hetty and John floated about, caught up in the festivities, and they seemed to put the rest of the unfortunate events of the day behind them. I heard her speaking to others, talking of how they would honeymoon for a week and then return to Petersburg where John would be stationed. At one point I saw John Pegram speaking to General Lee, nodding his head soberly as he listened to what the General had to say. I attempted to edge closer, but just got the last of it as General Lee said, "That road is crucial to us."

Again I knew Miss Van Lew's and my assumptions about the railroad and Boydton Road must be correct. After what Hetty said that morning there was absolutely no doubt about it. I stood in the corner alone, mulling it over, feeling the urgent need to let Miss Van Lew know, but also afraid to reveal the information. What would happen to Hetty and John if I told?

Hetty saw me standing idle by myself and managed to break away long enough to come say a quick hello. She rushed over to me with a bright smile.

"You look so beautiful!" I said. "And what a lovely ceremony."

"Thank you. I know you said I should enjoy it, but I must say it is such a relief for the wedding to be over."

"Constance mentioned you had some unfortunate difficulties getting to the church."

Hetty rolled her eyes. "Did we ever. You just wouldn't believe it, Serena. The fine horses and carriage the Davises sent over was of no use to us. John and I climbed into the carriage and the horses refused to budge, no matter how the driver urged them on. I've never seen anything like it. John had to rent a hired carriage, which is why we were so late."

"You must have been beside yourself!"

"I was. To have all of those guests waiting. I was positively mortified. Then just as I arrived at the church, my veil snagged on a floorboard and it ripped right in two. If the former incident with the horses wasn't enough, well, that nearly put me over the top. If it hadn't been for John calming me, well, I think I might have given up completely."

"You're Mrs. John Pegram, and that's all that matters now," I soothed.

"Hetty, dear," John called. He motioned for her to come to him and meet someone.

"I'm so pleased you were there today. You are such a kind person, such a good friend. Thank you. I must go to John now," she told me, giving me a quick hug before she left.

That night I wrote out a coded message.

General John Pegram, stationed in Petersburg, Virginia, has been given charge to fortify and defend the railroad as well as the main supply route of Boydton Road.

At last, something worth reporting. I imagined Miss Van Lew would be very pleased I had figured it out. Looking over the map in her study we had ventured a guess as to where the supply route might be, but now I had solid proof. I held the note in my hand, stewing over it for a time. I was torn. I felt Hetty had become a friend to me. Up till now, I considered myself a loyal person, the sort of person who would never betray another's confidence. But she didn't say it was a secret. She didn't ask that I speak to no one else about it. As a matter of fact, she was openly discussing it with a number of the wedding guests.

No matter how I tried to talk myself into it, I knew what I was doing was nothing short of betrayal. No amount of justification would make it otherwise. There was something to be said for my service in the army, foe fighting foe in open battle. It was so much nobler than the sneaky treachery I had fallen into while in Richmond. After a great deal of mental debate, I finally tucked the note into my apron pocket for safe keeping. I would try to figure out what to do with it after a good night's sleep. I couldn't deliver it tonight anyhow, so it was just the same if I waited until the morning.

Chapter 49

With Hetty's wedding behind me, my life fell into a monotonous routine of washing, rinsing, and hanging laundry once again. Pressing shirts with the heavy iron until my arms ached. Folding piles of laundry in neat and attractive bundles. All the while Zora stood over me, threatening, railing, and carrying on in such a way that I grew weary of her voice.

I told myself each morning as I woke, I was here for Sam. I was doing this for Sam. My husband needed me. This was a small sacrifice if it meant getting him back again. So she was unpleasant. So she was a trial to be borne. I wouldn't be here long. Like the inmates of Libby I counted each day and rejoiced that I somehow made it through another.

Elizabeth Van Lew was disappointingly silent. No news about Libby or the planned prison break. It made me nearly crazy, waiting like that. Again I was forced to bide my time, do nothing, and postpone any action until it was the right time. And as one week passed, and then another, I felt despair like a cruel tormentor. I could do nothing but continue on in Zora's service and remain at her mercy. As the days passed, she grew more hostile, more merciless.

One afternoon I stood next to the fire, stirring the large black pot with a wooden paddle, when she snuck up on me. To be truthful, I'm not sure if that was her intent. But whether it was her intent or not, she startled me. One moment I was stirring the pot, the next I was surprised by her, and I spun with my paddle drawn up ready to strike her with it.

Even after I saw it was her, I couldn't seem to calm myself. I felt a rush of energy, my heart hammering hard in my ribs, my stomach plunging, a terrible throbbing in my head. I brandished the paddle as if it were a weapon, ready to take her head off if she came one step closer. There was a moment when I might have killed her, but it slowly registered within my murky brain it was Zora. While I didn't like her, she was not the enemy.

Zora at first was very afraid. I could see the look of panic and dread on her face for a brief instant. But she was too proud to acknowledge I scared her. She tittered nervously.

"It's only me, Serena. You'd think I was the invading army come to take you away."

I didn't say anything. I slowly lowered the paddle, breathing heavily with a sense that I had crossed a boundary. My chin was down and my head cocked so that I was looking at her from the corners of my eyes, distrustful and still on guard. Our eyes locked, and an understanding passed between us. Her expression grew shrewd. She wore a cynical smile, and her eyes narrowed.

"I do believe I have misjudged you, Missus Barlow," she said with a silky smooth voice. "You may be a lot tougher than I gave you credit for."

I wiped my forehead with the back of my arm, shrugged and went back to stirring the laundry. "You may be right," I acknowledged. "Don't sneak up on me like that again."

"I'll make a note of it," she said.

"Did you need something?" I asked. What was she doing lurking about like that anyhow?

"I found this in your apron," she said. "I thought it may be important."

I eyed her distrustfully. She pulled a slip of paper from her pocket and held it out with her arm fully extended, waiting for me to snatch it from her hand. It was my message. The message I had encoded after Hetty and John's wedding naming Boydton Road as the supply route. I crammed it unceremoniously into my pocket and continued working.

"You found it, huh?" I said with an accusation in my voice.

"Is it?"

"What?"

"Important?"

"No."

She watched me. I ignored her.

"What is it?"

"I wrote it weeks ago. But it turned out to be of no significance. I forgot I even had it." She could tell I was lying. It takes a good liar to detect the lies of others. It is the honest people who can't believe anyone would deceive them. The deceitful ones, they are always mistrustful, considering everything suspect. We were at the same game, her and me.

"I figured you wouldn't leave something urgent laying around for anyone to find," she acknowledged with a cocked eyebrow.

"That would be very imprudent of me."

She laughed. "Waste of time, I suppose."

I thought she was referring to the fact that she made such a to-do over it, how she put on such a production of bringing it to me. I gave her a false smile with my teeth gritted. "Yes, it's nothing."

"I probably shouldn't have sent it through the laundry for Miss Van Lew then. I mean since it was nothing."

Chapter 50

I stopped stirring the laundry and stared at her with a sneer on my lips. "What?" I spat.

"Well, I found it, and supposing it was a message that needed sending, I copied it, and I put it in the laundry for Mary Jane," she confessed with repugnant false innocence.

"Why would you send it? You find a random piece of paper and your first inclination is to send it to Miss Van Lew?" I raged.

"How was I to know it was unimportant?"

I had a choice. I could press the issue, make it into something much more significant, or I could act as if it was nothing and give her no satisfaction in the matter. I determined I would say nothing else. I would give her no satisfaction.

"Oh, dear, I hope I haven't upset you."

"Not at all. I simply worry that Miss Van Lew might be troubled over naught."

"In that event, she'll determine it has no bearing on our work and she'll discard it. Right?"

"Absolutely," I agreed with a sneer.

"Glad that's settled then."

As she walked away I thought I saw a look of tremendous satisfaction on her face. She left me there and went inside. I took the slip of paper from my pocket and crushed it in my fist until it was a small compact ball. Then I tossed it furiously into the fire. It instantly burned away.

I've often wondered what it was like for Hetty that cold and colorless February day when she came back to Richmond on the train from Petersburg. Just a short two and a half weeks before she was the new bride of a general, written about in the papers, talked about by all of the young socialite girls who covetously aspired to be like her, her dreams of future greatness stretched out before her. No one envied Hetty now, a somber figure dressed in black, escorting a wooden coffin back home to be buried in the frozen soil. But it was red, Virginia soil. It was southern soil. It was the soil that John Pegram fought and died for.

When I read about the Battle of Hatcher's Run in *The Richmond Daily Enquirer*, I knew it was my doing. If I hadn't named Boydton Road, perhaps they would have surmised it anyhow after what Elizabeth and I pieced together from the letter I read in John Pegram's pocket. But then perhaps they would have gone with Vaughan as the supply route if not for the message Zora sent on my behalf. I felt the weight of responsibility squarely upon my shoulders. John Pegram was killed by a Minié ball as he stood at the front of his men defending the supply line. And Hetty, dear Hetty, was left a widow just eighteen days after her marriage to him.

Zora came home from the marketplace without the meat she went to purchase. There was none to be had. But she did have news, and so the lack of meat was forgotten completely in her haste to deliver her information to me. She rushed in waving the paper in my face with an excitement uncharacteristic of the old harpy. I was vexed by her blustering and grabbed the paper from her hand to get her to stop.

"You must read the headlines, Serena, for without you it certainly wouldn't have been possible," she said with a malicious smile.

I didn't know what she was talking about, nor did I wish to, because I knew if she was behaving in such a manner she was not doing it to be kind to me. It must be something she thought would hurt me. Right away I was afraid for Sam. Had they attempted the prison break and been caught? I straightened the paper and scanned the front page. There it was, the death of General John Pegram very neatly summed up in a few short columns. I was shocked.

"Looks as though your note was more important than you thought," she gloated.

I didn't know what to say. Whatever I said I was sure would be used in hostility against me. I sat speechless with a pit opening up in my stomach, yawning wide and cavernous, filled with both old and new regrets.

"What's the matter, Serena? You aren't pleased by it?"

Her words were meant to hurt and torment me. I shifted my gaze from the paper to her and regarded her for a moment, studying her in a concentrated effort to understand. How could someone take such delight in the misfortune of another? Why was she so spiteful, so insufferable? I couldn't imagine what she had experienced in life that would cause her to be this way.

"Why are you so hateful to me?" I asked quietly.

This caught her off guard. I don't suppose she expected my question. Maybe she thought I would lash out at her, scream, and throw a fit. I can't be sure what she was thinking. But she looked confused, her eyebrows furrowing for a brief moment, her mouth dumbly opened. Finally, she rallied her wits about her and responded.

"Whatever are you talking about?" she said with an air of flippant indifference.

"You know what I'm talking about. Do not pretend you haven't disliked me from the moment you set eyes on me. And to get back at me you would have a man go to his death and find satisfaction in it," I replied evenly.

Her eyes narrowed. "I had nothing to do with John Pegram's death. You wanted to play spy. Well, these are the consequences of it. *You* have that man's death on your hands, not me."

"What is it, Zora? What is it that makes you despise me so?"

"You seek to bait me. You seek to draw me in," she accused.

"I seek to understand you. I seek to find out once and for all why you wish me ill, why you have treated me so poorly, why you wish to vex me so. What crime have I committed against you to justify such treatment of me?" As I spoke, my voice grew hard and filled with passionate accusation.

"You cannot speak to me that way!" She cried. "You are in my home by my good graces. Without me you would have been living in the streets. If it had been up to me, that's where you'd be Miss New York. Come down here, thinking you're better than everybody else. Butting in where you don't belong, taking my place with Miss Van Lew and then Miss Cary. Well, I say there's no place for you here. You don't belong. High and mighty northerner putting your nose into things that are none of your business." She snorted with a mock laugh. "I told you you didn't have the guts to do what needed to be done. And I was right, wasn't I? I knew Miss Van Lew had you pegged wrong. I knew it from the start. She thought you would actually do the hard things. But I keep my ears open. I keep my eyes open. You thought you'd hide that note from me, didn't you? But I was smarter than you. Wasn't I, Serena Barlow? Wasn't I?"

"I believe you've confused cruelty with smartness, Zora. There's nothing smart in a single thing you've just said. Ruthless, yes, I'll give you that, but you are possibly one of the most thoughtless individuals I've ever become acquainted with." I got up from my chair, the newspaper in my lap dropping to the floor. I stepped on it to get away from her as she yelled and screamed and ranted to my back.

"I'm talking to you! You can't ignore me like that! Come back here!" she raged as she hurled insults and accusations at me.

I was done listening to her. I was tired of letting her have such an effect on me. While I decided I wouldn't allow her words to hurt me, I had to acknowledge that her actions left me completely ruined inside. She did what she set out to do, she made me guilty of John Pegram's death. If it wasn't for my note, if I hadn't betrayed him and Hetty, John would still be alive. I was responsible. That wasn't something I could just walk away from. I couldn't help but fear the consequences.

Just a few short days later Hetty sent for me.

Chapter 51

A courier came around in the morning. Zora met him at the door where he told her, "A message for Missus Barlow."

"I'll take it for her," Zora said.

He looked mildly uncomfortable, shook his head, and said, "I must deliver it to her personally."

She was annoyed, but seeing that he was not going to budge, stepped aside and called to me. "Serena, there is someone here for you!"

I came to the door, and as I didn't know what it could be about, I'm sure my expression was filled with suspicion. Zora was not going to leave. She wanted to know what it was about just as much as I did. I squeezed past her and waited expectantly.

"Missus Barlow?" he asked.

I hesitated. I felt that old familiar companion of fear and dread well up within me until it filled me and threatened to crowd out the air in my lungs. It burst into my throat and threatened to spill into my mouth. Was it Sam? That was the ever-present fear I lived with. Has something happened to him?

"Yes…" I replied.

"I have a letter for you," he told me, holding it out for me. I accepted the sealed letter from the boy, and he mumbled a parting, "Have a pleasant day," before he quickly disappeared.

I shut the door and studied the letter I held in my hand, uncertain if I wanted to open it. Zora was watching me with her shrewd and narrowed eyes. "Well, aren't you going to open it?" she said in an incredulous huff.

I broke the seal, taking my time over it as I unfolded the pages and straightened the creased paper. I could see that it was in the flowery handwriting of a woman with elegant hoops and flourishes. The body of the letter was brief and didn't fill the whole page. I looked from it to Zora who was eagerly anticipating my sharing it with her. I didn't want to. I didn't want for her to know my business. Whatever the letter was, it was meant for me and not her.

I had no desire to duplicate our last disagreement. The tension between us was painfully palpable. I was uncomfortable around her and did my best to avoid being in her company. I thought another argument would only serve to make it worse, but I also didn't want her to think she could cow me into doing whatever she wanted me to. When you dislike someone as I did Zora, anything they say or do appears to be negative and overbearing. It inspires in you suspicion and distrust over the smallest and most insignificant deed. I folded the paper back up, nodded politely to her, and said, "Thank you." And then I walked away from her. I noted, with dread, her very displeased expression as I left her and went to my room for some privacy. I had made her angry, keeping the letter to myself and not involving her.

I couldn't seem to make myself care. I chose instead to focus on the letter. I sat next to the window for light and opened it again to read.

Serena,

Due to unfortunate circumstances beyond my control, again I find myself in Richmond. You most certainly must know of my recent loss, and it is for this reason I write to you. I must speak to you. If it should be convenient to you to meet with me this afternoon at two o'clock I will plan on receiving you at my aunt's home at that time.

Yours sincerely,
Hetty

I wasn't sure what to make of it. I couldn't gage the tone in which she had written the note. Was it friendly or merely polite? Was there a veiled ominous feel to it, or was the notion propagated by a guilty conscience? It was neutral to the point that I couldn't read in what spirit she wrote it. Perhaps she knew I was the cause of her "unfortunate circumstances" and meant to confront me. What then? I was stewing in apprehension. What did she need to speak to me about? I didn't want to know and I certainly didn't want to face her. How could I face her after what I'd done?

Despite my anxiety, I knew I would comply with her wish. I didn't feel I could refuse. I really had no choice in the matter. Hetty beckoned, and I must heed her call.

Chapter 52

Shrouded in ebony layers of anguish that seemed to draw the color from her skin, she sat close to the window with her arm stretched the length of the armrest and her head resting against the wingback cushioning, her eyes unfocused as they looked out over the street. I waited at the edge of the room, watching her with empathy and fear. She didn't look up right away to acknowledge me, but she knew I was there. The maid announced me when I arrived. After what seemed an eternity, she spoke.

"I wondered if you would come." Her voice was so void of expression that I speculated what she meant by it. Was it a reproach?

"Of course I came." I said, but I didn't move from the doorway.

"We don't know one another all that well, only a short few weeks, and so this is awkward for you at best, I'm sure."

"I am here."

"It was foolish," she told me, her voice barely audible.

"What was?"

"Believing."

"I don't understand."

"I have always had the unfortunate trait of possessing blind hope. A belief in the best," she said. Still she had not looked at me. "Trusting."

"I don't think that is an unfortunate trait, Hetty."

"It is when you allow yourself to be gullible."

I grew all the more uncomfortable. No appropriate response came to mind so I thought it best not to speak.

"There were so many signs. Warnings… I should have recognized them. Perhaps none of this would have happened." Was she talking about me? Her words could have meant so many different things.

I took a few tentative steps into the room, drawing nearer to her. "I'm not sure I know what you're talking about."

"Little things. Things that seemed inconsequential at the time. Do you remember?"

"Remember what? I don't understand, Hetty."

"The mirror broke. For no apparent reason it fell from its frame and shattered on the floor."

"Yes, I remember that."

"And the clock on the mantel quit that morning. Someone had neglected to wind it I suppose. But it stopped. We used John's pocket watch to keep the time."

"It meant nothing," I said with a growing sense of dread.

"The carriage the President sent. The horses would not comply. They refused to budge. We had to call for another. And my veil. It caught on a nail and split right in two. You know they say a veil protects the bride from evil spirits?"

"Oh, Hetty…"

"I've never considered myself to be a superstitious person, but don't you think it's odd? Don't you think it all must have meant something?"

I realized she wasn't suspicious of me at all, as I had feared. She really had no idea *I* was the reason for John's death. She was blaming herself for what happened, attributing it to a series of unfortunate and unrelated events, and it made me all the more remorseful. I nearly couldn't bear the notion. I wanted to tell her everything, but if I did I would have no hope of rescuing Sam. He was why I was here. He was the reason for all of it. I wasn't going to jeopardize that. I couldn't.

I knelt next to her and began to cry. "I'm so sorry," I whimpered, bowing my head to her lap.

She put her hand to my hair and began to stroke it tenderly. "No one else understands," she whispered, the tears forming in her eyes. "But you do, don't you? You have lost more than I. You understand."

"I'm so sorry."

I looked up into her eyes and was surprised to see compassion. In that moment she was thinking of me, not herself. She was concerned for *me*. Who else would be so selfless at a time like this? It made me cry all the more. I knew I didn't deserve her compassion. I didn't deserve anything from her.

"Dear, Serena, how you have suffered."

I hastily wiped my tears away. "Do not worry about me. After what you've been through? Don't even give me a second thought!"

"He was mine for such a short time. It hardly seems real. Eighteen days. That is all. Eighteen days."

"I would do anything, anything to turn back time and change the course of things for you," I said with a pleading that only partly revealed the torture I felt.

"There is no going back, Serena. No going back."

"I'm so sorry. So sorry." What a half-wit. That seemed to be the only thing I could come up with to say.

"You may think it strange. After all it was only eighteen days." Her voice broke and tears flooded her eyes. "But I don't know what to do with myself now that he's gone. I don't know who I am..."

I didn't think it was strange. I knew exactly how she felt. I felt the same. Like the biggest piece of me, that made me who I was, was missing. With Sam gone, with Lucia far away, so small and vulnerable, without me there to care for her, I felt as though, if I were to look in a mirror, I would have no face, no features I could recognize. Who was I? I surely didn't think I was the sort who would lie, deceive, cunningly manipulate. I didn't think I was the sort who would betray and sacrifice lives for my own advantage. I believed I was a good person. How could I have so grossly misjudged myself?

It dawned on me that here sat Hetty Pegram in need, and I was thinking of myself. One more point to prove I was corrupted. I knew deep down I was fixated upon my objective of reclaiming Sam, to the extent that I was willing to sacrifice anyone and anything to reach that aim. After everything I had done to this woman, she at least deserved my full consideration. I forgot myself and focused on her. She needed comfort, and I would give it to her.

"You are Hetty. The brave, generous, and true person you've always been. The same Hetty you were before you became Mrs. Pegram. The same Hetty you must always be, because you know that no matter how it hurts, you cannot be any other. Life will go on, and you will go along with it. And you will make the best of it. That's all you can do."

The tears were falling down her cheeks and running into the collar of her gown, making it wet. She took my hand and squeezed it tightly. "Thank you," she said. We sat in silence for a good long while before I left her there at the window looking out over the street. I never saw her again after that day.

Chapter 53

Elizabeth waited until we were alone to proceed. Her maid left shortly after showing me in to the study, shutting the door quietly behind. I immediately felt a strange energy in the room, which caused my heart to hammer against my ribs, and I knew that Elizabeth must finally have news for me. I sat expectantly, wondering when she would reveal to me what this was about.

"The time has come," she whispered with an intense edge to her voice.

"Sam?" I asked.

Elizabeth nodded her head. "Yes."

"Tell me!" I pleaded.

"I've gotten word that it will be within the next several days," she informed me.

"Are you certain?" I dared to hope, to allow optimism to flood my senses as I sat with her. For the first time in a long time I felt joy. The kind of joy that makes your heart skip with anticipation.

"If all goes well."

"And Sam?"

"Is yet alive as far as I know."

"Oh, God be praised. God be praised," I moaned pathetically. I couldn't recall ever feeling such relief.

"You must speak of this to no one. Not even Mrs. Vandyke. Do nothing that would jeopardize the success of their escape."

"I won't!" I promised. It didn't even occur to me that I didn't trust Zora Vandyke, and she would be the last person I would confide in. There was no trust between the two of us, and our affiliation was now deteriorated to an uncomfortable silence. I stayed with her because there was no place else for me to go, and she tolerated me because she had agreed with Elizabeth Van Lew that she would keep me. I suppose the two of us deserved one another.

The last few days we barely even acknowledged the other's presence in the rooms we occupied together. This very evening we ate dinner without so much as a single word exchanged between us. I ate each bite, actively avoiding any accidental eye contact. I didn't even want to eat, but I felt refusing to eat might bring Zora some satisfaction, and I certainly didn't want that.

I was grateful, not only for the potential of being reunited with my love again, for seeing Sam would be a dream come true, but also for the promise that I'd be done with her. It brought me such cheer to think I would never have to see her hateful face again. Sam and I could go home. I would hold Lucia again. He would see her for the first time and witness for himself what a beautiful creature we'd created together. It brought me such elation to picture it.

"You must be prepared to act," she continued, breaking into my thoughts. "The time is far spent, and there won't be another chance like this one."

Chapter 54

Rose saw the end was near. He could feel it in his bones. When there was nothing to do but contemplate; without the distractions of social events, studies, the burdens of running a household, or even food, you came to an understanding, an awareness, which was nearly impossible to reach otherwise. They were like the monks thousands of miles away, living in their monasteries in the mountains of Tibet, who deprived themselves of their own free will in order to reach a higher awareness. Although some of the prisoners turned to God, others chose to adopt the belief they were forgotten and forsaken, to curse God for their misfortunes. Strangely enough, it tended to be those who believed they suffered for a cause that held on, gritted their teeth, and endured with determination. While those who had no objective, no purpose to their plight, slowly gave up, gave in, and succumbed to their surroundings.

At any rate, Rose had observed and prayed and worked long enough to realize that it must inevitably be over soon. It was yet to be determined if it would end in victory with the success of their mission, or if it would end in bitter defeat after the months of laborious work in wretched conditions. The anticipation was more than the men could bear. But Sam could see it was eating Rose alive. For the last several days Colonel Rose insisted he be the one to dig, taking the shifts of others so he could personally oversee and work on the tunnel. Ever by his side was Hamilton.

The other men were eager as well, but for Thomas Rose and Andrew Hamilton it was a personal battle with dirt, air, rats, and self-will. Sam thought he should intercede and try to convince the Colonel to take a night off for fear he would kill himself in the work, but when he looked Tom in his bloodshot and swollen eyes, he thought better of it. Sam knew there would be no convincing him to rest. And Sam could feel it too, that last burst of energy when one has the finish line in sight after a hard, treacherous race. The truth was, he felt the same. He was ready to be done with Libby as well.

Sam was standing watch the night of February eighth with Hamilton at the hole fanning in air and Isaac Johnson safely upstairs sleeping. Sam witnessed Isaac's deterioration since choosing to stay in the cellar instead of trying to explain his absence at roll call. The darkness and the rats and the stagnant air had done their work. He was frail, sickly, close to death. At night he snuck back up to the main floor to sleep with the others in order to get away from the terrible conditions he was living in here below.

The night wore on in the same manner it always did. Sam was so tired he nearly fell asleep upon his feet several times. He would jerk to attention and scold himself for being lax with his responsibilities. Sometime in the darkest part of night Tom Rose squeezed himself from the tunnel with a weary but triumphant expression upon his face. Both Andrew and Sam scurried to his side, helping him up from the ground. Before Tom could say a word, Sam knew. He could sense it.

"I've broke through!" Tom Rose cried softly. Sam could hear the raw emotion in the other man's voice and felt its effect upon him. Tears came to his eyes. He was glad that the room was so dark. He didn't want them to see his weakness.

"Where? Where does it lead?" Hamilton questioned him.

"Right where we aimed on it leading. I was standing in the shed just beyond the fence not five minutes ago."

"God be thanked!" Sam said in a sigh. He took Tom by the hand and gripped him tightly as he reached his other hand up and clutched his shoulder. "We've done it! You've done it!"

"You must tell us everything," Major Hamilton pled.

"The tunnel exit is in the perfect location. Right inside the wall of the shed. I worked my way out just as the sentry was announcing the time. One o'clock in the morning. I went out the shed door right up to the gate at the fence, lifted the bar, and let myself out. There I was standing on Canal Street. Can you imagine? Free as a bird. I strolled down the street a little ways to see what I could see. Not a soul approached. I finally thought I should come back and share the good news. So I went back through the gate, locking it behind myself, and then back into the shed. Before I went down the tunnel I moved a barrel over the opening, so no one would happen upon it. And here I am."

"We must tell the others," Sam replied.

"And we will," Hamilton agreed. But he paused, as though he were afraid of how Sam would react to his next statement. "But not tonight."

"What?" Sam was surprised. Sam looked from the Major to Thomas Rose in a confused state, not sure what to make of it. Why wouldn't they tell the others? Tom hastened to smooth things over.

"He's right, Sam," Tom said. "It will be light soon. If we tell them and they make a run for it, we'll be found out for sure. All that hard work for nothing."

"We wait. We tell them in the morning. That will give us time to prepare. If we head out at the earliest possible moment once it gets dark tomorrow, we have ten hours to get a start. We tell them now, the fools might chance it and get us all caught."

Sam knew what Andrew Hamilton was saying was true, but the thought of waiting another day was a thing he didn't wish to contemplate. There was the tunnel, beckoning to him, promising sweet liberty.

"Wait?" Sam swallowed hard, rubbing his hand over the back of his neck in agitation. "I'm a fool too then. For I'm of a mind to crawl out that tunnel right now and never look back. Let's be done with this place. Let's get while we can," he begged.

"Sam, you know that would be folly. You'd be rounded up and brought back in short order. If we wait until tomorrow night, that's our best chance at success."

Sam felt his stomach, in dread, twist within him. Yes, they were right. He knew they were right. He slowly nodded his head in agreement. It *was* the best thing to do. The only thing to do. While his head understood, his heart rebelled. He laughed as though it were a lark, a great jest. The tunnel lay just a few feet away, but it may as well have been miles.

"I suppose we try to get some sleep then," he suggested, growing resigned to the fact that he would have to have a little more patience than he cared to.

"Take heart. Come tomorrow night we will be free men!" Tom Rose exclaimed.

Chapter 55

In the early morning hours, before the guards were about, Major Hamilton called the small group of tunnel workers together. They congregated near the hearth, where the secret opening lay just beyond, and huddled cautiously to hear what Hamilton had to say. Sam noted that their eyes betrayed the anxiety they surely must feel.

It was either very good news or very bad. There was a general air of tension that kept them from feeling unbridled hope. How many times had they tried and failed? As far as they knew this would be yet another disappointing letdown. He observed how they watched, attempting to discern by any small clue as to whether it would be victory or defeat.

"Today is our final day in this place," Hamilton told them in a soft murmur that they strained to hear. "Colonel Rose has completed the tunnel."

A cheer went up, alerting the other prisoners to their meeting. Both Rose and Hamilton pushed their hands down and did their best to quiet the eager men. "Shh. Keep quiet!" Tom warned.

The men were too thrilled to be silent. They were slapping one another on the back, boisterously shaking hands and laughing. Sam thought it was like seeing children who had just been told they could have anything they like at a candy store. He felt the infectious excitement, like a rush, run through him. Strangely enough he had an immediate headache from it. Yet the grin on his face could not be forced away. He could feel the throbbing in his cheeks from it.

"We all did our fair share of the work," Rose said. "So now we must determine how we leave Libby. Major Hamilton and I thought the only fair way to do it would be to draw straws."

"You and the Major did more work than the rest," Sam injected. He would have done anything to get out of that reeking prison, but his sense of fairness still remained. The other men chimed in that they agreed with Sam.

"It's only fair the two of you go first. Besides, you out- rank us all," Sam added.

The two men exchanged a look, shrugged their shoulders, and nodded their agreement. What Sam had said was true. They didn't argue the matter, wasting time with modesty, they pressed on. Thomas Rose held out his fist with straws gripped tightly. Each plucked a straw and examined it. Sam felt fortunate when his was measured to the others. He would be leaving earlier on.

All the day long he struggled to keep himself still. He attempted to rest upon one of the empty cots, but he was too excited by the prospect of escape to sleep. The hours seemed to trail along at a reluctant pace, determined to drag themselves out in a painful and lingering crawl. All the while, Sam pictured in his head the route. He would climb down the rope, make his way to the dark hole, and wiggle through the tight and unforgiving space until he reached the shed. From there it was just a short distance to freedom.

Sam was surprised the guards hadn't picked up on the change in energy in the rooms. News such as this was too good to keep to one's self. Sam didn't share it with anyone, afraid it may curse their good fortune. But others did. Like a fire to kindling, word spread. A good majority of the men who knew nothing about the secret tunneling below their feet now conversed about it in urgent whispers.

There were plans being made, men attempting to trade for things they thought they may need once they were out. Sam grew more worried as the day went on. Too many people knew. Too many men were talking. As evening set in and darkness began to fall, the anticipation grew to near hysteria. Under the guise of normalcy the men settled in for the night, laying restlessly about the rooms, struggling to stay still and quiet.

Finally, Hamilton and Rose went to the stove and began the process of removing the bricks. It had been determined that since they were the masterminds, the orchestrators of the whole operation, they should be the first to embark. Thereafter the other diggers would take shifts that were assigned to them by the lots drawn. Each shift was to wait fifteen minutes before heading down to the cellar and crawling through the tunnel. Sam would be among the third group to leave.

Once Tom and Andrew were gone for a time, the next group got up from their spots and silently headed for the cellar. And that is when it seemed to go all wrong.

Chapter 56

The dam gave way and the flood waters broke through. Not just two or three of the men, as planned, got up to go to the cellar. It was closer to half a dozen. It hadn't been even five minutes when another group got up from their spot on the floor and went toward the hearth. Was it less than five minutes? Another group got up to leave.

Sam waited patiently for his turn, but disappointingly found there would be none. These men were going to make a run for it, whether they helped with the tunnel or not. They didn't care whether they were ruining it for anyone else. Surely with the deluge of men making an exit, suspicions would be aroused, and everyone would get caught if it kept up. He didn't know what to do.

There was a line forming by the stove, a line of men who were going to escape. Come what may, they were determined to get out. Sam couldn't wait any longer. He was desperate, like the rest of them, and so he got up and took his place in the line. Better to have a chance at escape than being the bigger man and politely waiting his turn. He had worked too hard and sacrificed too much to stand by and let the opportunity pass.

There were still some who were oblivious to what was going on, some who had not heard the rumblings of the tunnel and escape. But a majority of the men were now competing for a spot in line. Sam knew they were leaving too close together, being too quick to send another man through, but he was powerless to stop it. If he tried to intercede, he was afraid there would be a commotion and the guards would then most certainly be alerted.

He went with the flow and prayed that he would get out before the fools got them all discovered. An hour or more went by before he got his chance. It was like second nature to him now. He descended the rope and landed with a thud upon his feet. With urgent self-assurance he counted the paces to the wall, bent down and searched for the opening with his fingers.

There it was, his route to freedom. He went in head first and began working his way through the narrow passage, just big enough for his body to forcibly squeeze into. Clawing, wiggling, working his way through, he made his slow progress along the burrow.

It seemed never to end. At one point Sam began to panic. What if he was stuck here for good? He couldn't move. He couldn't breathe. He felt as though he were slowly suffocating to death. The darkness wrapped around him like a spider's web, and he forced himself to fight the terror, to keep moving forward.

When Sam's head emerged above ground, the cool clean air rushing to his face, filling his lungs. It was sweet victory at last. Using his arms, he pulled himself from the hole, crawling onto the ground before he righted himself and stood to his full height. Slowly his eyes adjusted to the dim interior of the shed.

Crates were stacked precariously about him. He picked his way through to reach the door. From the door to the open gate it was just a short piece. He stumbled out into the street, stopped and stood for a moment in the weak light of the street lamp, looking down one stretch and then turning to look down the other. Which way should he go? He decided that the best way would be toward the river. He would follow the river.

Chapter 57

For three long and sleepless nights I waited. There on Canal Street, near the gates of Libby Prison, I kept my station, sitting on the hard wagon bench and keeping Dandy at the ready. Or as ready as I could. Throughout the night the horse would sleep, his almost humanlike snoring nearly making me fall asleep too.

As tired as I was, I fought to stay awake. I was terrified that I would miss something if I didn't remain alert. The first night was a disappointment. Nothing. For some reason I had worked it up in my mind to believe it would happen then. It had to happen then. I was so weary of waiting. I expected it with such certainty that I was nearly shocked when the morning approached and nothing came of it.

The second night, I was certain too. But there was the previous night's failure. So while I was expecting the best possible outcome, I was also planning on the likelihood I would be frustrated again. And I was. In order to keep watch and keep awake I paced back and forth along the shadow of the street, where I was sure I would not be spotted by anyone.

Now as the third night commenced I felt an exhaustion I could scarcely combat. Numbness had taken over my mind. My limbs felt too heavy to lift. I was tired to the point that I feared I couldn't make it through the night without falling into a slumber.

It was just growing dark when I pulled the wagon to the place I had occupied the two previous nights. Sitting on the wagon seat, I had a clear view of the prison walls in either direction. I hated that ugly building, those horrid red brick walls. Unlike previous nights, I expected nothing. I expected a long night of struggling against sleep.

For a fleeting moment I thought of the Apostles, asked to keep watch as Christ prayed in the garden. I always wondered how they could so unfeelingly sleep through the terrible suffering of the Savior, when he had pled with them so earnestly to keep watch with him. How could they rest and leave him alone as they did? For the first time I had some empathy for them.

In the silence and gloom, I nodded, my head falling forward with a jerk. I came awake, snapping my neck back in alarm, wondering how long I had slept. As my blurry vision attempted to focus, I spotted them. Two dark figures lurking near the prison's tall brick outer fence. They paused there for a moment, seeming to be in conversation before they split up and headed in opposite directions.

Where had they come from? Was it the prison? Or were they just passers-by, out late and on their way home? I couldn't be sure. I climbed down from the wagon and made my way cautiously to where they'd been standing. I noticed that the prison gate was slightly ajar. My heartbeat accelerated when I understood. It would be tonight. Sweet mercy, blessed relief, it would be tonight.

Taking up a position behind a lone and rather sparse tree planted at the sidewalk in front of the prison I waited. Some time went by before a few more men came trotting out of the gate. I watched, trying to determine if Sam was among them. I couldn't be sure. Not only was it dark, but they were dressed alike in Union uniforms. They approached me, still unaware that I was there.

As they drew near, I whispered, "Sam?"

The two were spooked. They recoiled from me like startled rabbits, ready to bolt. I expect they weren't planning on company. Being on high alert, fearing discovery, they thought for a moment a guard had detected their movements. It wasn't until they saw me, a harmless lone woman, that they seemed to relax a bit. I tried to appear as non-menacing as possible. I held my hands up in front of me to show them I had no ill intent.

"I'm looking for Sam Barlow," I said in a hiss.

They didn't say anything, just backed away from me and took off at a trot down the walkway. I could do nothing but watch them go. I receded back to the shadow of the sparse tree, my frustration mounting. If I was honest with myself, the frustration was not so much from the men being unwilling to answer me as it was to mask my terrible fear. I didn't want to acknowledge it. I couldn't, because then I would have to do something about it. If I ignored it, distracted myself with some lesser emotion, I could stay where I was and keep to my objective.

Very shortly another man came through the gate and around the corner. Judging from his height I knew he was not Sam. I didn't even bother with him. I watched him disappear into the night without a word to him. A steady stream of men flowed consistently from the prison walls as they exited the tunnel, came out of the shed, and made for the street. I did my best to be patient, but each time I tried to inquire after Sam the men either bolted from me in fear or shrugged their shoulders and told me they had no knowledge of him.

One fellow told me, "Sam? I can't say where he is. Don't know." He seemed sorry that he couldn't help but was eager to get away from the prison and said this as he hurried off.

At least the man knew Sam, and there was some hope that he would be among those to escape. I would estimate close to fifty men came out of those walls, one or two at a time as I waited there for several hours. I grew irritated, thinking perhaps it wouldn't happen after all when I didn't see Sam right away. I gave up hiding behind the tree and drifted nearer the fence, just a few feet away from the gate. If the men didn't respond to my constant inquiry after Sam, I would draw closer and inspect their faces for myself. Their grim, haggard appearances betrayed their suffering, their terrible story of neglect and abuse. I shuddered under the gaze of hollow eyes and empty expressions. It *was* just as bad as they had made it seem in the papers. Of that I had no doubt.

It was nearly two in the morning when I heard the next set of feet approach Canal Street. I didn't bother saying anything. I just waited for the man to come out and stepped up closer to inspect his face, as I had the others. He didn't anticipate having company. He came around the corner in a hurry and ran right into me. The shocked expression he wore was a mix of fear and complete and total surprise.

Sadly, I didn't recognize him. He had a full beard, his cheeks lean and sunken, and the skin beneath his eyes drooping and puffy at the same time. His forehead appeared wide and boney. The eyes themselves were not as I remembered, although the same hazel color. They seemed to be bottomless, like a murky, deep cavern with no reflection of light. It was just the darkness of the night, I told myself. His clothing, torn and dirty, hung loose and ample upon his too thin frame. He was nothing but skin and bones. Everything about him was distorted into hard lines and angles, his features magnified by the lack of plumping fat to soften his edges.

His eyes grew wide, fluttering back and forth in his sockets as recognition registered, his mouth drooping open in shock. I could tell from the way Sam looked at me that he didn't believe what he was seeing. He thought it some cruel trick perhaps, or he had finally lost it and the mind which threatened to crumble for so long had finally given way. I put my hands to his chest to keep him at arm's length as I scrutinized his face, trying to make sure it was him. Could it really be Sam? I wasn't certain; although I recognized his voice, there wasn't much more that rang true to me in his looks. I could have been looking at a total stranger for all I knew.

"Serena?" he gasped. "Serena, is it really you?"

"Sam?" I was cautious. I shamefully realized my face must betray the horror mingled with disbelief I was feeling at the sight of him.

"Serena!"

"It is you," I breathed. "I can scarce believe it, but it is you."

Sam put his hands to either side of my face, cupping my cheeks with his lean fingers. "You're here?"

"Yes, Sam."

It was too much. Tears welled up in his eyes as he continued to study me. Then he dropped to his knees, pressing his body to mine, his face hidden against my belly as he bawled like a baby, his frame shaking in uncontrolled spasms. His arms were clutching me close, as though he were afraid if he let me go I would disappear, and he would find it was all a dream. I bent my shoulders forward and wrapped my arms around his neck, my own tears slipping down my face to anoint his head as I put my lips to his hair again and again.

"It's me," I whispered soothingly. "It's me. I've come for you, Sam. I'm here."

I can't say for sure what I was feeling just then. It didn't seem real. I was relieved, but I was also dazed. Here was Sam, finally in my arms. Yet, I recognized right away that everything about him was altered. The man I knew was not this man. As he sobbed in my arms, so vulnerable, so breakable, the fear I had experienced earlier transformed. I was no longer apprehensive about being caught outside Libby prison in the dead of night. I was frightened of him. I was frightened of losing us.

The past lay behind me, inviting and familiar, and the future stretched before me in painful uncertainty. I was agonizingly aware a choice was being presented to me in that moment. I must let the past go and do my best to forge ahead and make a new future with Sam, or I could stubbornly hold on to that yesterday which was departed and gone. Like a flash of lightening, burning with destruction, the scene I witnessed of the mass graves in the fields of Bull Run blinded my vision. I did not want to live among the dead.

I couldn't let him see. I had to hide it. The only thing I could think to do to conceal my fear was to reassure him. And that is what I did. I told him again and again that it was going to be all right, although I didn't know for certain myself if it truly would be.

Beneath the halo of the street lamp, without even attempting to hide ourselves, we were fixed in that manner until someone ran headlong into us and startled us from our trance.

Chapter 58

Another inmate made his way to the street and found us smack in the middle of his escape route. I gasped, startled by the intrusion. The other man managed to exclaim, "What in blazes?" He backed away slowly and then turned in the other direction, disappearing into the dark.

Now that I had come back to myself, I realized what danger we were putting ourselves in, dallying for all to see out in the open. I reached down and tugged on Sam's arm, trying to pull him to his feet. "Come," I said. "We must go."

We hastily crossed the street, making our way to where I had left Dandy tied with the wagon. "Here," I told him, drawing him to the back of the wagon. I lowered the gate to the wagon bed, exposing the crawl space just big enough for a man to lay on his back. I had packed it with straw to try and make it a bit more comfortable, but I was certain it afforded little relief from the hard wooden planks. "Climb in."

He eyed the small space apprehensively. "What's this?"

"Your father made it. A secret space for you to hide," I explained urgently. "Quickly, Sam. Time grows short."

Sam reluctantly climbed into the back of the wagon, pulling himself backward until his feet disappeared within the darkness. I shut and latched the gate, ran around to the front, and climbed up to the bench. Dandy had been sleeping and responded slowly to my urgent tug on the reins.

I headed up Capital, doing my best to look as though I should be there. Only a few blocks from the prison was Elizabeth Van Lew's beautiful mansion. I kept the wagon to the side of her home, across the street. As I had done before, I slipped quietly into the yard and worked my way to the back door in quiet secrecy. I knocked twice, briskly enough to be heard. It must have been the noise that broke the late night silence, but a dog began to bark in the distance.

After a few moments one of the servants came to the door, still dressed in their nightdress. He was older, his hair graying. His expression was purely startled as he looked at me, and then suspiciously looked past me and about, as though he expected someone else to be waiting in the shadows.

"What business you got here?" he asked gruffly.

"I must speak with the mistress."

"She sleepin'. Can't be disturbed."

"Please! Tell her it is Serena Barlow. Tell her it is urgent," I pled.

"I ain't rousin' her out of bed at this ungodly hour. You must be plumb outta your mind. Go on, git!"

"I must speak with her. I'm not leaving until I do. The longer I am out here for all to see, the more likely I am to stir up attention."

He was fit to be tied. Again I saw him scan the yard behind me. Grudgingly he finally let me in. I stood near the door, venturing no further into the dark room. He disappeared for a moment. After what seemed like a very long time, Elizabeth's maid appeared. I could see she was not pleased with me. Her lips were pursed and her brow furrowed.

"What are you doing here?" she asked.

"I must speak with Miss Van Lew," I told her urgently. I was thinking of Sam out in the wagon, alone and in a terrible condition. I needed to hurry.

"She told you not to come here without being asked," the maid said with a firm and insistent edge to her voice.

"I know, but it is an emergency. You must understand, I have no choice."

"You wanna get Miss in trouble?"

"Of course not. But…"

"We don't want no trouble and you surely brung it. You go on and get now."

"If I can just speak to her. I need her help."

"I done told you she ain't to be disturbed."

I stubbornly refused to take no for an answer. I set my jaw, my teeth gritted in determination. I went to move past her, thinking I would go and wake Miss Van Lew myself, but she stepped in front of me and blocked my way. Now the older man who had opened the door came forward with a warning look in his eyes. He stood next to the woman, and the two guarded the way so that I couldn't get past them.

"It's time you be on your way," the man said with an angry nod of his head.

"You tell Miss Van Lew I came. She knows where to reach me," I said, hastily backing up toward the door and turning to leave.

When I got back to the wagon, I could have cried. I climbed back up onto the wagon bench and put my head into my hands feeling overwhelming defeat. Sam was back there, hiding in the secret place, depending on me, and I had no idea what to do. One thing was certain, I couldn't wait out here in the open. That was sure to be a fatal mistake.

Chapter 59

Under different circumstances I might have relished the look on Zora's face. Desperation had driven me to her cottage near the river. I left several nights before with the intent never to return, sleeping in the wagon by day and keeping watch at the prison by night. I hadn't seen the woman in nearly three days, and now here I was banging on her door, rousing her from her sleep in the wee hours of the morning. She was cautious when she opened the door, still half asleep and not sure what to make of any of it.

"Serena? What…what are you doing here?" she stammered in confusion.

"I had no place else to go," I admitted. I pulled Sam's arm, putting him in view of her.

Now her confusion gave way to a determined shake of her head. She was not going to help me. She was not going to let Sam stay. "No!" she sputtered. "No!"

"This is my husband Sam. I got him from Libby, and I need a place to keep him for a day or two," I tried to explain.

"What are you trying to do, get me hanged?" she raged.

"He's too sick to move. And I have little doubt we'll be caught if we set out now. It will be morning soon, and they'll have discovered he's gone."

"Get off my property."

"Serena," Sam tried to intervene. He tugged at the sleeve of my dress. I ignored him.

"I'm only asking for a few days, just until he gets on his feet."

"I won't have him. I won't have you," she replied, cutting off the end of my sentence.

"Zora-" I began.

She went to shut the door. I knew I couldn't let her. I stuck my foot in the jam, preventing her from shutting it completely. This made her angry. She gasped in outrage as she opened the door again with the intent to push me out of the way. She stopped short when she saw Sam's pistol in my hand. That is when the fear came to her eyes. She took a step back, her hands raised in a defensive motion.

"I am not leaving," I said firmly. I was so very tired, at my wits end, and she had pushed me too far. In my frenzied state I fully intended to use that gun if I had to.

I took Sam by the hand and pulled him through the door. He seemed just as surprised as Zora to see me with the weapon. I motioned to a chair near the fireplace where the remains of a charred log were smoldering. "Sit down," I said.

She didn't say a word, only did as I told her to, backing up reluctantly and sitting down with an abrupt drop. I stood over her with the barrel still aimed at her, not sure what to do now.

"After everything I did for you," she said accusatorily.

"What did you do for me? I worked like a slave for you. I figure I paid my dues," I replied coolly. Sam watched our interaction with confused and narrowed eyes, unsure of himself as he stood defensively near the door.

"Serena, we should leave, before there's trouble," he whispered.

I sniffed, shifting my attention from Sam to Zora. "There's food in the kitchen," I told him as I was eyeing her, choosing to ignore what he said. He hesitated for only a moment and then went over to the kitchen and began to frantically rifle through the cupboards. He pulled out a bag of cornmeal dipped his hand in and began eating the meal from his hand. I watched him devour the raw meal and thought my heart might break.

"Stop holding that gun on me, you fool," Zora said, bringing my attention back to her. "There's no reason for it. I'm not going anywhere."

"I don't trust you."

"I may not like you. I may have even wanted you out, but I didn't want you dead or nothing," she said with a sneer.

Meanwhile, Sam was scooping up pats of molded butter and popping them in his mouth. Next he descended upon a pot of beans and began to eat those too. He was about halfway through the pot when he stopped suddenly. He rushed to the dry sink and began convulsing and vomiting. I left Zora and hurried to his aid. There was nothing I could really do, but I stood next to him with my hand on his back.

"Sam, are you all right?"

Of course it was silly of me to ask. He was too busy throwing up everything he had just eaten to respond. I quickly got him a cup of water and when he was finished, I gave him the cup. He sipped at it briefly, but then sat it down, putting his hands on the table to brace himself.

"Sam?"

"I need to lay down," he murmured.

"Come to the bedroom," I said, taking his arm and guiding him down the hall. About halfway to the bedroom Sam's legs went to liquid and he fell to the floor in a crumpled heap.

"Sam!" I crouched down next to him, but he was unresponsive as I tried to slap his cheeks and shake him awake. "Sam!" I cried again.

"Help me!" I screamed at Zora. "Please!"

She got up from the chair and came to help me. You may wonder how the two of us got a grown man down the hall and into bed. But Sam had lost so much weight he was really very light and easy enough to lift. I took his arms and she took his legs and we carried him to the bed and laid him there.

"What's happened to him?"

"I don't know," Zora replied.

I was borderline panicked. "What should I do? What should I do?" I was wringing my apron, pacing the floor. "I meant to only sleep here for the night and be gone." I stopped my pacing and looked to Zora. "I need a doctor."

"You must be joking," she scoffed. "You call a doctor and he will report you. Your Sam will be back in prison come daybreak."

I glared at her. "You'd like that wouldn't you," I accused.

"Shut your mouth, you simpleton. I'm not the enemy."

"Aren't you?"

"No."

"What shall I do?" I moaned.

"I know a woman…" Zora began.

"What woman?"

"She deals in herbs and midwifery."

"And?"

"She is known for discretion," Zora informed me.

"You think I'll let you leave. That's what you think?"

"Someone has to go fetch her."

"I'm not senseless enough to let you leave."

"Suit yourself. You don't have to trust me, but he'll die without my help."

"Bear in mind, if I am caught…if it doesn't end well for me, well, it won't end well for you either, Zora."

Chapter 60

In the early hours of the morning, an ashy veil of light just beginning to spread over the horizon, Allison Cosgrove came stealthily to the cottage by the river. She had an odd odor about her, which I noted as she passed me when she entered the front door. She was taller than me, thin and boney. Her hair was done in a thick loose plait, wispy around her lean oval face. Her dress was old style, worn and threadbare. Overall there was a sense of antiquity about her, although she couldn't have been more than thirty or thirty-five.

"Where is he?" she asked.

I showed her down the hall and into the bedroom. I had taken Sam's boots off, and his coat too. Then I attempted to cover his dark blue trousers, the mark of a Yankee soldier, with the quilt on the bed. He lay there looking like a corpse against the pillow.

"You understand I deal mostly with expectant women?" she asked, looking from him to me.

"Please…we need help."

She nodded and then went over to him, beginning by rolling back his eyelids and looking into his eyes. She slid her fingers down the sides of his face and then pressed them firmly beneath his jaw to his neck. I watched her look him over and waited to see what she would say.

"What brought on his illness?" She asked.

"He hasn't been able to eat. A stomach ailment. Last night he began eating and then he threw up and then he went unconscious and hasn't woken since."

"Perhaps the food was too much for his system."

"Can you help him?"

"I don't know." She was hesitant. Possibly, afraid that if she said no I would lose my composure.

"I have money," I offered eagerly. "Yankee money."

Her eyes narrowed, and she looked at me strangely. I wasn't sure if it was suspicious or disbelieving. "You're asking me to fix a man who looks to me on the verge of death. His pulse is weak, and he's nothing but skin and bones."

"How much?" I asked, understanding dawning on me. She was extorting money from me. It had been a mistake to call on her. But what choice did I have? I would do anything, anything to help Sam. Everything I had done thus far was only proof.

When Allison left, most of the money I had, money I planned on using to get Sam and I home, went from my pocket to hers. "If he should wake, feed him as if he were a babe. Begin with liquids--broths, warm milk, thin porridge. Once he masters these things begin giving him puddings--corn, blood, and the likes. Eventually he should be able to eat more solid foods."

"If he should wake?" I said aghast.

"I made no secret I am not a proper physician," Allison huffed.

"Will I be able to move him?"

"Move him?"

"Take him on a trip. His aunt lives in Georgia, and I must take him there to recuperate," I lied.

"I don't believe it would be wise," she replied in disbelief. "This is the best place for him to recuperate. If you move him I doubt he would make the trip."

My heart sank when she said this. I couldn't bear the thought of being stranded here while the manhunt for the escaped yankees ensued. We would be trapped like fish in a net. I loathed the idea that I would remain at Zora's mercy. Allison left shortly after.

I went back to the bedroom where Sam lay in the bed, sitting in a chair close by to watch him. The last three nights of sleeplessness weighed heavy upon me. So very tired was I that I could not keep my eyes open any longer, and I dozed in the chair, my head heavy upon my chest. I do not know how much time passed, only that the next thing I knew there was a loud and brusque knock at the front door.

Chapter 61

I heard Zora in the other room, her feet crossing the floorboards to the front door. I heard the door opening and then Zora asking, "Yes?"

"Sorry to disturb you, ma'am but we are out and about looking for some Yanks this morning." My eyes darted from Sam to the door where I knew they would be coming shortly to take my husband away again.

"Yanks?" Zora said, sounding amused.

I clutched the pistol I had in my hand, thinking I may have cause to use it soon. "That's right, ma'am. We had some of that ruffian from Libby Prison escape last night," they informed her.

Another voice, still male, chimed in. "You ain't seen anything, have you now?"

"You can't be serious. No one escapes Libby," Zora flattered them.

"Afraid so. May we look through the house here, make sure all is well?"

"I give you my word I haven't seen one of the scoundrels, but you are welcome to look," she said. I heard her step aside to let them in. "Don't mind my cousin. She is ill and resting in the bedroom," Zora said.

I was frantic as I pulled the sheet from the bottom of the bed, lowering Sam's feet to the ground, then moving to the other end of the bed, taking the sheet from that end and gently lowering his head to the ground. He was now on the floor between the bed and the wall, hidden from view. I jumped onto the bed, covering my body with a blanket, my hand in my pocket with a finger on the trigger.

If it came to it, I would use the pistol. I would get rid of those soldiers. Shortly they came down the hall and through the door. I groaned when I saw them. "Zora?" I asked, doing my best to seem groggy, disoriented.

"It's all right, dear cousin. These men mean no harm," she said soothingly.

"What's the matter with her?" one of the men asked.

Zora then acted as if she were confiding in them, her voice dropping to a whisper. "The doctor says the poor dear is suffering from Cholera. Why, I've never seen anyone as ill as she, the lamb. He's advised me not to come into the room with her; it is, after all very contagious. But who else will care for her if not me?"

At this I began coughing violently, moaning and carrying on in the most pathetic manner. The two soldiers exchanged terrified looks and backed away from the door. I reached my hand out toward them despairingly. "I feel so hot," I complained, although it was a chilly February morning.

"Thank you for your cooperation," one of the soldiers said, his voice high pitched and eager. "But we have much to search and a great deal to do in a short time," the other said hastily.

"Zora?" I called out.

"I'll be right back, sweet. Just let me see these men off, and I'll take care of your needs," she said, in a voice she had never used with me before. Indeed, a voice I never heard again. For she quickly resumed her gruff demeanor the second the two were gone.

"I want you out of my home as soon as you can make preparations," she seethed when she returned from letting them out.

Chapter 62

Once Sam was settled back into bed, I bathed him from a wash basin and dressed him in fresh clothing that I had taken from Zora's piles of wash. For days I sat by his side, praying to God he would wake up. I rarely left his side, keeping watch in the chair next to the bed.

It was late evening, the room mostly shrouded in shadow. I sat dozing in the chair when I heard him speak to me. "Our child…" he said, his voice gravelly and raw.

I smiled, although I was crying too, relief and joy flooding me. "Our child is well," I assured him. "Not the son you had wished for, but a very fine daughter who looks a great deal like you."

"A daughter," he said in satisfaction.

"She wears your dark hair, your square chin, and thankfully your ears," I said.

"Her name?"

"I hope you will approve. I had to choose alone you know," I said with a lighthearted chuckle. "Her name is Lucia."

"Lucia," he repeated. "I like it."

"Good, because there is no going back now."

I did as Allison the midwife had bid me. I gave him warm milk, porridge, broth and the like for three days before I decided there should be no more waiting. It was time to go. Rumors prevailed that

Richmond was soon to be moved upon by the Northern armies, and with this fear, many were leaving the city in a hurry. I thought it was sad to think many of them had come in much the same panic looking for protection.

At any rate, I used it to my advantage. I packed what little I had, putting Sam in the back of the wagon in the hiding place beneath the false bottom. Zora was more than eager to watch me as I made the preparations. But when I went to say goodbye she had a cloth sack filled with bread and bottled beans and dried apricots. She handed them to me resentfully.

"We may have had our differences," I said diplomatically, "But you have my sincere gratitude, Zora." Although I didn't like her, my appreciation was sincere.

"Don't feel obligated to visit me any time soon, Serena," she said bluntly.

"I don't believe I'll be this way again, Zora."

There were never more blessed words than when I was able to say to Sam, "We are home." As we crossed the borders from the South to the North, back on friendly soil again.

Chapter 63

Easter Sunday was celebrated at my home on April 15, 1865. There were two reasons to rejoice that warm spring day. The first was the miraculous resurrection of our Savior after three days in the tomb, and the second was that we had received word just days before of the surrender at Appomattox Court House by General Lee, effectively ending the War between the States. And although one far out ranked the other, I still counted them both miracles.

The war was already over for Sam and me. He was not fit to return to the army after Libby, and I didn't speak of any battles or what was transpiring out in the battlefields because I didn't want to upset him or cause him any unneeded stress. I sought to make his environment as pleasing and carefree as I could, not wishing to bring the least degree of anxiety upon him. All I wanted was to provide the best possible care for him so that he could get better. I had thought not to invite anyone over that Sunday, because I didn't want too much excitement, but Sam had insisted on it. He wanted to bring our two families together in our home. He wanted to celebrate.

I had been right to worry about the excitement and strain it might cause. While it was enjoyable to visit and be surrounded by family, it was also exhausting. The children ran in and out the door, laughing loudly, shrieking as they chased one another in a game of tag, rolling in the grass, and swinging on the swing as we women cleared the table. My mother and Sam's mother, Jersha, were taking plates of leftover lamb, potatoes, parsnips, pickled beets, brown bread, and bottled beans back to the kitchen to be divided among households.

I knew that it had taken a lot for my mother to come. She spoke very little and concentrated on keeping her hands busy as we cleaned up. I could tell that she was intimidated by Sam's mother, who spoke easily, carried herself with poise, and seemed perfectly comfortable in her own skin. There was something very charming about my mother-in-law's ability to blend in seamlessly with any crowd. She spoke her mind in a way that most women could not get away with. Although it was sometimes quite blunt and far too honest, she could easily spar with the best of them and manage to remain endearing despite her directness. I liked her very much, but didn't want to seem too favorable toward her for my mother's sake.

Jersha floated back and forth between the table in the dining room and the kitchen carrying a stack of dirty dishes. She dumped them into the soapy water of one of the basins in the dry sink, rolling up her sleeves in a determined manner. At that point she must have spotted one of her children up to mischief out the window. Jersha opened the backdoor wide and hollered out, "Stop that or I'll come after you with my spoon!"

I carried two pie plates in, setting them on the small table against the back wall. "Mother, your chess pie was the best I've ever tasted!" I praised, hoping it would give her confidence.

She managed a forced smile. "No better than usual," she said modestly. I realized that I had made a mistake. I had drawn attention to her, and that was something she did not care for.

"Accept the compliment, my dear. The pie was exceptional," Jersha said, taking a cleaned plate and dunking it into another basin to rinse before stacking it on a towel.

Mother looked slightly alarmed by Jersha's no-nonsense admonition. I felt uncomfortable for her. I searched frantically for a way to change the course of the conversation.

"John tells me you've a new foal," I said to Jersha as I rearranged slices of pie into separate pie plates so that everyone would have a sampling to take home.

"Yes, it is so. What a little beauty he is too. The spitting image of his father. I suppose he will be a great help at the mill when he grows big enough."

Mother seemed to relax when the focus was removed from her. Jersha prattled on about the foal, which I had no objections to. I liked hearing her speak. She had a soothing voice that commanded attention. We finished cleaning the table, drying and putting away the dishes, and finally had a moment to sit and rest.

"I'm going to check on the baby," I told my mother and Jersha. It wasn't the truth. I was going to check on Sam. But I felt foolish telling them my real purpose. Sam's mother gave me a knowing smile that made me want to blush. My mother simply nodded her head and went back to sipping her cup of coffee.

I went to the parlor looking for Sam. The two fathers sat conversing with one another, talking politics and planting. I drifted in, spotting Sam with his legs stretched out before him, his feet crossed at the ankles, in the arm chair John had brought over shortly after Sam had returned home. He said Sam ought to have a comfortable chair to recuperate in, as he unloaded the upholstered wing back from his wagon to bring into the house.

I felt bad that everything we owned had been given to us, but I was too humble to turn away his gift. And I knew that he was right. Sam should be made as comfortable as possible. I hovered over Sam as he slept with Lucia cradled against his chest, his arms enfolding her. She slept too, her little fist curled around the fabric of his shirt, her lids fluttering every now and again, as though she were trying to force herself awake but didn't have the strength to pull it off, and then she would give a shuddering sigh and sleep on.

"Perhaps I should have him go lay on the bed," I said.

"Let him sleep, daughter," my father protested.

"Don't you think he'd sleep better on the bed?" I asked.

"Leave him be. He's not made of china, stop fussing over him." He and John gave one another exasperated looks and then chuckled over it. I wasn't sure if it was for my benefit or theirs. No one wanted to acknowledge that Sam had come back changed. To look into his sunken eyes and hollowed face one would have to acknowledge what had happened to him. And the thought of what happened to him was unbearable. The truth was that Sam was fragile. He had begun to gain some weight back, but his health was not completely restored, and he had terrible digestive issues that plagued him much of the time, making it difficult for him to eat anything but the blandest of foods. I couldn't help but worry over him, just as much as I worried over my darling baby girl.

I humored them with a smile. "Made of china..." I said shaking my head and rolling my eyes.

Just then Sam opened his eyes. He saw me standing over him, and a slow grin formed upon his lips. "Happy Easter, Dearest," he said in a drowsy tone.

"Happy Easter," I replied. He reached for my hand and kissed my palm with a lingering and sweet kiss. "Would you like to go lay down on the bed? I can take the baby."

"No. I fancy holding her a bit longer," he said.

"Would you like me to fetch a blanket? Would that make you more comfortable?"

"No need. I'm fine."

Just then Rosa and Lilly, Sam's youngest sisters, burst through the front door in a flurry of excitement. "Someone's coming down the lane," they squealed in near unison.

I went to the porch, waiting to see who it was. Aida pulled her buggy right up to the porch steps, pulling the reigns hard to stop the horse. I smiled pleasantly.

"Have you come to wish me a happy Easter?" I asked.

She was out of breath, her bonnet hanging down her back, her hair in fly-away wisps all about her face. I should have known right away that something was amiss. After all Aida was a careful sort, everything in its proper place, neat and tidy, the model of decorum. Not at all the sort to drive up haphazard in a state of excitement as she had. She didn't answer me right away, which set me on edge.

My smile melted. "What is it?"

"The president has been assassinated!" she cried. And then Aida fell apart. She took a shuttering breath and dissolved into tears. "Abraham Lincoln is dead!"

"No," I whispered in disbelief. "How?"

"He was shot yesterday at Ford's Theater and, after suffering through the night, expired early this morning."

I can't describe adequately how I felt at that moment. My mind took note of the smallest details, the smell of lilacs, Stanley spinning aimlessly on the rope swing that hung from the maple tree just growing full with new spring leaves, Aida balling helplessly as the horse pawed at the ground, and yet none of it seemed to register. I felt an emptiness that seemed to open and expand within my chest. It was as though I didn't understand any of it, as though none of it made sense, and yet all of these things were familiar to me.

I was in complete shock. I could scarcely believe it. I knew that she wouldn't make such a thing up, but how could it be? After the joy and elation we had felt at the surrender, the final end to this cursed war, it was incomprehensible the distress and sorrow I felt in contrast.

I had never met President Lincoln, only saw him the one time from a far off distance shortly after joining the army, but I took his loss so very personally. It was as though I had lost a dear and beloved friend. Someone had shot and killed my president! *My* president!

I realized then, that there would never be an end to war, to the hatred and brutality that fuels conflict and strife. There was no safety or security to be had, because there would ever be a battle raging in the hearts of conspiring men. It was a constant as old as time, beginning with Cain who slew his brother Able over a trivial thing called jealousy. It ever was and ever would be.

Abraham Lincoln was an ideal, a symbol, a dream of a united people, all free, all one. After seeing what I had seen in the war, I shouldn't have been so naïve as to think that these things were actual possibilities. With the death of that man my eyes were opened. I saw how fragile and temporary hope can be.

Chapter 64

When I finished it felt as though the room were full of the participants of my story, crowding round the table, lingering in the corners. One by one they had collected there over the course of the day, resurrected by my memories of them. Perhaps Mr. Franklin could sense it too. He wore a very sober expression, attempting a smile, but unable to quite master it. "Extraordinary," he finally said.

"I hope I have not disappointed--that my story *was* worth the long trip after all," I replied, doing my best to keep my emotions in check. I always grew sentimental when I spoke of that Easter Sunday.

"One of the most captivating I've had the pleasure of hearing."

"If you would be so good as to keep me updated on the board's ruling I would be most grateful," I told him, doing my best to change the subject and master my emotions at the same time.

"It's not my place to say, but I can see no reason why you shouldn't receive the pension you've applied for."

"You must understand I wouldn't make such a request if it weren't necessary. I really didn't wish for anyone else to know about me and what I've done. But times are hard, and I can't see another way."

"I don't mean to appear rude, but may I ask what misfortune prompts you to do so?" Mr. Franklin inquired with concern in his voice.

I hesitated. It was not my practice to discuss personal matters with strangers. And yet, I had just told this man my most private and guarded secrets. Why shouldn't he know all of the truth? The results of the culmination of all of the events I described so earnestly to him and how they affected my life.

"Sam was never the same after Libby."

Mr. Franklin pursed his lips and nodded thoughtfully. "I see."

"He did his best to earn a living and provide for me and the children, but he steadily grew worse over the years. I did what I could on the farm. I did what I could to get by, make sure the children were well cared for. But…he cannot and should not be laboring for a wage anymore. He just isn't able to work any longer. His health won't permit it, and his pension is hardly enough to survive on. Quite simply, I need the money to keep the farm and to care for Sam."

"It is only right," he said with strong conviction. "You have done remarkable things. I don't know any woman who could claim the same."

"There are plenty of women who could claim the same. Women who have fought to keep their farms and care for their children too. If I had a penny for every widow I knew, well…I wouldn't need a pension."

"I'm sure. I just meant to say if you need help, you should have it." His voice was soft and considerate.

"Mr. Franklin, while I appreciate your sentiment, you have it all wrong. This isn't about me being a man or a woman." He looked confused, which compelled me to clarify. I didn't want there to be any mistake about what I was trying to communicate to him. "This is about me being a soldier. I fought in the war alongside other soldiers," I continued, pulling my shoulders back and looking him squarely in the eye with pride. "I am not asking for help. I don't expect handouts, although Lord knows I've had my fair share to make it through. What I am asking for is rightfully mine. Just as Sam gets a pension, I should too. I was a soldier. I have earned it."

"Well stated, Mrs. Barlow. I apologize if I have offended you."

"I'm not offended. I know you must feel pity for me. But I don't want you to. Life gives us each unique tribulations that we must wade through. I am no different than anyone else in that respect."

"Yes, but you've shouldered a great burden."

"It was a burden I asked for. All that I wanted was to be with Sam, to be useful to him, to take care of him. I got that wish. I got that wish and much more. If Sam had been taken from me, it would have been a far worse burden to bear. So many did not come home. I could have been one of the wives who never got to hold her husband again, like poor Hetty. And because of Sam I have five beautiful children, all sensitive, compassionate souls, all hard workers that can be relied upon in matters of importance, all believers in God, and all upright citizens. Two daughters and three sons," I said proudly.

"Yes, but surely you didn't hope to take care of Sam in this manner."

"It wasn't exactly what I had in mind when I was a girl and wished only to be useful to him, to make his life easier and be his constant companion. But we rarely get what we want the way we want it, Mr. Franklin. I have learned the hard way that life is made up of a series of terrible ironies. It is given to us to make the best of it, to try to put it straight or, in most cases, to just do what we can with what we have and learn to be happy in spite of it."

We parted at the front door. I waved good bye to him as he put his hat on his head and walked down the lane, no doubt on his way back to town. I was alone. Yet, I was never really alone. *They* stayed behind. They did not belong to him, they belonged to me. I could feel them congregating around me, watching him leave over my shoulder. They were never very far away, silent and grave, like gloomy effigies of shadow and dust. The guilt and the nightmares who were once flesh and blood, now housed in the corridors of my mind along with the frightening images I had grown used to over the days, months, and years since. All of the men whose lives I had taken. Jack Monroe was there with his ever sneering smile, along with brave and noble John Pegram, the nameless men of Salem Church, their faces still pristine and clear in my mind, the boy in the cherry orchard with his fearful death face, a throng who remained irrevocably connected to me. I would do my best to forget them once more, and one by one they would leave until summoned again.

I heard Sam calling from the bedroom, his voice with its ever calming effect upon me, deep but gentle. "Serena?"

"Coming, Dearest," I replied, turning away from the door to go to him. He needed me. That need was the one thing to give me purpose, to keep me going. I needed him too. "Coming."

The End

Acknowledgements

In trying to be historically accurate, I must make a confession. I took the escape from Libby Prison and moved it forward a year so that it would fit into my story. The great undertaking of breaking out of Libby actually took place in 1864, not 1865. Otherwise, I attempted to make it as close to fact based as I could while adding in a fictional character.

My research was based upon the book *Libby Prison Breakout* by Joseph Wheelan and the firsthand account *My Experience As A Prisoner of War, and Escape From Libby Prison* by William B McCreery in order to reconstruct the events surrounding the men who dug a tunnel and broke out of the infamous prison.

You may also note that Hetty Carr Carry was an actual person, as were the events surrounding her marriage to John Pegram. Although, Serena was not the reason for his unfortunate demise.

About The Author

Tracy Winegar enjoys cooking and gardening in her free time. She loves all things vintage and considers several family heirlooms to be her prized possessions. She's also always on the lookout to score pieces to add to her growing Jadeite collection.

Tracy lives with her husband and four beautiful children in Treasure Valley Idaho.